STRANGER
THAN TRUTH

Also by Vera Caspary

The White Girl
Thicker Than Wwater
Laura
Bedelia

STRANGER THAN TRUTH

A Novel

VERA CASPARY

First Edition published 1946 by Random House.

Copyright © 1946, 2013 by the Vera Caspary estate

ISBN: 978-1-5040-2911-7

Distributed in 2016 by Open Road Distribution
180 Maiden Lane
New York, NY 10038
www.openroadmedia.com

FOR GEORGE SKLAR

*Severest of Friends and
Best of Critics*

CONTENTS

Part One
THE WILSON STORY by John Miles Ansell

Part Two
TESTIMONIAL by Grace Eccles

Part Three
WHOSE TARTAN? by John Miles Ansell

Part Four
THE SERPENT'S TOOTH by Eleanor Barclay

Part Five
TO A GENTEEL LADY by John Miles Ansell

Part Six
A SHORT HISTORY OF HOMER PECK by Lola Manfred

Part Seven
THE TERRACE

No character or incident in this book is drawn from life.
It is all fiction—except the idea.

STRANGER THAN TRUTH

PART ONE

The Wilson Story

by John Miles Ansell

"Buried truth is ever in conflict with its dark surroundings. In its restless movement toward the light, it causes ferment and revolution in the social environment, and neuroticism and disease in the individual."

My Life Is Truth
NOBLE BARCLAY

CAPTAIN RIORDAN TOLD ME THE WILSON STORY in September. We were sitting behind a bottle of Canadian rye in a Third Avenue bar. He drank and I paid. I considered this a good investment because Riordan's stories were always better when he was mellow.

I had recently become editor of *Truth and Crime*, and was still new enough to believe I could improve the magazine. *Truth and Crime* was just another of the fact-detective magazines, filled with hashed-over newspaper stuff and old police-blotter cases, served up with sensational titles and pious crime-does-not-pay endings. The Wilson story had no ending, so I decided to use it as an Unsolved Mystery of the Month.

Instead of assigning it to a staff writer, I handled it myself. Although I had to use the *Truth and Crime* formula, I felt that I had written it so that an intelligent reader might find something more in it than the conventional mystery. I saw it as a bit of Americana, a comment on a curious phase of our national culture.

On Thursday morning, November 22, 1945, I was sitting in my private office in the Editorial Department of Barclay Truth Publications. It was my first private office and I was still new enough to enjoy seeing my name and the title, Editor, in gold letters on the door.

I was feeling good that morning. Righteous. Our February issue was to go to press that day, and all but one story had been sent via the Production Department to the printer's. The January and December issues had gone to press under my authority, but they had been filled with old stuff, stories ordered by my predecessor and not to my taste. The February issue was my own job, the first all-Ansell number, and I felt like a proud papa putting his firstborn to bed.

The telephone rang.

"The Production Department," Miss Kaufman said. "They want to know why your Unsolved Mystery hasn't come through."

I took the phone. "Look," I shouted, "what are you worrying about? You've got everything except the Unsolved Mystery and I'm expecting to get the okay on it any minute now."

There was a rumble at the other end of the wire.

"Don't blame me," I said. "I sent that script through three weeks ago. It's in Barclay's office now, and as far as I know he's using it for toilet paper."

The rumble at the other end of the wire grew ominous.

"Look," I demanded, "can I help it if Mr. B. holds up the works? He's boss here, he made the rules, he knows when we go to press. Look," I continued as the rumbles grew louder, "here's my secretary. She's just come back from Barclay's office. What did they tell you about the Unsolved Mystery, Miss Kaufman?"

Miss Kaufman who had not been near Mr. Barclay's office merely raised her bushy eyebrows.

"Good news!" I shouted into the phone. "Mr. Barclay's secretary told her he hadn't had time to get to the script until this morning, but he's just finished reading it and he's crazy about the yarn. I'll have his okay any minute now, and I'll get it to you pronto. How's that?"

Just then an office boy came in and dropped into my In Basket an envelope decorated with red stickers which meant *Rush* and yellow stickers which meant *Scheduled for Current*.

"Just keep your pants on," I told the rumbles. "The script's here now. We'll send it right over."

Miss Kaufman had opened the envelope. She grabbed the telephone. "Mr. Ansell will call back in a few minutes," she told the Production Department. Then she handed me the manuscript. Attached to its upper right hand corner was a green sticker. Green stickers meant *rejected*.

"What the hell!" I said. "They can't turn down this story."

"But they did," said Miss Kaufman and handed me a memorandum typed on blue paper. It read:

Memorandum
From the office of: Edward Everett Munn
To: John Miles Ansell
Date: 11/22/45

Ref: Ms. 1028-TaC

In accordance with our editorial policy, cannot allow publication of above ms. Have read myself and called attention of Mr. Barclay to such objections as would offend readers. Would suggest you substitute material discussed in conferences, Dot King or Elwell cases, more nationally known and of wider interest. Hope this does not seriously interfere with your schedule.

E. E. Munn
Enclosure: Memo to N.B.

"Hope it doesn't seriously interfere with our schedule! That son of a bitch!" I said. "He's been holding it in his office until the last minute, so he can put me on the spot."

"What are you going to do about an Unsolved Murder?" asked Miss Kaufman.

"The Elwell case! Dot King! As if every true-crime magazine in the country hadn't reprinted them a dozen times. I'm going to tell Edward Everett Munn . . ."

"Don't shout so, Mr. Ansell. They can hear you all over the office."

"What do I care? Let's give the stooges and spies something to report. I know when I've got a good story and I don't intend to have it sabotaged by a cretin who ought to be collecting garbage . . ."

"Please, Mr. Ansell."

"Yes, yes, I know they're listening. I hope there arc no garbage collectors around because I don't want to insult their trade. Garbage collectors are good honest efficient men and I'm sure they'd never let E. E. Munn into their union. Do you know the real unsolved mystery, Miss Kaufman? How he ever got the job of Supervising Editor and how he manages to hang on to it. Solve that and you'll win the love of all those who slave in this jute mill."

Our private offices were private in name alone. They were divided from each other and from the General Office by frosted glass partitions that stopped three feet short of the ceiling. Loyal employees said that this was a health measure, allowing free circulation of air, but cynics hinted of espionage. The older Barclay editorial workers were a discontented lot.

"Before you shoot off your mouth about what's wrong with other people," Miss Kaufman remarked, "maybe you'd better find out why they've turned your precious story down."

She handed me a carbon copy of the memo that Edward Everett Munn had sent the publisher. I tried to read it, but I was angry and the lines seemed to blur. I took off my glasses and looked around for something to wipe them with. As usual my handkerchief had disappeared. Miss Kaufman found a square of pink cotton and wiped my glasses.

"Thanks," I said gruffly.

"Read it," commanded my secretary.

Memorandum
From the office of: Edward Everett Munn
To: Noble Barclay
Date: 11/22/45

Ref: Ms. 1028-TaC
In order that we have on record our objections to above ms.—Unsolved Mystery, Feb. '46—I herewith submit the following reasons why said ms. is unfit for publication:

1. The crime is unknown. Has it not been definitely decided *in conference* that the chief sales feature of the Unsolved Mystery is popular knowledge of the featured crime?
2. Satirical tone of article. It is not the object of Barclay-Truth Publications to point out the ironies of life, nor to assume a derogatory tone toward matters which our readers do not see in the same light as so-called sophisticates. This is not the *New Yorker.* Our readers are serious-minded, thinking men and women.
3. Frivolous attitude toward alcoholic beverages. Editors should be conversant with our policy in this matter.
4. Facetious remarks about correspondence schools. The writer evidently forgets that many of our best friends and oldest advertisers are reputable institutions of this nature. Is it not in bad taste as well as financially unsound to criticize a large group of advertisers?

Inasmuch as the above embodies several angles of destructive criticism, we have offered constructive advice in the attached memo to the editor.

E. E. Munn

Enclosure: Memo to John Miles Ansell

I crushed the memo into a ball and aimed it at the waste-basket. Miss Kaufman fished it out. "For our files," she said.

"You don't think I'm going to take that hogwash seriously?"

"What can you do?"

"For once in the history of Truth Publications, Miss Kaufman, an editor is going to fight for his magazine."

"But your job, Mr. Ansell."

"Think I'm afraid?"

"What about the forty a week you send your mother?" asked Miss Kaufman. Then she smiled and added, "You'd better comb your hair, Mr. Ansell. And straighten your tie."

I whirled around. I embraced her. She was on the wrong side of forty and her breasts would have been a bumper crop in any harvest. "Kaufman, old girl, you're tops." I kissed her full on the mouth.

"None of that. I'm a respectable married woman."

I combed my hair, straightened my tie and took off my glasses. "Good or bad, that story's going into the February issue. I'm fighting to the finish."

She handed me the crumpled memo. "Take this along. Don't ever try to rely on your memory, not around here. Well, good luck, little David."

"Don't you worry, I've got my slingshot with me."

Typewriters stopped as I crossed the general office. Everyone who had listened while I shouted my opinions of Munn watched as I opened his door. I held my head high, thrust out my chin, stood straight, so I'd seem taller. This time, I told myself, Ansell triumphs. Come back with your shield or on it. People have always liked you, John Miles Ansell. You've never had to speak French nor play the piano, and everyone hates Edward Everett Munn, that is, everyone who is young and healthy and intelligent and right.

"Good morning, Mr. Ansell. Would you like to see Mr. Munn?" his secretary asked.

"No, dear, I've come to ask your hand in marriage. Will you make me the happiest man on earth?"

Pale lips tightened. Munn's secretary never laughed at my jokes. She was anemic and not very bright. People said she was Barclay's third cousin. The editorial department was a garden of nepotism. Poor relations blossomed all over the place.

"Mr. Munn is tied up now. He'll be free in a little while. Won't you sit down?"

I did not like being confined in a small space with that case of pernicious anemia, so I asked her to send for me when Mr. Munn was ready. I strolled out, trying to look as debonair as possible, for the eyes of the General Office were still upon me.

Instead of returning to my own office I sauntered along the linoleum, past the offices of *Truth and Health* and *Truth and Beauty*. In front of the door lettered *Truth and Love* I paused. The door was open.

"Hey, Ansell," boomed a rugged female voice.

I straightened my tie once more, smoothed my hair and entered jauntily. The effect was wasted. The smaller desk stood empty and Lola Manfred was alone with the manuscripts.

She noticed my wandering gaze. "Eleanor's downstairs in the Studio," Lola said. "I always relegate to her the duty of posing models in those amorous photographs which prove so conclusively that our love tales are life experiences. What's this I hear about your entering the lists and challenging the doughty Munn?"

"News travels fast around here."

"You said it." Lola ran her hands through hair dyed the color of a Christmas tangerine. "What's the matter anyway? Can't you take a rejection?"

"When I was a freelance writer, I used to eat rejection slips for breakfast."

"Then what's the shooting for?"

"It's not the rejection," I said. "It's the principle."

"What principle?"

"I'm supposed to be an editor," I said. "At least that's what I was told when they hired me. And then, just when I've started getting my monthly routine working, they hold up a manuscript for three weeks and don't let me know it's rejected until the day we go to press. How do you like that?"

"It wouldn't be the first time in the history of this dump," Lola said wearily. She swung around in the swivel chair, bent over and opened the lower drawer of her desk. Her voice, which ordinarily boomed over the frosted-glass partitions, softened. "Close the door."

"Why?"

Lola had dainty hands and the movement of her thumb was incongruous as she jerked it toward the door. I closed it. As I returned to the desk, I saw with a start that Lola had pulled a milk bottle out of the lower drawer. I was more shocked than if I had seen her take a whiskey bottle out of a desk owned by Noble Barclay. Lola's reputation was not precisely milky.

She pulled off the paper cap, tilted the bottle against her mouth. She grimaced as if the milk were so distasteful that she drank it on doctor's orders. When she handed me the bottle I noticed that her long drink had not drained out any of the cream.

I smelled it.

Lola laughed. "Isn't it clever? One of the boys in the Art Department painted it for me. He even put some yellowish paint on the top as if the cream had risen."

I gave her back the bottle. "Not in the office," I said.

"Is that a principle, too?"

"I like to get my work done. You can't write well or make decisions when you're foggy."

"Edgar Allan Poe drank like a fish and I bet they'd never print his stories in *Truth and Crime*."

"I can make the grade without alcohol," I said.

"But what's the advantage?" asked Lola and took another drink.

She put the bottle away, and leaned so far back in the swivel chair that I was afraid it would tip over. "Now that I've got my strength back," she said, "I'd like to know just what principles you're prepared to defend so vigorously."

"I was hired to do a job. When I first came to talk to Barclay about it, he said he wanted me because my stuff was different. He said I had a touch you don't often find among detective-story writers. He wanted me to lift the magazine out of its present rut and make it an outstanding monthly."

"You're not by any chance alluding to *Truth and Crime*" Lola sneered.

"Look," I pleaded, "there are hundreds of ways of handling a crime story. After all, crime is as much an indication of the state of our civilization as our laws or our codes of conduct. After all, a murder story has social significance."

Lola groaned.

"I don't mean to be pompous," I protested.

"How old are you?"

"I'll be twenty-six in March."

"Poor lamb."

I do not like to be patronized. "I have no illusions," I said. "I'm not naïve. I know what kind of magazines Barclay's getting out. But I was hired to put some pep into an ailing circulation and, damn it, I'm going to try."

"Has your rejected manuscript social significance?"

"Not in the conventional way. There's a bit of comment that Munn thinks is satirical, but if he and Mr. Barclay insist, I'll take it out. What they don't seem to understand is that I'm trying to give our readers something new and fresh."

"What's so new and fresh about it?"

"It hasn't been in any other detective magazine or Sunday supplement or murder anthology. That's the trouble with most of our stuff; it's hashed-over and dull to our readers. They're detective-story fans, they probably know all the good murders."

"Is this such a good murder?"

"Nothing extraordinary, except for one angle. The victim. He was . . ."

Lola yawned. My arguments had bored her. "Is the story good enough to lose your job over?"

"Why don't you read it? Then you'd see my point."

"Good God!" she cried. "It's bad enough to read what I'm paid for. Why did you take this job in the first place, Ansell? Was it to put social significance into *Truth and Crime* or to make a hundred dollars a week?"

"A hundred and twenty-five," I boasted.

"Most of the hacks around here would consider that principle enough for anything."

"I'm not so cynical that I can't believe you can't make a decent living and be true to your principles, too."

"If it's social significance you want to get into your stories, you'd better quit here and go to work for *The New Masses*. If it's principle, the place for you's a garret where you can starve comfortably. But before you give up that hundred and twenty-five berries and a job where you can get out a magazine with one hand and hoist drinks with the other, you'd better learn the difference between a principle and the desire to get your own way."

Lola's drinking, I decided, was directly related to the cynicism with which she approached her job. Not that I blamed her for finding

Truth and Love distasteful. Lola Manfred had once written some good poetry.

She laid her hand gently upon my coat sleeve. "Are you sure you know what you're fighting for?"

"I refuse to be pushed around."

"I hope when you're shivering in your garret that principle will warm you."

"But suppose I let them set a precedent this time, how much authority can I expect in the future?"

"Does it matter?"

"Does it matter!" I cried.

She blew her nose daintily on a soiled handkerchief. "What makes you so different, Don Quixote, from your fellow prisoners in this steam-heated dungeon? Why should you enjoy the luxury of getting your own way when the rest of us make daily obeisance before Munn and kiss Barclay's noble prat?"

"I've never noticed you indulging in those rites, Lola."

"I don't have to. They can't fire me. I happen to know where the body's buried."

"Perhaps I'd better find myself a body."

"It oughtn't to be hard. There are probably plenty of 'em rotting in the crypts."

The door had opened softly. Someone was standing behind my chair. I turned hopefully, but it was not Eleanor. Munn's secretary had come in. She smiled contemptuously and said, "He'll see you now, Mr. Ansell."

I started out. As I held the door for Munn's secretary, Lola blew me a kiss. "Come back when it's over and I'll provide consolation." She jerked her thumb toward the lower drawer and winked.

"Come in, come in," Munn called jovially. "Sit down, won't you? Are you comfortable there? Let me pull down the blind. I'm sure you don't want the light in your eyes."

That was Munn, glib and unctuous. The smile was too quick, the voice too smooth. He loved himself, he was a success, a male secretary who had become a big executive. He had a clown's mouth, red as paint and curving like the crescent moon. When he laughed the muscles of his cheeks never moved. It was as if his mouth had its own life, independent of his face. His hair had grown thin. A peak descended to his forehead but on the sides it scalloped off. He had angular eyebrows and narrow, restless eyes. His desk was neat, the blotter spotless and all of his papers filed into one of those leather folders called a "Work Organizer." On the wall hung numerous photographs lovingly autographed by Noble Barclay.

He offered me a cigarette.

"I don't smoke Turkish," I told him and took out my own. He leaned over to light one for me. I waited for him to open the conversation.

After a while he said, "You wanted to see me about something, Ansell?"

"You know damn well what I've come to talk to you about." I waved the crumpled memo. "We're supposed to be going to press today."

He nodded. "I've noticed before, Ansell, that you always wait till the last possible moment before putting through an important story."

"I wait? Look, Munn, that story was held in your office for almost three weeks. Look at the date on the manuscript. You're on top here, you're the Supervising Editor and General Manager. Why did you hold the story until the day we go to press and then reject it with a sappy memo? For once in your life, Munn, someone's asking you for a reason."

Munn watched his smoke rings drift toward the ceiling. "I don't quite understand your complaints, Ansell. Most of our editors find that the organization functions efficiently."

"Damn it!" I shouted. "You can't do that to me. You know I can't put the magazine to bed without an Unsolved Mystery."

"Have you no other copy to substitute?"

"The illustrations have been made. The plates are all ready."

"We can get cuts made over night. Have you no other Unsolved Mystery, Ansell?"

I jumped up. I stood before him. I pounded on his desk with both fists. "There's nothing wrong with that story. Why the hell are you sabotaging it?"

He nodded toward the crumpled memo. "You're aware of my objections."

"I don't entirely agree with you, Mr. Munn."

"I'm sorry, Ansell."

Out in the General Office, the typewriters were clicking again. I heard laughter to my left, which was the direction of the *Truth and Love* office, and I wondered whether Eleanor had returned from the Studio, and what Lola had told her. Would Eleanor also think me a solemn young fool, or would she admire a man who fought for his rights?

"Look," I said to Munn in a moderate conversational tone, "I don't want to be stubborn about this. You're right about that correspondence-school stuff. I've no illusions about the purpose of our magazine."

"Our purpose, Ansell, is to disseminate truth in a form that will appeal to popular taste."

"Yes, of course, Mr. Munn. But the advertising . . ."

"Advertising helps finance our periodicals, Mr. Ansell. Without it, we should be obliged to operate on a much smaller scale and we could not bring our message to so many people."

"I understand that. And I'm quite willing to cut out all the cracks about correspondence schools. I'll simply state that this particular course was a phony and not to be compared with the accredited educational institutions which advertise in our incorruptible publications."

I saw my mistake at once. Humor of any kind baffled Munn. He was one hundred per cent literal and any remark that hinted of irreverence toward Noble Barclay or Truth Publications was a personal affront.

I hurried to cover up. "Look, Mr. Munn. Where the liquor is concerned, you haven't a leg to stand on. How can we, in our editorial columns, pretend that liquor doesn't exist, when three of our magazines are running wine ads?"

"I believe that you were absent from the conference at which we discussed the matter."

"I didn't miss the piece in *Truth and Health* that said that wine, taken at meals in moderate quantities, is a vitamin-packed food and provides an antidote against the craving for stronger liquor. And in the next issue of *Truth*, I understand . . ."

"I didn't know that you were so well acquainted with the contents of our other publications."

"Such a drastic change in policy can't go unnoticed. Look, Mr. Munn . . ."

"*Look*, Ansell. I'm astonished at you, a professional writer, abusing the English language in that manner. You ask me to look. What am I to look at? Don't you mean to employ the verb, to listen?"

I was going crazy. You could never argue with Munn. He was always like that, going off the main path, scooting down some dark alley.

"Listen, if that's what you prefer, I'll merely mention that there was liquor in the murder victim's glass. I won't say what kind of liquor."

"Do you consider that consistent with our policy of strictest truth in every detail?"

"I'll cut all mention of liquor out of the story. It has nothing to do with the murder anyway. Will that suit you?"

He crushed out the cigarette, rolled the stub against the bowl of the ashtray until the paper was empty. He rolled the paper into a tiny ball, threw it into the wastebasket and emptied the ashes into a covered tin receptacle. "I dislike the odor of stale tobacco," he said and wiped his hands on a paper handkerchief which he had taken out of his desk drawer. Then he threw the handkerchief into the wastebasket.

"We were talking about a manuscript," I reminded him. "The Unsolved Mystery, the murder of Warren G. Wilson. Remember?"

"I've finished talking about it."

"I haven't."

At this point I should have given up. I knew that Lola had been right. It was not principle I was fighting for, but authority. Just the same, I went on fighting.

"Compromises are useless, Ansell. Need I remind you that you're wasting time? The story has been rejected. Definitely."

There was a long silence. He had dismissed me and he waited to enjoy the spectacle of my retreat. I sat tight. Who was he, Edward Everett Munn, to turn me out? For a moment there, I had wavered and been willing to call quits.

"Look, Munn," I said, and when he frowned, I didn't bother to change the verb. "I've offered to take out everything you object to in the story. Even without the comment which I think gives it quality, we'll be offering our readers something fresh. I'll make the cuts now, and send you the manuscript by lunchtime. If you'll okay it immediately, I can get it to the printer's this afternoon."

"And if I refuse?"

"I'll send it through anyway. As editor, I'll take the responsibility."

He rose. Sitting down he seemed insignificant because his head was small and his shoulders narrow, but when he stood on his incredibly long legs, he looked like a middle-aged boy on stilts. "Very well, there's only one thing for us to do. We'll take it up with Mr. Barclay."

He lifted the mouthpiece of his interoffice phone. "It's Mr. Munn," he told the instrument. "Very important."

A female voice shrilled through the box. We waited a few seconds and the female voice shrilled again. "He'll see us now," Munn said, smiling because the boss had not kept him waiting.

No typewriter ceased its clatter as Munn and I walked through the General Office. There was not a split second's lapse in the rhythm of the machines. Discipline never slackened when Munn was in the office.

He walked ahead, the shepherd leading the lamb to slaughter, the warden taking the condemned man to the death house. Before the door of Barclay's office, he stopped and leaned over to whisper something. His breath smelled of peppermint-flavored mouthwash. "Has it ever occurred to you, Ansell, that your stubbornness might lead to disaster?"

It certainly had occurred to me, but the disaster I had in mind was the loss of a good job, not the horror and tragedy which came as the result of my determination to get my Unsolved Mystery into the February issue.

At that time I did not consider the Wilson story anything out of the ordinary. The murder was not particularly exciting. It was the background of the victim—as much as was known of it—that interested me. I had no other reason for writing the story, scheduling it for the February issue and sending it for approval to Noble Barclay.

I have a copy of the manuscript in my files, and since it is the focus of a much stranger story, I am including it here, just as I wrote it and submitted it on November fifth to the Reading Department, the Supervising Editor and Barclay.

Here it is:

* * *

No. 1028—TaC
11/5/45
Sched: Feb.
Author: John Miles Ansell

The Unsolved Mystery of the Month

DEATH OF THE MAN WHO WAS NEVER BORN

They did not immediately see the body. It lay face downward in the narrow channel between the wall and the bed. The right arm was extended. The man had apparently fallen while reaching for the telephone.

It was nine o'clock on Sunday morning, May 13, 1945. The body had been there since Friday night, for it was on Saturday morning that the chambermaid, the bath maid and a bellboy had noticed the sign on the door: *Do Not Disturb.*

On Monday morning the sign was still there. The chambermaid had notified the housekeeper. The housekeeper had telephoned the desk clerk. The desk clerk had reported to Mr. Frederick Semple, manager of the hotel. Accompanied by the desk clerk, the housekeeper and the chambermaid, Mr. Semple approached the door of Suite 3002-4. Before using the pass key, Mr. Semple pressed the electric button, knocked at the door and called the tenant's name. There was no response, and Semple, followed by his retinue, entered the apartment.

Drawn curtains repelled the sunlight. Bulbs burned in three silk-shaded lamps. The electric phonograph's motor throbbed. Evidently the machine had been burning up current since the last of the records had dropped into the well. Pillows were heaped at one end of the wide couch and close by stood a coffee table with cigarettes, ashtray, French brandy and a snifter, not quite empty.

Beyond this room a short corridor led to bedroom and bath. The bed had been turned down and on the night table were shell-rimmed spectacles, a copy of Saki's short stories and a thin gold watch which had stopped at 5:20.

At the far end of the room a desk had been overturned. A portable typewriter lay on its carriage, legs upward like a helpless animal. Pens, pencils, paper and carbons were scattered on the desk and spilled on the floor.

And in the narrow channel between the bed and the wall lay the tenant with a bullet in his back.

An hour later, Mr. Semple, quivering from shock and thinking of the effect of scandal upon the conservative bankers who operated the hotel, told the police what he knew of the late tenant.

His name was Warren G. Wilson and there had been nothing in his way of life to suggest a violent end. He had occupied his suite for five years and three months, and never in that time had his activities created any of the problems which distress the managers of exclusive hotels. Servants remembered his generosity and regarded his passing as the loss of a friend. He had spent most of the time in his suite, reading in bed or lying on the couch, listening to his records.

According to the Coroner's report this inactivity had been due to illness. Pale flesh had been stretched meagerly over Wilson's bones and his lungs were so embroidered with scars that it was remarkable that he had lived long enough to be killed by a shell fired from a .22 automatic.

He had entertained few visitors. Hotel clerks remembered Mr. Thornhill, Mr. Henning and Mr. Bendas, middle-aged gentlemen who shared Wilson's hobby of collecting first editions. That his bent was literary was proved, not only by these friendships and his library, but by the collection of writing materials stored in his cupboards. That Wilson's ambitions were unfulfilled was shown by the absence of manuscript.

An examination of his bookshelves showed that he had been a man who admired style, and it can be assumed that he was a perfectionist who wrote three lines on Monday, added two commas and a semi-colon on Tuesday, on Wednesday took out a comma, spent Thursday criticizing what he had written, threw it all in the fire on Friday and spent Saturday thinking he had done a hard week's work.

There had been a woman. She had come to the hotel infrequently, but had never left her name at the desk because she returned with Mr. Wilson after he had dined out. Two elevator boys said she was good-looking, but neither could remember whether she had been blonde or brunette.

On the night of his death Wilson had dined out, but had returned without a companion. While he sipped French brandy and listened to his favorite phonograph records, a Negro pianist was playing boogie-woogie in the suite across the hall. For on that night, Wilson's neighbors, the only ones who shared the thirtieth floor of the tower with him, were giving a party. More than sixty people rode to the thirtieth floor that night. Strangers were not asked their names, for the hostess in 3006-8 had informed the desk that guests were not to be announced.

No stranger stopped at the desk that night to ask the number of Wilson's apartment. The murderer had evidently known that his victim occupied Suite 3002-4. To the busy elevator boys all passengers bound for the thirtieth floor were party guests. One boy, a new employee, hired only the week before and unfamiliar with the hotel guests and their regular visitors, told the police he remembered a nervous lady who dropped her pocketbook as she got off at the thirtieth floor. He had bent over to pick it up, but the lady had swooped down, grabbed the bag and tucked it under her arm in a most belligerent manner. All the boy could remember about this lady was her plaid coat.

The hostess in Suite 3006-8 could not recall a guest in plaid. Her party had been formal. A plaid coat would have been as inappropriate as a top hat at a baseball game. The police decided, therefore, that the plaid coat might help identify Wilson's visitor. It was not much of a clue. Plaid coats were all the style that season.

To make the search more baffling there was the report of Jean Pierre Hyman and the conflicting opinion of his head-waiter, Gus-tav. Mr. Hyman is the owner of the French restaurant that attracts so many gourmets to his modest but expensive quarters on East Twelfth

Street. Jean Pierre remembered the lady who had sometimes dined in his restaurant with M. Wilson. She had been young and fair, and on her last visit, ten days before Wilson's regrettable death, had worn a new spring coat of red, blue and green plaid. She had been, according to Jean Pierre, a dainty blonde.

Although he did not like to disagree with the boss, Gustav, the headwaiter, insisted that Wilson's girl friend had been a willowy, radiant brunette with soulful dark eyes. Yet Gustav and Jean Pierre were agreed on one point. There had not been more than one young lady.

The police found themselves seeking a girl who was either blonde or brunette and who wore one of the hundreds of thousands of plaid coats circulating in New York. It was a tough assignment, but Captain C. Allan Riordan of the Detective Bureau vowed that he would not rest until he had discovered the lady in plaid who, on the night of May eleventh, might or might not have been carrying a .22 automatic in her pocketbook.

Meanwhile Captain Riordan and his staff sought other information. Somewhere in the fertile ground of Warren G. Wilson's past lay the clue to his strange death. Why was he, a man of gentle disposition and quiet habits, the victim of premeditated murder? What rage or grievance could inspire the death of a man known to have been a connoisseur of wines and salads, an admirer of Prokofiev, Debussy, Mahler, Saki and William Blake?

One fact about Wilson baffled Riordan as much as the identity of the lady in plaid. No one knew the source of Wilson's income. On the second day of every month he had deposited in his checking account two thousand dollars in cash. It was highly irregular, but his bankers had asked Wilson no questions. Since the '29 depression there had been a number of eccentric depositors who, fearing revolution, had converted their assets into cash which they kept in safety-deposit boxes.

None of the vaults in New York had a box registered in the name of Warren G. Wilson. And in those sacred cells where gold and bonds and cash are locked away, no record, no clerk, no guard recalled a customer of Wilson's description who unlocked his box on the second day of each month. The Department of Internal Revenue had no files on Warren G. Wilson.

In their search for a death clue Riordan's men investigated every known facet of Wilson's life. His barber, his tailor, his friends among the collectors of first editions were questioned. No one had known him very long and none was aware of his origin. Some remembered his allusions to Arizona, New Mexico, the desert; and the police discovered, too, that he had once worked in Chicago.

In a corner at the bottom of the bookshelves Riordan found the strange clue. Not a death clue so much as evidence of the strange birth of Warren G. Wilson. For he had not been born at all; he had been conceived more than twenty years earlier over a bootleg Martini in a Chicago speakeasy.

The birth clue that Riordan found on the bottom bookshelf was a series of loose-leaf pamphlets in an imitation-leather binder that bore the title:

BUSINESS DYNAMICS

A Success Course in Salesmanship,
Merchandising and Finance
by
WARREN G. WILSON

This was the pretentious title of a correspondence course of thirty lessons sent out in envelopes labeled, *From the Private Office of Warren G. Wilson.* Warren G. Wilson was President of the Warren G. Wilson Foundation, Chicago, 111. The course cost seventy-five dollars and students paid at the rate of five dollars for two lessons a month.

The thirty lessons covered a wide range of subjects, varying from such abstruse material as Dynamics of Business to such practical advice as Personal Appearance: A Business Asset. In the writing of these lessons Mr. Wilson had shown himself a man whose knowledge of human nature was derived, not from experience alone, but from the works of Locke, Mill, Henry George, William James, Pelman of Pelmanism, Emile Coué, Horatio Alger, Jr., Sigmund Freud and the author of *Letters of a Self-Made Merchant to His Son.*

Most interesting to the police were those pages of reminiscence

23

wherein Warren G. Wilson's advice to students was rich with nuggets of wisdom culled from conversations with the great tycoons. Surely among the bankers and financiers of whom he had written with such intimacy there would be one who could recall Warren G. Wilson and furnish a clue to his early life. But all of Wilson's magnates were dead long before the year of his copyright.

Who was Wilson? The name had an irritatingly familiar sound. Even Captain Riordan, when he first took over the case, remarked that he seemed to recognize it. In his effort to discover what had happened to Wilson in the years between the copyright and the murder, Riordan sent men to a place which must have seemed alien to detectives, the Public Library. There, in magazines published in 1920 and 1921, were advertisements of the Success Course. In all of the ads the fame of Warren G. Wilson, businessman and financier, was so taken for granted that anyone unfamiliar with the name would have been ashamed of his ignorance.

From these advertisements in popular-science and mechanics magazines, health and success magazines and monthly journals dedicated to self-education, the trail led back to Chicago.

In the '20s Chicago was not only the world's capital of bootlegging and gangsterism; it was the hub of the mail-order business, the Athens of the correspondence course, the seat of education guided by sages learned in the art of ballyhoo and in the science of installment collection. For five dollars down and five a month they offered instruction in everything from ballet dancing to psychic healing. These were not counted as rackets; they were legal business institutions and the U.S. mails were their sales routes.

Every advertisement carried a guarantee. You learned what the master taught or your money was refunded. Warren G. Wilson did not guarantee success; he promised that if you had not "increased your earnings nor advanced your position within six months after *completion* of the course" every cent would be paid back to you. This was a common trick among the correspondence schools. Few suckers asked for refunds; fewer completed their courses. The lessons were sanctioned by the Interstate Commerce Commission and the Better Business Bureaus, and allowed to be distributed through the mails because they actually contained certain concrete details. In addition to instruction on the quick, easy way to success, Wilson's course included penmanship, double-entry bookkeeping, typing, elementary shorthand, insurance tables, tariff regulations, compound interest and stock-exchange rates.

Research into its history proved that the Warren G. Wilson Foundation which had guaranteed success to its students was itself a financial failure. The first advertisements had appeared in 1920 and in 1922 its offices were closed.

Through records in the files of the magazines in which Wilson's course had been advertised, Captain Riordan discovered the name of the agency which had placed these ads. It had been a one-man company and its owner, now vice-president of a respectable New York agency, told Riordan all he knew about the Wilson business but asked, for the sake of his reputation, that his name be kept out of the story.

This man, the reputable but nameless advertising agent, remembered the conception and assisted at the birth of Warren G. Wilson. The name was chosen deliberately. In 1920 many Americans believed that Woodrow Wilson was one of the great martyred Presidents, while others thought he had run the country onto the rocks and that it would be saved by Warren G. Harding. The author of the lessons, owner of the business, so-called president of the Foundation, was a Mid-Western youth named Homer Peck.

Peck had been an advertising copywriter. He had been brilliant at it, made a great success, and older advertising men had prophesied a wealthy future for him. But Peck had demanded more than prophecies and promises. When his employers refused to raise his salary he quit his job and went into business for himself. Over cocktails served in teacups Peck had outlined the idea for his correspondence course to his friend, the advertising man. Neither considered the business shabby. Both had majored in the subject of mail-order education by writing ads for schools of signal engineering, scientific farming, sign painting and photoplay writing.

Of Peck's personal life the advertising man knew little. Peck had lived in a cheap apartment on the near North Side in the Bohemian arty neighborhood bordering Chicago's so-called Gold Coast, had written short stories which no one would publish, and had an affair with his stenographer, a slim, radiant young girl who wrote poetry. The advertising man had admired Peck's ingenuity, considered him a cockeyed genius and expected him to make a fortune. He was surprised, he said, when Peck decided suddenly to give up the one-room office pretentiously called The Warren G. Wilson Foundation of Business Dynamics. With a little effort and a few thousand additional dollars, the advertising man believed, the Warren G. Wilson Foundation might have flourished.

But Peck, as the advertising man remarked, was too much of a genius to care about making money. He enjoyed his ideas too much ever to achieve solid business success. On the day he closed his office he had lunched with the advertising man. Failure had not depressed Peck. His mood had been optimistic. Raising the teacup that held his Martini, Peck had proposed a toast to his next venture, which, he promised, would make that ex-giant of finance, Warren G. Wilson, look like a worm under the sidewalks of Wall Street.

The promise was never fulfilled. The advertising man never drank another cocktail with Homer Peck, and but for the settling of accounts heard nothing of Warren G. Wilson until he read of the murder.

This is all the New York police have learned about Homer Peck. A Chicago bank account closed in November, 1922, advertisements in old magazines, an advertising agent's recollections of a client's failure—nothing more. The loft building in which Peck had his office has been torn down and a skyscraper erected in its place. The speakeasies where Peck and his friend held their conferences are gone, too. Even the blatantly wicked Chicago of their day, the taxi wars, bootlegger battles, get-rich-quick schemes, the blue-sky mail-order courses are memories of an era that goes down in history as preface to the Great Depression. And only a corpse with a bullet wound in his back brings back memories of the great jazz era.

Whose was the body? What strange and secret events led to the death of the man who was never born? What became of Homer Peck whose agile but none-too-scrupulous mind created the fabulous Warren G. Wilson? And where into this pattern of mystery does the girl fit, the girl who is neither blonde nor brunette and who rode to the thirtieth floor on the night Wilson died? These are the questions to which the police seek answers. These are the only known facts about a murder committed last May and still unsolved.

The case is not closed. Captain Riordan is determined to solve the mystery. Somewhere out of the dark shadows of the past, there will emerge one bright truth to shed its light upon the mystery of Wilson's death and to reveal the identity of the man who concealed his failure behind the name of a correspondence-school professor who never existed.

* * *

That was the Wilson story, just one in a long series of Unsolved Mysteries. Perhaps, in fighting to get it into the February issue, I was stupid. Perhaps subtleties escaped me. I had no idea then that I was suspected of knowing more than I had written into the manuscript. As I followed E. E. Munn along the corridor to Noble Barclay's office, I honestly thought I was defending my rights as an editor.

We had to wait a while in the reception room before Mr. Barclay would see us. His secretary, Grace Eccles, bestowed upon us the smile reserved for those privileged to enter the private office.

"He'll be just a minute," she said. "The Senator's on the wire."

She popped back into the glass-enclosed den that guarded Barclay's privacy. We were left with the strangers in the reception room. There was an air about the place, a sense of feudal grandeur. On the oak-paneled walls hung pictures of Noble Barclay and his family. Laid out on the big oak refectory table were current issues of the five magazines, *Truth*, *Truth and Health*, *Truth and Love*, *Truth and Crime*, and *Truth and Beauty*. On a velvet-covered table lay a single copy of *My Life Is Truth*. Beside the handsome portrait on the dust jacket was the information that this was Copy No. 6,182,454 of Noble Barclay's immortal work. Bookshelves contained each of the seventy-six editions in sixteen languages, including Japanese.

Oblivious to the strangers' uneasy stares, Munn stood before the great window, his head thrown back as though he were praying secretly or exulting. I wondered whether he rejoiced because he had me in a spot, or whether he was merely rehearsing for our scene with the boss.

The strangers crouched humbly on the carved Italian bench at the dark end of the room. There were five of them, shabby and self-conscious; a middle-aged woman with a furtive sniveling boy of ten or twelve; an elderly couple who sat as if they were paying for space on the uncomfortable bench; and a hunchback who offered his abject grin as appeasement for his ugliness. These were true believers who would sit all day on the hard benches to catch a glimpse of Noble Barclay.

"Ready now," cooed Miss Eccles.

She pressed a button, the latch of Barclay's door was released, and the strangers stared enviously as we were admitted to the holy place.

Barclay stood at the window looking down upon the rainy street. His back was toward the door. We walked to the center of the long office, but a thick carpet muffled our footsteps. I cleared my throat. Munn frowned and shook his head, but it was too late. Barclay's meditations had been interrupted. He turned.

"How are you, Ed?" he said to Munn. And to me, extending his hand, "Glad to see you, boy. Sit down. What can I do for you?"

He was big and affable. Under a mane of sleek white hair his features were tanned and strong. His tweeds were bulky, but he was built for sturdy fabrics. The heavy wool did not hide the strength of his shoulders.

"It's about the Wilson story, isn't it?" he asked, looking straight into my face.

Munn had pretended not to know why I burst into his office. Barclay used the frank approach. "I thought this stormy petrel would beat his wings against my window."

"You know about it, Mr. Barclay?"

"I've read the story. A great yarn, boy. Ask Ed what I said about you last night." His glance demanded response and Munn bared his teeth in a phony smile. "I wanted to talk to you myself, but I came into the office late this morning. Mrs. Barclay and the twins just got back from the Coast and I had to meet the train."

"I don't understand, Mr. Barclay, if you liked the story . . ."

"Liked it? That story was great. Great writing. Guts and punch. And I liked the way you went after the stuff yourself. You weren't content just to rewrite the printed stuff; you had to find out how the wheels turned. That's the spirit we appreciate, lad."

"Let's get down to facts," I said. "You think it's a good story, but Mr. Munn says we can't run it. He sent you a memo. Have you read it? Do you agree?"

"Hold on," laughed Barclay. "Munn and I talked this over last night before he dictated that memo. I'd have used simpler language myself, but Ed can't get over that course he took in Business English."

This was a sly dig. Barclay winked at me. Munn laughed mechanically.

"I just don't understand, Mr. Barclay."

"Policy," put in Munn.

"Hadn't we agreed on one of the better-known murders? Dot King, the Elwell case, practically historic, you know," Barclay said.

"Our readers know the stories."

"You made that observation at the last conference, but it was ruled out, if you remember."

"It was my opinion that we decided to use old stories when we had nothing better. I got hold of a new story for you."

"I admire your initiative," Barclay said.

The noon bell rang. I wondered if Eleanor was going out or whether the rain would keep her in the building.

"All I want, Mr. Barclay, is a good reason why you object to the Wilson story," I said earnestly.

Munn played with his cigarette case. He did not smoke in Barclay's presence.

Barclay cleared his throat. "I like the way you handle a story, John, but I don't like certain angles of this one. It's the character, the man who was murdered. People are only interested in a story when the characters are exciting."

"Don't you think there's something exciting about a man who got two thousand dollars a month without doing a lick of work for it?"

"If we knew the source we might be interested," Barclay answered. "Background and color, the underworld, for instance. Something colorful."

"An expensive bachelor apartment at the edge of Greenwich Village," I said. "Mysterious woman dines with the man in expensive French restaurant. What's dull about that?"

"The man himself. Character. Character's the basis of interest in any story. This character—what's his name? Thompson? Thompson was dull. He did nothing with his life. No one cared whether Thompson lived or died."

"Wilson," Munn said.

"Look, Mr. Barclay," I pleaded, "we've carried five different versions of the Rothstein case. Rothstein was a gambler. He cared for nothing but money. He was cruel, coarse, greedy and we knew nothing about his character. Elwell was also a gambler, he . . ."

"They did something with their lives, something active, even though they were dissolute. Thompson was an idler. He spent his money on a lot of dusty old books. He had no friends, no woman loved him."

"There was the lady in plaid."

Munn coughed.

"It's funny," I said. "You tell me Wilson's an uninteresting character and yet when you talk about him—even though you seem to forget his name—you get as angry as if he were real and you had something against him."

Barclay laughed. "What do you think of this lad, Ed? Obstinate as Granddaddy's mule. It's a spirit I admire. Tenacity. I knew from the minute I met you that you were the sort of fellow we wanted for Truth Publications."

"Then you'll run the story?"

"No."

"That's that," Munn said. The clown's mouth curved in triumph.

I was angry. Barclay had been flattering me, telling me I was a genius, a man of iron. For that he expected me to fawn and wag my tail and accept defeat gracefully. I wasn't built that way. Job or no job I had to know the reason for my defeat.

"It seems to me, Mr. Barclay, that you and Mr. Munn have some other reason for rejecting this story, something you don't want me to know."

Munn dropped his cigarette case. Barclay spoke into the telephone box on his desk. "Tell the Senator I'll be a few minutes late." He hung up and turned toward me. Our eyes met. I waited. He said, "How long have you been working for us, Ansell?"

"Four and a half months."

"Four months? And I've been running these magazines almost twenty years. Munn has been with me for much of that time. Do you, after three months, presume to tell me that you know more about the business than I do?"

"Remember the war," I said. "The people who got their countries into it always answered criticism by saying they'd been governing a long time and knew more about it than those who warned them that they were heading for disaster."

Munn slid forward in his chair. He was prepared to speak, but Barclay waved him to silence. Rising, the boss came over to my chair and looked down into my face with a candid unwavering glance. "You've been pretty frank, young man, in asking my reasons for rejecting your story. But let me ask you: Why are you so determined to run it?"

I was surprised. The question was too simple for that dramatic build-up. "It's a good story. It's one of the best Unsolved Mysteries we've ever had. You said so yourself, Mr. Barclay."

"I said it was good. I didn't say it was the best. When a man wants something very much, his desire is likely to exaggerate, even to twist and pervert, the truth."

"But you said you liked it."

"When you're in a tough spot and feel the world's against you, John, do you ever stop to examine the causes of your grievance? I don't mean the surface causes or what you believe is the other fellow's reason for thwarting you. What I'm asking is that you search yourself and dig deep for the elements of your discontent."

"I've read *My Life Is Truth*, Mr. Barclay."

Barclay nodded. He began to speak again glibly as if he were repeating phrases he had learned by heart. "It's not always a simple matter to discover the truth. We've got to dig deep to find the heart of weakness. What's the core of that obstinacy, young man?" He paused and looked down at me in an eager, good-fellow manner. Since I did not answer he went right on. "Don't be afraid of your weaknesses. All men are weak, none of us is perfect. Your pride won't let you accept another man's decision. Why not? Isn't stubborn pride a blanket covering hidden shame? What weakness have you buried, so that you've got to be too proud and obstinate to obey orders?"

His eyes were fixed upon my face. His smile was gentle but his manner compelling. I felt myself blush. This made me angry. I clenched my teeth and doubled my fists.

Barclay turned away as if he wished to save me embarrassment. Munn and I watched him cross the office to the door of his private lavatory.

"Stand up, John. Come here." Barclay had opened the lavatory door.

I knew what was coming. So did Munn. He grinned as he rose and stretched himself with an attempt at nonchalance. The inside of the lavatory door was a mirror. Barclay held the door open at an angle which reflected the three of us. It was cheap, a sideshow effect, but successful. The stilts which Munn used for legs gave him a full six feet and Barclay was two or three inches taller. I stand five foot five in my shoes.

Barclay spoke softly. "You've got to face it, lad. It's resenting the big fellow and wanting to show you're stronger that's made you into a little fighting cock who thinks he can whip the giant roosters."

Munn smiled and hummed softly.

Barclay's hand found my shoulder. "Sore, aren't you? Not that I blame you. Pretty fresh of old man Barclay to bring this up. What the hell business is it of his?" He caught my eye, smiled ruefully. "You see, I can tell what you're thinking. And I'm right about you. All the trouble you've ever had with other people is because you've made up your mind you won't be dominated. You're going to show them. You're going to knock us big fellows right down into the gutter so we'll have to look up to you. Right now, John, you feel like telling me to go to hell, don't you?"

It was true and I shook my head.

"Say it aloud. Say, 'Go to hell, Barclay. It's not your business that I'm a pint-sized runt.' You don't know, fellow, how it's going to help you to tell me right out loud what you feel." He spoke gently. His eyes had grown moist with earnestness. "Don't be ashamed because you're not satisfied with yourself. All humans aspire to perfection. We all loathe our imperfections; we hide them as if they were sins. No man can escape the essential truth about himself; no man is ever free of shame and resentment until he sees the truth fully and shares the truth." He raised his head and looked about, blinking as if he had come out of darkness into sunlight.

Munn watched, titillated by my embarrassment. The lavatory mirror reflected his smirk. Barclay noticed and closed the door.

"You've read my book, John. Then you know me for what I am. No man since Cain has ever loathed himself so violently as Noble Barclay. And look at me today," he smiled as if he and I alone knew the story which had been printed in 6,182,454 copies and sixteen languages. Then, because I had not offered the expected response, he asked in a subdued voice, "You've read the Introduction, haven't you?"

"The Introduction," Munn said pontifically, "is the greatest document on human despair ever written."

"We're keeping you from lunch, aren't we, Ed?" Barclay wet his lips.

Munn's grin faded. In some subtle way which he could not understand the dog had displeased the master. He shook his head, mumbled something about liking to have his meals on time, and left, tail dragging.

I wondered whether I ought to leave, too, but Barclay was not through with me. He seated himself on the big red leather couch, and indicated that he wanted me to sit beside him.

"Angry?"

"No," I said.

"Why do you lie about it?" He threw back his head and laughed. "If you weren't sore, you wouldn't be human." Leaning forward, his big, square-fingered hand on my knee, he whispered, "I was right though. Confess it. You hate being a runt, don't you?"

Rain beat against the windows. The room had grown dark. Barclay switched on a lamp. His movements were powerful and precise. He let his hand fall to my knee again and his dark, restless eyes searched my face. The lamplight made me feel naked.

"Go on, say it. Tell me I was right. You've always wanted to beat the big guys, haven't you?"

"I guess so."

"You'll feel a heck of a lot better when you've said it aloud. You won't be sore at me anymore. You'll know that I know what's at the bottom of John Ansell, just the way I know Ansell knows what's at the bottom of Noble Barclay."

Although I had read that ultimate essay on human despair and knew the brighter facts about his regeneration, I was not so sure I knew what was at the bottom of Noble Barclay. Sincere prophet or clever charlatan? Twenty weeks after I had come to work for him I was no more certain than at my first interview.

To keep him from eavesdropping on anymore of my inhibitions I said quickly, "Okay, you're right."

"Good for you, John!" He extended his hand. His face was ingenuous, shy and happy. He clasped my hand with a powerful fist. He had won the round, but his pleasure in triumph was so naïve that I was not only free of resentment but glad I had acknowledged my shame.

He had too much sense to rub it in. Our interview was over. "Sorry we can't lunch together, but the Senator is waiting. Some other time, I hope." He put on his camel's hair coat, fished a pair of pigskin gloves out of the pocket, smoothed his white hair. As we went out he graciously held the door for me.

We parted in the reception room. At the door of his private elevator, Barclay gave me a mock salute and a friendly grin. I felt fine. As I walked through the deserted general office, a lonely stenographer eating lunch out of a paper bag looked at me and smiled. My self-esteem grew. I was a pint-sized runt and I wasn't afraid to say it aloud. I was a good guy; people liked me. Noble Barclay was sorry he couldn't have lunch with me. My hand was sore from the clasp of that big fist.

On my way to lunch I hurried, whistling, through the tunnel that led from the foyer of the Barclay Building to Ye Olde English Grille. The tunnel was damp and cold as if the wind and rain had penetrated its stone walls. I heard women's voices, became aware of dark silhouettes.

A bulky shape blocked my path. Until she spoke I did not recognize my good friend, Miss Kaufman. She told her cronies to go on while she stopped to ask about the Wilson story.

"It's out," I told her.

"Why?"

"Mr. Barclay doesn't want to run it."

"Doesn't he like it?"

"He thinks it's great, one of the greatest stories ever written for *Truth and Crime*."

"Then why won't he let you run it?"

I couldn't answer. After all that had happened it was still an unsolved mystery.

Miss Kaufman's questions had shattered me. I felt inadequate and no longer the sort of man whose smile brings sunshine into the lives of lonely stenographers. The glow had faded and Barclay's approval was no more than an ironic symbol of my defeat.

As I entered the Grille, Barclay employees stopped eating to stare at the man who had defied the boss. From the round table at which the editors ate, Lola Manfred beckoned. I did not hurry to the seat she had saved for me. Through the smoke and steam of the restaurant I saw that Eleanor was not in her accustomed place.

A waitress noticed and, with a jerk of her thumb, guided my glance. Although the Grille was situated in a structural steel building, it had been decorated to look like a seventeenth-century English inn. Heavy beams and plaster columns divided the room into a series of dim caves. Lights were hidden in lantern-like fixtures shaded in cloudy amber.

Eleanor waved. She sat alone at the small table. She had on a black suit. It was tailored and severe, but there was nothing severe about Eleanor. She wore a white blouse with a lace collar and a bib or frill of lace cascading down the front. As I came close I decided that today I would tell her I thought her the most beautiful woman on earth.

"Hello," I muttered as I stood awkwardly beside the table. Opposite her a tilted chair showed that a seat had been reserved.

"Would you like to sit here?" Eleanor said.

"Thanks." I tried to be nonchalant, as though I ate lunch with her every day.

"Were you fired?"

"Oh! That's it. I'm the man of the hour. Everyone in the place is talking about me."

She smiled. "You hardly made a secret of your feelings about the Munn memo. What happened?"

"I wrote a story and thought it was good. Your father doesn't want to run it."

"Why not?"

The waitress handed me a bill of fare. I pretended not to know what I wanted. Eleanor's question embarrassed me. I had been crazy about her since that August noon when she had first smiled at me across the table where editors and privileged editorial assistants lunched. Evidently Eleanor had liked me, too, for she had gone to lunch with me the next week. I had taken her to a quiet, expensive restaurant and everything had been wonderful until I asked her about her father, her life with the Truth-Sharer and how it felt to be the Truth Girl. That had been a terrible mistake. She was sensitive on the subject. Since then I had been obliged to find excuses to visit Lola Manfred in the *Truth and Love* office, hoping Lola's assistant would be there. Sometimes at night I waited in the corridor until Eleanor came along, and rode downstairs with her in the elevator and made excuses about dining in Greenwich Village, so I could sit beside her on the bus.

"Why wouldn't Father let you run it?" Eleanor persisted. "What kind of story was it?"

They had piped-in music at the Grille. A brass band played the *Fledermaus* waltz. Dishes clattered on tin trays and all around us people were watching. We were the most interesting couple in the place, Barclay's daughter and the guy who had defied her father and her father's Number One stooge. I did not mention the Warren G. Wilson story to Eleanor that day because I wanted to talk of something pleasanter than my quarrel with her old man.

I said, "It must be Thursday. What's there about Thursday that always makes them play Viennese waltzes?"

"All right, skip it. But you weren't fired?"

"Would you care if I had been?"

Eleanor looked over my shoulder at Lola Manfred. They exchanged some sort of signal.

"What's that about?" I wanted to know.

"I won a dollar on you. I bet you wouldn't be fired. Lola was sure that Ed Munn would stick his knife into your back."

"I'm glad I didn't take any bets on myself. I'd have been on Lola's side. For a while I was seeing myself in the Sunday *Times*—'Young Man, Editorial Experience, Will Travel . . .'"

"Were you frightened?"

"Frightened isn't the word. Realistic."

"I'm glad you weren't fired, but I'm gladder that you risked it. Most of the others around here—" her scornful glance included them all, Henry Roe of *Truth Magazine*, Tony Shaw of *Truth and Beauty*, Lola Manfred, the associate editors, sub-editors, readers, and Edward Everett Munn who was eating health salad at a side table "—most of them think only of their jobs. They show off a lot and sometimes they laugh at Father. But when they get upstairs they're afraid to express their opinions. They're yes-men. You'll never be a yes-man if you live to be a hundred."

I was glad I had defied Munn and stood up to Barclay. Eleanor admired me. I ate up her praise like a two-dollar minute steak and begged for more. "Yes-men don't die in gutters. I'm looking for a nice sunny gutter with running water."

"I'd rather have you die in the gutter than be like those others."

She said it defiantly, as if she were telling her father and all the yes-men how she felt about gutters. I thought of her standing up to Munn and the office stooges, defending and praising the lone rebel, John Miles Ansell. I wanted to thank her by saying something gallant and wonderful.

"You're looking extra beautiful today. More beautiful than yesterday or last week or the first time I saw you."

"Don't kid me. I'm not even pretty."

Eleanor's face was a contradiction, delicately modeled with a fine, faintly aquiline nose, almost hollow cheeks and a broad firm jaw. The jaw saved her from fragility. I liked the contrast between the delicate nose and the definite chin. Her eyes were set deep and heavily shadowed. At the first glance they seemed dark, but it was always pleasant to discover and rediscover their gray transparency. The shadowed eyes gave her a dark look so that she seemed like a brunette, but her skin was pale ivory and all the small curls around her forehead fair enough to show she had been born blonde.

"You're dazzling."

"Because I bet on you?"

"Eleanor," I began. "Eleanor . . ."

"Yes?"

"Eleanor, we ought to celebrate tonight, you and I."

"Celebrate what?"

"Gutters. Or not getting fired. Anything you like, just so we celebrate."

She laughed again. Eleanor was glad I had asked her out to dinner. All the time I'd been seeking excuses to visit the *Truth and Love* office and waiting in corridors, Eleanor had expected me to ask her for a date. And I had thought the warmth and graciousness was just natural charm, that she would have greeted any other man, Henry Roe or Tony Shaw or even Edward Everett Munn, with the same measure of enthusiasm.

"Tonight then, Eleanor?"

"Tonight."

We ordered ice cream and drank two cups of coffee, so that we'd have an excuse to linger at the table. We sat through *Tides from the Vienna Woods, Southern Roses* and *Vienna Blood.* When we left the restaurant was almost empty. I pulled out Eleanor's chair and held her coat. When my hand brushed against her arm she quivered slightly and pulled away.

The strains of *Vienna Blood* followed us through the tunnel.

"May I have the waltz, Madame?"

"You're crazy."

I held out my arms and we waltzed down the tunnel. She had always seemed tall to me, but when we danced together I noticed that the shoulder of her plaid coat was lower than my shoulder. This fact delighted me. Tall girls make me sensitive about my size.

Eleanor gave me her address and told me to call for her at seven. I went back to the office and phoned Jean Pierre's. I told Gustav to save the best table and select the choicest duck. I told him we'd start with champagne cocktails. I owned the world.

The phone rang. It was the Production Department.

"They want to know when the new Unsolved Mystery's coming through," Miss Kaufman said.

"So they've discovered my Pyrrhic defeat?"

"Everyone in the office always finds out your business before you do. Once when I was working on *Truth in Pictures*, Mr. Barclay decided to kill the magazine. Mr. Munn was supposed to tell the editor, but he forgot, and a whole issue was printed before anyone let us know we didn't exist."

"Wasn't he fired?"

"Mr. Munn is never fired. Production's still on the wire, Mr. Ansell. What shall I tell them?"

I promised Production the new copy that night. I should have started working at once, but I felt good and stood idle, my hands in my pockets while I whistled *Vienna Blood*. "Something's happened to you, Mr. Ansell." "What makes you think so, Miss Kaufman?" "You ought to be furious. Working like you did on that Wilson story, checking all the details yourself and writing it so well, and then they want you to substitute some old piece of junk that you throw together in a couple of hours." "That's life. Get me the file on Dot King, please." The Unsolved Mystery was an advertised feature of *Truth and Crime* and had to be included in every issue. There was no time now to get a staff writer on the story, so I decided to write it myself. Fortunately we had used other versions of the case and had the facts on hand. And there were pictures left over from a story in *Truth and Love*, June, 1937. We used a stock layout and sent the photos to the Production Department with Rush stickers on them. We had to get a Rush release on the story, too. Since he had got his way about the Wilson piece, Munn graciously allowed the new manuscript to go through his office, sight unseen. We needed a sight-unseen release from Mr. Barclay so that we could send copy to the printer as fast as it came out of the typewriter.

"You'd better get Mr. Barclay's release yourself, Mr. Ansell. You know Grace Eccles. If I ask a favor she'll probably stall until Mr. Barclay's gone for the day and she can get me blamed for inefficiency. But if you ask her, we'll have it in five minutes."

"What makes you think so?"

Miss Kaufman raised a shaggy eyebrow. "You're an attractive young man."

"Okay," I said. "I'll exercise my charms."

Mr. Barclay's secretary smiled at me over her typewriter. She was a scrawny female with a rough skin that she tried to conceal with layers of cosmetics. The structure of curls on her head looked like carved mahogany. She swung around in her swivel chair, clasped her long white hands and looked expectant. I leaned over the desk as I told her that I needed help in overcoming an insurmountable obstacle, and added plaintively that this was an appeal to her well-known generosity.

White hands fluttered. "Anything I can do for you, Mr. Ansell, will give me the most profound pleasure."

"Would you have the courage to approach Mr. Barclay and ask him a favor for me?" I gave her my most soulful glance. "I need a sight-unseen release on the Unsolved Mystery. We're using the Dot King story . . ."

"I know all about it, Mr. Ansell," she put in quickly, so I should know that no detail of office business escaped her.

I handed her the release form. "Tell Mr. Barclay I promise to make the story exactly like all the other stories we've ever run. And I positively guarantee, Miss Eccles, not to use any dirty words."

"Oh, Mr. Ansell, what a sense of humor! You must teach me to laugh." Miss Eccles trilled her pleasure like an intoxicated canary. Sighing, she settled down to business again. "I'll bring this in to him myself, just as soon as he's off the wire. He's on the phone now. Washington, you know."

While I waited I wandered around the reception room, looking at pictures of Barclay and his family. One of the old photographs showed him, magnificent in bathing trunks, displaying his muscles to an adoring little girl. She was skinny and soft-boned with the long legs and puny arms of early adolescence.

"Someone certainly enjoyed his luncheon," cooed Miss Eccles.

I kept my face toward the wall.

"I congratulate you on your taste, Mr. Ansell. What a lovely human being! So sane, so healthy, so democratic. And not afraid of life, is she? *His* influence, don't you think? As the twig is bent, the tree's inclined."

"Look, Miss Eccles," I said, turning from the picture and hurrying toward her desk. "You can help me a lot if you will."

"Anything for you, Mr. Ansell. There may be obstacles and handicaps in the way of our desires, but what is achievement without struggle? Let me offer you my hand over the rough places."

She held out her hand, letting it droop gracefully at the wrist. I needed a few seconds to recover. Waiting, Miss Eccles performed a few more Delsarte exercises with her hands.

"Miss Eccles," I began slowly, "can you tell me why Mr. Barclay rejected the Warren G. Wilson story?"

Miss Eccles' hands fell like rocks. Her chest was as flat as a washboard and in action it looked even duller.

"The Warren G. Wilson story," I repeated.

The washboard continued its rise and fall. "I don't know what you're talking about, Mr. Ansell."

"Come, come. Nothing in this office escapes your vigilant notice. The Wilson story, the Unsolved Mystery of the Month, the story the boss rejected . . ."

A buzzer sounded. Miss Eccles picked up the release form and started toward Mr. Barclay's office. "He's off the wire. I'll see about your release. You needn't wait, Mr. Ansell. I'll send it over by boy."

I went back to my office. The Dot King files were waiting on my desk. I had a lot of work to finish that day. Four thousand words before I had dinner with Eleanor. I decided to leave at six, so that I could change and shave before I called for her. If the story was not ready, I'd return late that night after I had taken Eleanor home.

The red-haired office boy brought me the release form signed by Noble Barclay. I tried to concentrate on Dot King, but it was a tired story, long unsolved, and who cared?

"Miss Kaufman, what do you think of the murder of Warren G. Wilson?"

"It's an Unsolved Mystery. Unsolved Mysteries stay unsolved. The murderers are never discovered."

"Am I crazy or could there be some personal reason for Mr. Barclay's not wanting the story printed?"

Miss Kaufman's cheeks grew fruitier. "I've seen five editors leave with nervous breakdowns. They're always the nice ones." She marched out of the office carrying a towel and her soapbox.

In two minutes she was back. "Something's going on around here. The Ladies' Room has been locked for twenty minutes."

"Must be hard on the ladies," I remarked, and started typing noisily to show that I had settled down to work.

I wrote two sentences. Rain beat against the windows. It had been pouring for two days and everything felt soggy. Wind shrieked through the airshaft: I jerked the paper out of my typewriter, crushed it and threw it in the wastebasket. It was then twenty past four and more than two hours since I had seen Eleanor.

"I think I'll have a cup of tea," I said guiltily. There was no reason why I had to offer excuses to my secretary, but I was ashamed because I should have stayed at my desk until I had done a little work on the Dot King story.

As I crossed the general office I noticed the silence. No typewriters clicked. The stenographers had left their desks to crowd in the narrow corridor that led to the Ladies' Room. I crossed to the *Truth and Love* office.

The door was open. Lola Manfred was there, smoking and reading a manuscript, her feet on the desk. She looked at me through a haze of smoke and asked, "Would you want your wife to confess her premarital experiences?"

"I have no wife and she's had no pre-marital experiences."

"You can never tell," Lola said. "In *Truth and Love* the man always thinks the girl is undefiled and then she's neurotic or ill and has to dig out the truth, confess to him in a dim room, otherwise their marriage has no chance. Secrets are a festering sore, Johnnie. You've worked for Truth Publications long enough to . . ."

"Where's Eleanor?"

Lola looked around the office as if I had asked for a paper clip. "I don't know. She's been gone for a long time. Are you in love with her? I hope . . ."

I escaped. The crowd around the Ladies' Room had been increased by office boys, advertising solicitors, bookkeepers from the offices on the floor below. The superintendent of the building passed me. He carried a giant ring from which hung a single small key. I thought of the key ring that Mr. Semple, the hotel manager, had carried on the day Warren G. Wilson's body was discovered.

The superintendent pushed through the crowd and thrust his key into the lock of the Ladies' Room door. Somebody cried, "Oh!" as Grace Eccles came out. She stood in the door, startled by the glances and exclamations of curiosity. Then she raised her head and swept through like a queen of tragedy while humble stenographers and bookkeepers' assistants cleared a path.

A few seconds later Eleanor appeared in the door. Her face was like marble and her painted mouth looked black. I spoke to her, but she passed without a sign of recognition. She had grown taller and more brunette. I tried to catch hold of her arm, but she curved through the crowd and disappeared.

The girls whispered and chattered. Some went into the Ladies' Room. Others returned to their desks. Typewriters began their clatter. The door of *Truth and Lave* was closed tight.

I went back to my desk. The storm had lightened, but raindrops still trickled down the window. I put a fresh page in my typewriter, but I could not work. I was thinking about murder. Between college and the Army I had earned my living by writing crime stories, but murder has always been a remote horror, no more terrifying than ghost stories told in a lighted room. Warren G. Wilson's story had moved closer. He had been no criminal whose way of life called for violence, but a man of my own sort, bookish, fond of music and good food. I could no more imagine an enemy plotting his death than I could believe that someone should want to murder me.

At last I started to work. At five-fifteen, when other Barclay employees were washing their hands and covering their typewriters, I had written exactly one page. Miss Kaufman offered to stay and work with me.

"Never mind," I said. "I'm not staying. I have a dinner date and I'll come back later. Leave word for the night man that I'll want to get in."

An office boy dropped an envelope in my basket. It was a manila office envelope with a blue memo form inside. This is what it said:

Memorandum
From the office of:
To:
Date:

Dearest J.A.

Please forgive me but I can't possibly make it tonight. Give me a rain check, please, and don't be angry. I know you'll understand.

E.B.
P.S. Don't ask why. Don't ever.

I was stunned. Why should I understand? What did Eleanor think? I'm not psychic. It was our first date and I had been stood up. Why? She had seemed enthusiastic, as if our first date were important to her, too. Now I was to understand a crazy, incoherent note. Mine not to reason why, mine not to make reply. Hell, I wasn't the brave six hundred.

"I'm going to find out. No woman can do that to me. Understand, my neck! What does she think?"

In this mood I stormed into the *Truth and Love* office. It was empty. Neither Eleanor's plaid coat nor Lola Manfred's frowsy fur cape hung on the costumer. Both desks were neat, both typewriters covered.

Miss Eccles was at the telephone when I rushed into her office. She held one hand over the mouthpiece while she said, "This is an important call. Long distance. Could you wait outside, Mr. Ansell?"

I waited, pacing the corridor. People were leaving the office. Their coats and raincoats were damp from the morning's downpour. Everything smelled musty. Tony Shaw stopped to tell me that he was hurrying to meet an actress for cocktails at the Plaza.

The light in Miss Eccles' office was switched off. I left Tony and ran in, turned on the light and caught Miss Eccles with her coat and hat in her hands.

"Trying to sneak out on me, Miss Eccles?"

"No, indeed. I completely forgot about your wanting to see me. I usually take this at night," she nodded toward the door of the private elevator. "The other's so crowded, you know."

"What did you tell Eleanor in the Ladies' Room?"

Her pale eyes blinked and the washboard chest began to rise and fall.

"What did you tell Eleanor, Miss Eccles?"

Barclay's door opened. He had on the camel's hair coat, the pigskin gloves, and in his right arm he carried an expensive briefcase.

"I'm leaving now, Miss Eccles. How's it coming, Ansell? You got my release, didn't you?"

Miss Eccles' eyes followed hopefully as he crossed the office. But he had no more duties for her that day, and did not think of asking if she wanted to ride with him in the private elevator. As the automatic doors slid open he called, "Good night," and the doors closed.

Miss Eccles chattered, struggling for breath. "A great man, a wonderful human being, absolutely devoted to his work. It's a privilege to work with him, to be so intimate with one of the great figures of our day, a man whose name will live in history and whose philosophy . . ."

"Look, Miss Eccles, I don't care about his greatness. I want to know what you told Eleanor in the Ladies' Room and why it happened just after I'd asked you about the Wilson story."

She gave me the look of a stricken doe. I was ruthless. Grabbing bony shoulders I shook her until her teeth chattered. Her face was stricken, and I remembered Lillian Gish's face in an old movie, *Broken Blossoms*.

"Tell me."

"The secret is not my own."

Her body remained rigid, but her head turned on the thin stalk of her neck. She looked at the wall that was broken by the copper and chromium door of Noble Barclay's private elevator. This door opened.

"I think I'll leave this," Barclay said, gesturing with the hand that held the briefcase. "Can't work tonight. Wife's just home from California, you know." For emphasis he set the briefcase upon his secretary's desk. "Going home, Grace? I'm driving uptown, can I give you a lift?"

He waited at the elevator door. She glanced at me over her shoulder, and it was as if the angels had swooped down and rescued her at the very portals of hell. This time the elevator door closed with a bang.

I worked until seven o'clock, went downstairs and had two Martinis and two lamb chops at the Grille. When I returned to the office there was no sign of life in the place. All the lights had been turned out and the darkness was like something solid. I switched on a small light and hurried to the *Truth and Crime* office.

Noble Barclay did not ask his editors to work in sordid surroundings. "One incentive for joining us," he had said when I came to talk to him about the job, "is the cheerful atmosphere of our offices. We believe that creative people are more productive under harmonious influences. All of our private offices have been done over recently by one of the best interior decorators in the business, under Mrs. Barclay's personal supervision."

My office represented the decorator's blue period. The walls were gray but the chairs had been upholstered in some shaggy blue material, the picture frames and lampshades matched, and even the Thermos jug and drinking glass were of a harmonizing blue plastic. The effect under artificial light was melancholy.

On my blue desk blotter lay the first page of the new Unsolved Mystery. For a practiced hack like me it should not have been hard to finish the story. I had only to paraphrase one of the old versions, dress the skeleton lushly with descriptions of the kept woman's apartment, jewels, wardrobe and pantry, add some hot passages about her lover's caresses, and then take the joy out of the titillating paragraphs by emphasizing the wages of sin. Our readers were always happy to ponder virtuously the joys of evil.

I was bored but conscientious and managed twelve pages of the drivel. As I paused to rest and smoke a cigarette, I found myself thinking of Miss Eccles and how her pale lips had worked and her stricken eyes had narrowed as she told me that she was guarding a secret. It was Barclay's secret, I was sure, and I was positive, too, that he had not returned to leave his briefcase but had been listening behind the elevator door while I questioned his secretary. For a man like Noble Barclay, the millionaire, the famous author and publisher, the Messiah in the camel's hair overcoat, the whole thing seemed absurd.

I had tried to understand Barclay; I had read his book and considered his philosophy. But to me he was a caricature philosopher, Superman combined with Freud, Dale Carnegie selling Buchman's Moral Rearmament according to the methods of Bernarr MacFadden. Barclay's creed was like Buchmanism without God; like MacFadden minus muscles. Instead of prayer he used auto-suggestion and self-hypnotism.

I finished my cigarette and automatically lighted another. The storm was over, the night air clear. A high, angry wind whined through the airshaft. My tongue was heavy, my throat dry and I felt as if I had just awakened with a bad hangover.

The water in the blue Thermos was cool and refreshing. I lit a fresh cigarette and read the page in my typewriter. It seemed remarkably good. Suddenly my typewriter began to move away. The wall behind it retreated, too. My desk had begun to rock, the floor to tip, the whole building to pitch like a small ship on a furious sea. Clinging to the arms of my chair I lifted myself like a cripple. At the first step my legs unhinged and I slid along a glazed surface.

After centuries of darkness I lay in a berth on an express train headed for a rock cliff at the rate of ninety thousand miles a second. We hit the cliff; I was not crushed to death but lifted, gently, out of the berth and carried on clouds through unending space. A siren clanged. Fire engines, I thought, and then I was the siren, the fire engine, the rubber-tired hack. My body was moldy from years in the grave, but I was not dead because my eyes discovered streaks of moving light. My siren clanged again; the blue streak changed to a white radiance and the radiance was shattered into a million trillion slivers.

A weight lay upon my chest and the thing that clasped my wrist was a human hand. Remote and pontifical a voice sounded.

"We can't be sure until we've got the analysis but I saw one just like this when I was interning. Bichloride of mercury. The patient died."

PART TWO
Testimonial

by Grace Eccles

"Truth should not be hoarded like miser's gold but shared as freely as the warmth of the summer sun. But the only Truth that is yours to spend and share is the Truth About Yourself. The secrets of another person's life are his own, and while you may be aware of the harm he is doing himself and others by hoarding them, his secrets are no more yours to give away than his home, his money and his personal possessions."

My Life Is Truth
NOBLE BARCLAY

When the history of this generation is written there will appear high upon the roll call of contemporary immortals the name of Noble Barclay. I have had the singular honor of associating for seven years with this great man, five of which were spent in such close intimacy that I have often wondered if his wife knew him as well as his secretary.*

Others have worshipped the genius of Noble Barclay. I have constantly and consistently adored the human being. Not only had he formulated and originated a new creed for living, but he practiced what he preached to the final word. Cynics there are who doubt his sincerity, but I, who had better opportunity than any other to observe his smallest actions, have never seen him deviate from a rigid interpretation of his philosophy.

Let me first introduce myself, Grace Jacqueline Eccles, forty-seven years of age (in this as in everything else, I am completely truthful), independent, self-sustaining, mentally and morally free.

---

* Miss Eccles' confession was written at my request. I had to flatter her extensively to get her to do it, and I have not yet told her why I wanted her version of the story. J. M. Ansell, June, 1946.

What a contrast to that Grace Eccles of a decade ago! Not only was I inhibited and narrow-minded, but also unemployed. The latter was not wholly my fault. Our country was in the midst of the so-called Depression. Few positions were available and those were usually bestowed upon younger girls of obvious charms who looked as if they would perform other than the conventional duties of a private secretary.

At this time, depressed, melancholy, unsure of myself, and devoid of feminine sex pride, I was indeed a sorry-looking individual. I did not make the most of myself. Instead of drawing attention to my best features (many friends have told me my hands are a fit subject for a painter), I thought only of my deficiencies, foremost among which was a poor complexion. At that time it was pallid and marred by acne due to a malady from which I constantly suffered. I was too modest then to admit that I was victim to the commonest of Nature's tricks, but now today, free and without guilt or shame, I can say aloud that I endured the tortures of constipation.

Even in these dark hours, however, my normally unselfish nature asserted itself. Unable to help myself, I tried to help others. There lived in our neighborhood a girl younger than myself and more unfortunate in that she was blind. According to stories whispered by scandalmongers she had none to blame but herself for this tragic fate. It was said that she had consorted with a married man whose vengeful wife waited one night until her husband and this girl came out of a bar and dashed acid in the girl's face. As a result of shock and

remorse the girl went almost insane but she was saved by the tender nursing and devotion of her dear mother. Her eyesight, however, was lost. She was taken to see several world-famous specialists, but they shrugged their shoulders and shook their learned heads. The optic nerve had been destroyed and she would never see again.

In addition to this tragedy the girl also suffered the belief that her face was hideously scarred. This was untrue but no one could convince her. In her mind's eye this girl saw a countenance so distorted that none could look upon it without revulsion. As she had been extremely pretty and consequently a vain person, this cross was almost too heavy for her frail shoulders.

I tried to bring some brightness into the life of this tragic creature, and whenever I was not immersed in personal melancholy or seeking employment, I spent my time reading aloud to her. One day by a coincidence, which some would call a minor accident but which I prefer to think of as a divinely guided miracle, a copy of *My Life Is Truth* came into my hands. I had picked it up by mistake, leaving the copy of a light novel by Kathleen Norris.

I glanced over the Introduction. It was strong meat. At first I was dubious for it seemed that no mortal could suffer what Noble Barclay had gone through in the first fifty-seven pages. What inspired me to go on reading was the reaction of my audience.

When I had come to the last sentence in the Introduction (just the Introduction, not even the philosophical portions) this girl said to me in a trembling voice, "Grace, it's absolutely true what people say about me. I have been lying to my dear mother and my good friends. I was fooling around, as they say, with Mr. L. Not only that, but I tried to take him away from his wife. God help me, I never confessed this to a living soul but you, Grace, but I swear it's true. I feel much lighter now that I've said it, as if I'd cast off a heavy load."

Unfortunately her mother entered at this moment and we shut up like clams. Although her mother had been a devoted nurse, she had never ceased abusing her daughter for immoral conduct. I left immediately, the precious book clutched tight in my tremulous hand.

While I was helping my sister wash the supper dishes our telephone rang. It was the blind girl. Her mother had gone to an Eastern Star meeting and she wanted to talk to me. I hurried to her at once, bringing Noble Barclay's immortal work. We did not read much, however, because I listened while she poured out her heart. She confessed everything about her relationship to Mr. L., from the first caress to the pleasure she had experienced in intimate association and her evil desire to get rid of his wife. At times her emotion was so great that I had to bring her blackberry cordial from the bathroom cabinet. But she was almost in an ecstasy, and to make a long story short, she not only recovered her sight miraculously within twenty-four hours, but soon afterwards married a prosperous automobile salesman, and is now living happily in Birmingham, Alabama.

My own miracle, while not so sensational, worked such a change in my sensitive and shrinking nature that timidity was transformed to self-confidence, foolish and desperate fears were overcome, and within a fortnight I found myself the incumbent of a part-time job. In addition I was cured almost immediately of the malady from which I had suffered for so many desolate years, and my complexion soon afterwards became clearer.

All this happiness and good fortune were due to a single cause, my belief in Truth as expounded by Noble Barclay. Day and night I sought some way of expressing my gratitude. A second miracle brought me that opportunity. I happened to hear through an employment agency that there was a vacancy in the Stenographic Department of none other than Truth Publications. I applied at once for this position, and when the Head of the Department heard that I was not only one of Mr. Barclay's followers, but would be satisfied with $16.50 a week, I was hired on the spot.

For more than a year I was but a cog in the wheel of his vast enterprises. I confess now that I was shocked to discover that many employees were not believers in his principles, and wondered why he did not insist upon belief as a prerequisite of employment. How narrow-minded of me and how much broader his policy! He would never make arbitrary rules for his help but was willing to give all the same opportunity. The Head of the Department was such a cynic that I felt privately that she did not deserve the honor of that position which she managed to hold because she got maximum work out of the girls and found many excuses to dock those who were guilty of small infractions of the rules.

Once again I was the vessel of what others may call chance or coincidence, but which I prefer to think of as a small miracle. Why was I lucky enough to be sitting in the office eating a box lunch when Mr. Barclay suddenly was seized with the desire to dictate while his secretary was enjoying his noon meal at a restaurant!

Up to this moment I had not met Mr. Barclay personally. With his almost omnipotent glance he noticed my tremors. "You're not afraid of me?" he asked in the kindest voice in the world.

"I adore you," I replied humbly.

This rejoinder from a member of the cynical Stenographic Department must have startled him, but he was self-contained and with infinite patience and tolerance, he asked my name. That was not all I told him! Careless of his valuable time, selfishly concerned with my own emotions, I poured out the whole story of my conversion. Ringing a bell he summoned several of his aides, and asked me to repeat for them the story of my introduction to his philosophy and the incidental episode concerning my ex-blind friend. They asked her name and address, promising they would not embarrass her with publicity anent her previous affair and assuring me that they meant only to confirm my happy story.

A few months after this, destiny called me to the position which I have enjoyed for seven years. It was not long before I gained Mr. Barclay's confidence and was able to keep him informed daily as to the undercurrents in the office, the crude and impolitic remarks of the envious and cynical, and the true nature of those who pretended to admire their employer. With an increase in my responsibilities came several substantial raises in salary. Mr. Barclay is more than generous with those upon whose loyalty he can depend.

Let me add here that in his personal life as well, I found Mr. Barclay generous to a fault. Among his multitudinous friends, none knew that every month he privately and secretly gave away two thousand dollars in cash. So great was his modesty that none knew of this except I, who kept his personal checkbook. These secret philanthropies were never entered as anything but petty cash withdrawals and he never tried, as many would, to deduct the sum from his income tax. Once when I questioned the practical value of his scruples he took me to task by reminding me that the recipients of such charity would be embarrassed were their names known to anyone except himself.

"How grateful they must be for your generosity and understanding," I remarked.

"We cannot always expect gratitude, Miss Eccles."

I am often filled with melancholy as I ponder the cynicism and distrust with which others regard the nobility of this man. But I comfort myself with the thought that he is so big that our little natures do not distress him overmuch. Someday all humans will learn to face and acknowledge Truth, and then war and illness will disappear from the earth, and there will be no more drunkenness or poverty, and life will be one sweet song.

Because I have been so close to this great man, Mr. John Ansell has asked me to contribute a chapter to his book on Noble Barclay. That this request flattered my humble person I admit frankly, since I have had little time in my life for literary pursuits. I admit also to some bewilderment anent the subject of my reminiscences. Why does Mr. Ansell particularly request my memories of the "incident" regarding Mr. Warren G. Wilson? But, as Mr. Ansell suggests, it is ever the duty of one who knows the truth to challenge the spread of rumor.

On that fatal Friday in May, I returned from luncheon at my usual time. No sooner had I entered my office than the telephone rang and one of the switchboard operators informed me that she had a message for my chief. A Mr. Warren G. Wilson had called to say that the date was on and he expected Mr. Barclay at his apartment that evening. As is my habit, I went into Mr. Barclay's office and made a notation on his desk calendar.

Mr. Barclay had been lunching with the Senator, and did not return to his office until 4 p.m. A few minutes afterwards he buzzed me.

"Where did this come from?" he demanded and pointed to the lone message on his calendar pad.

"It came while I was at luncheon. I received it from the switchboard," I replied.

"Thank you, Miss Eccles," he said briefly. Jerking the page off the calendar pad, he tore it into minute particles and deposited them in the wastebasket.

Evidently Mr. Barclay communicated with Mr. Munn on the inter-office telephone, for I had hardly returned to my desk when that individual came hurrying through my office and disappeared into the private sanctum.

My duties were interrupted a second time when Mr. Barclay commended me to summon his daughter. Eleanor was not at her desk in the office of *Truth and Love* Magazine. I was to locate her immediately. After a few unsuccessful attempts I discovered that she was in our Photographic Studio, helping to pose models for illustrations. A few moments later, in response to my request, she hastened through my ante-room and disappeared, also, in her father's office.

Their conference did not break up until after six o'clock and I saw no more of them that day. The incident, no doubt, would have been erased from my mind had not a curious coincidence followed. That being Friday, the next day was Saturday. Mr. Barclay was absent from the office. Certainly a man so unstinting of his energy was entitled to an extra half holiday each week, which he usually spent in the country with his wife and small sons, while faithful myrmidons kept watch over his affairs from nine until 1 p.m.

Eleanor was also absent that morning, but unofficially. She had simply failed to appear in the office. For that reason I was involved in an argument with the Photographic Studio. Shortly after I had settled at my desk, Mrs. Harden, who is in charge of the Studio Property Room, telephoned to inquire about a gun.

Yes, a gun. This may sound melodramatic but it is a comic facet of our work in the confessional magazine field. Since many of these stories published in our magazines are true confessions of crime, it is necessary in posing illustrative photographs to use firearms. And in order to have this equipment when necessary, we have an ever so amusing little arsenal adjacent to the studio. Although the guns are not loaded, they are considered lethal weapons and when an editor or sub-editor or assistant, in posing pictures, wishes to use such property, he signs a requisition. The love story that Eleanor was working on evidently required the pictorial display of a .22 (what this is, I confess, I have never been certain). The point was that she had this pistol in her hands when summoned to her father's office.

Mrs. Lola Manfred, Eleanor's superior on *Truth and Love* Magazine, reported that the gun was not in the office they shared. She suggested to Mrs. Harden that Eleanor might have carried the gun into Mr. Barclay's office and left it there. Hence, I was involved in the search. No gun was visible. I hunted high and low, but was unable to find anything of that description.

Let me say here, before any further suspicion is engendered in the reader's mind, that the gun was discovered that very Saturday morning on a window sill in the Photographic Studio. Mrs. Harden had telephoned Mr. Munn about it, asking if he had seen the gun in Eleanor's hand. He replied in the negative, but offered to assist in the search. Shortly after the weapon was discovered and we all had a big laugh over our "gun hunt."

It was not until the following Monday morning that I learned from the newspapers that Mr. Wilson—yes, our own Mr. Warren G. Wilson—had been murdered. In self-defense, let me remark that it seemed perfectly natural for me to comment on this to Mr. Barclay.

"Did you see the morning papers?" I inquired. "Aren't you shocked about your friend, Mr. Wilson?"

Mr. Barclay, usually the most considerate of employers, snarled at me. "Never mention his name again, Miss Eccles." Not content with that he stamped across my office to the door of his sanctum. "Not to me or anyone else. Do you understand?"

"But, Mr. Barclay," I argued, trying to explain what I considered a normal interest in the sensational occurrence.

"You are never to speak Wilson's name again, neither to me nor anyone else. I never knew the man. He was trying to annoy me. You'll forget the whole incident, Miss Eccles."

It was easier to pledge my word than discipline my unruly thoughts. Each day thereafter Mr. Wilson's name was in the newspapers. I was almost ill with worry. Mr. Barclay's admonitions to silence contradicted the most elementary precepts of his creed. The only explanation with which I could satisfy my gnawing curiosity was that he was shielding another. I repeated and repeated over again his wise words regarding the sacredness of the secrets of others. I realized then that I, also, must conceal what I knew in order to shield some unknown innocent. The pain of such concealment was sweeter when I realized that I suffered for another's sake.

Months passed. The name of Warren G. Wilson was almost buried in my unconscious mind when John Ansell, unwittingly, I believed, chose his murder as the subject for the Unsolved Mystery Department of *Truth and Crime* Magazine. I was not surprised when Mr. Barclay rejected the story. I though the matter would be buried for the nonce. But Mr. Ansell was a rebel in our midst. Challenging authority, he demanded a reason for the rejection of his story. When Mr. Barclay withheld the answer to his impertinent questions, Mr. Ansell tried to force the information out of me.

But Grace Eccles was too clever for him. Using feminine wiles I made a tactful excuse about a telephone call and managed to get rid of that inquisitive little gentleman. Although I gave him no reason to suspect that his questioning had unnerved me, I felt quite ill and knew I could not continue with my duties unless I unburdened myself partially or wholly of the heavy load that had been fermenting within me. The pressure was too great for my fragile consciousness to bear.

Let me add here that I suspected no one of intrigue. At this time I sought nothing more than relief from the pressure of self-distrust. What guilty untruth about myself was I hiding behind the suspicion of others? It would have been most salutary to discuss this matter with Mr. Barclay himself, but since that day when I had promised never again to mention Mr. Wilson's name, I felt that to seek his confidence *on this particular matter* would be tactless.

While I was pondering the matter and watching office personnel through the glass window of my own little domain, I noticed Eleanor Barclay among the girls going to the Ladies' Room. This seemed divine coincidence. Who was more worthy of my confidence than his own daughter, and who could be trusted more completely to guard his interests? In indulging my need for a session of Truth-Sharing with Eleanor Barclay, I felt no qualm of disloyalty.

I followed her to the Ladies' Room. It was my presence, I am sure, that quickly cleared the place of all the stenographers who waste company time smoking and dawdling before the mirrors.

"Eleanor, I must speak to you," I said, locking the door.

"Is it necessary to barricade ourselves?" she inquired flippantly.

"Please do not be cynical, dear," I admonished. "When you know this organization as well as I do, you'll realize how many two-faced people there are in the world. There's no other place in this office where you can be sure of complete privacy."

"But somebody may want to use the toilet."

"I shan't be long," I promised. "I sorely need a short session of Truth-Sharing."

"Is it really necessary?" she asked ungraciously. "I want to leave early today. I'm going to have my hair. done. I've got a dinner date, a particular dinner date, a dinner date I've been wanting for months."

This was inconsiderate, since I had frankly appealed to her for sympathy, but I generously overlooked it on the score that youth must have its fling.

"I have something more important than a dinner date to discuss with you," I rejoined.

"Well, make it snappy," she retorted.

I was careful at the start to explain that I suspected no one of deceit, but was merely trying to purge myself of unworthy emotion. But I had hardly begun to describe my actions in relation to the telephone call when she interrupted.

"Is it true the switchboard operator made a mistake on that call, and gave the message to Mr. Barclay instead of me, or was it you, Grace, playing one of your little tricks?"

Needless to say, I was shocked. "I was not aware until now, Eleanor, that you were acquainted with this Mr. Wilson."

Her cheeks wore an unbecoming flush. "He was calling me," she said. "That's how it all started. But I hope you don't think it has anything to do with the murder."

"Why, Eleanor!" I exclaimed. "That thought never entered my mind. It was simply that your father showed so much emotion over the incident and was so vehement in forbidding me ever to use Mr. Wilson's name again that I . . ."

"Why don't you do what you're told?" she interrupted harshly.

"I have never mentioned his name . . ."

"What do you think you're doing now?"

"Truth-Sharing," I reminded her, "is different. Confessions are sacred. You know as well as I that the secrets of another person's heart, no matter how freely offered, are not yours to disperse."

"Okay," she snapped. "What else do you know?"

Oral truth-sharing has always been an effective cure when I am troubled. No sooner have I purged myself of foolish secrets and distressing fancies than I realize that their only substance was my own fallacious imagining. I felt a great deal better and would have flitted gaily out of the Ladies' Room had not Eleanor caught my arm and squeezed it painfully.

"Now that you've shared with me," she admonished, "never, never, never in your life mention this to anyone else." Her excitement was so intense that she threw her cigarette into one of the wash bowls and leaned against the wall, her face as white as the tiles.

Girls had begun to pound on the door, demanding admission. I took the cigarette stub out of the wash bowl where she had thrown it so thoughtlessly, creating a bad example for the untidy stenographers. With utmost sympathy I tried to help Eleanor unburden herself of those dark secrets that were obviously causing such conflict in her psyche. My efforts were rewarded with a proud and stubborn glance. Locking herself into one of the compartments, Eleanor refused to speak to me or to answer any of my sympathetic questions.

There was more rude pounding on the door and remarks of a vulgar nature were shouted through. Gently I addressed Eleanor, but no answer drifted from her compartment.

I stooped and spoke softly, fixing my eyes upon her thin stockings and frivolous, high-heeled pumps. "Eleanor, my dear, if there's anything buried in your unconsciousness, speak of it, share it with me. Don't let pride or shame inhibit you. Buried truths are festering sores, you know. Share the truth with your old friend . . ."

"Go to hell," she answered ungraciously.

Just then the janitor opened the door. I made my way through the throng of gaping stenographers and returned to my office. I did not see Eleanor again that afternoon but was informed that she had left without finishing her work for the day, probably to have her hair set for that dinner date.

In spite of her lack of sympathy this little session of Truth-Sharing had purged my spirit. For me the unpleasantness would have been completely over had not Mr. Ansell burst into my office a second time that day and demanded to know what information I had imparted to Eleanor in the Ladies' Room. When I refused to

VERA CASPARY

answer, he laid his hands upon me savagely. Had it not been for the fortunate coincidence of Mr. Barclay's appearance, I might have been the victim of brutality.

It was almost as if Mr. Barclay had known instinctively of my predicament. Was it mere chance that ordained my rescue? I prefer to think there was something deeper in the coincidence of Mr. Barclay's taking his briefcase with him that night and then suddenly remembering that he would not need it and deciding to return it to the office. My spirit had cried out to his, silently, and without perceiving the direction of his guidance, he had opened the elevator door at the crucial moment.

His powers of intuition must have perceived my distress, for upon leaving his briefcase upon my desk, he kindly invited me to ride uptown with him in the limousine, a privilege which I do not often enjoy. Such typical Barclay generosity was manifest in another of his kindly gestures the following day when another unfortunate incident darkened the atmosphere of the Barclay Truth Publications.

The office that morning was in a state of the wildest excitement. One of the scrubwomen, arriving at ten o'clock the previous night, had discovered Mr. Ansell unconscious on the floor of his office. Had not the night man summoned the ambulance so promptly and the doctor been so efficient in rendering first-aid, we might have lost our *Truth and Crime* editor.

Mr. Barclay did not arrive at the office until noon that day. Upon seeing me his first words were, "He's all right. Let them know it outside."

"Who's all right?" I inquired, not crediting Mr. Barclay with knowledge of the unhappy situation.

"Ansell," he answered briefly.

"Oh!" I exclaimed. "Then you've heard about it?"

"Where do you think I've been all morning?" he demanded and hurried into his private quarters.

A few moments later I received a summons via the buzzer.

"Will you get me some cash, Miss Eccles? I haven't a penny in my pockets."

"My, someone has been extravagant," I observed, treating the mat-

62

ter in a light vein. "Only yesterday afternoon I cashed five hundred dollars for you."

"Must I answer to you for that?" he asked with unusual severity.

"I was just making an observation," I remarked. "I do not mean to be inquisitive. You've probably been over-generous again. I've been wondering a bit about your penchant for giving away money ever since last May when we quit drawing that monthly two thousand dollars for personal charities."

The expression of his face was enigmatic. I hastened to fetch his checkbook. When he had signed a check and I had sent it down to the bank, he instructed me to ask Mr. Smith to come to his office immediately.

"Which Mr. Smith?" I asked, since there were several of that name among his acquaintances.

"Sometimes you're very irritating," Mr. Barclay rejoined in a manner unlike his usual magnanimous self. "Mr. Smith of the Barclay Building Grille, of course."

I considered this unjust inasmuch as this particular Mr. Smith had never stepped foot into our offices. Heretofore his transactions had been negotiated entirely with the leasing agent of the Barclay Building, a subsidiary corporation. Instead of accosting Mr. Barclay with these facts which would have cleared me of his charge of obtuseness, I humbly performed my duties. Ten minutes later the required Mr. Smith entered the private office.

"I've good news for you, Smith," Mr. Barclay said as he shook hands with the restaurateur. "Ansell has promised not to sue. I've persuaded him to keep the matter quiet. No one will know except a few employees in my office and they will be requested not to spread the story. Of course, Smith, I'm sure it's not your fault, but I urge you to be more careful in future."

Mr. Smith professed not to know what Mr. Barclay was talking about. I could tell by his manner that my employer was not "taken in" by Mr. Smith's pretense of innocence, however. What transpired further I am in no position to say, as Mr. Barclay informed me that my services were not required. Twenty minutes later Mr. Smith left smiling and apparently pleased by the magnanimity of Mr. Barclay.

Again my buzzer sounded. This time Mr. Barclay wished to dictate the following memorandum:

Memorandum
From the office of: Noble Barclay
To: All Employees
Date: 11/23/45

For the sake of our tenant, the Barclay Building Grille, and our friend, Mr. I. G. Smith, its proprietor, I am requesting you not to repeat the rumor that Mr. Ansell was poisoned by eating shrimps at the Grille. Mr. Smith exercises the greatest care in preparing the dishes served in his restaurant, and would never allow food to be set before a customer if there were any question as to its freshness.

Unfortunately, it is not always possible to judge seafood. The shrimps cooked yesterday in the Barclay Building Grille kitchens showed no sign of deterioration, and no one was more surprised than Mr. Smith himself to learn that Mr. Ansell's sudden illness was blamed upon the food served in the Grille.

Since Mr. Smith is not only our tenant but a good friend to all of us who eat in his restaurant, I appeal to your sense of good sportsmanship in asking that you use all possible discretion in keeping the story from spreading.

"Make ten copies and circulate them through the office," Mr. Barclay instructed. "Have them signed by every employee and then have every copy returned to me with the signatures."

"Yes, Mr. Barclay," replied this humble servant.

While I was typing the memo, Eleanor burst into the office. She greeted me as if our last meeting had not ended in an impasse.

"He's all right, Grace!" she cried, as if I had inquired as to some party's condition. "All he needs now is a short rest and he'll be back at work. You can't imagine how I feel."

"Are you by any chance alluding to Mr. Ansell?" I inquired.

She nodded vehemently. "I thought I'd die when I heard he'd been poisoned. I guess I have a melodramatic mind because I . . ." She paused at the brink of revelation and changed her mind about voicing it. Shrugging her shoulders, Eleanor babbled on, "What a relief to learn it was only seafood! Hasn't Father been wonderful?"

"Noble Barclay," I replied, "is always wonderful."

"They called him early this morning to tell him one of his editors had been found half dead in his office. Father rushed to the hospital at once, and told them to do everything they could for Johnnie. I've never seen Father so wonderful."

"I am glad," I observed, "that you appreciate your father." I would have said more, but Eleanor, with that rudeness that is characteristic of her and which, I am sure, she must have inherited from the distaff side, fled from earshot.

Since I am in the habit of eating a light breakfast I take my lunch early. As soon as I had finished typing the memo and had sent it, with complete instructions, to the various Department Heads I wended my way downstairs to the Grille. Seating myself at my usual table, I consulted the menu. My regular waitress approached me and asked, "How about shrimp Creole, Miss Eccles? It's very nice today."

"How dare you?" I cried with the utmost indignation. "Do you think it in good taste to jest when one of your patrons almost lost his life by eating your contaminated shrimps yesterday?"

The waitress seemed surprised. "Shrimps! Yesterday?"

I was annoyed with Mr. Smith for failing to inform his employees of the unfortunate affair of Mr. Ansell's shrimps. Although I had typed the memo requesting employees not to spread rumor outside of our office, I considered it my duty to inform the waitress lest she hear of it through unreliable sources and indulge in idle gossip.

"But we didn't serve shrimps last night," she insisted. "We haven't had a shrimp in this place for over a week."

I tried patiently to argue with the stubborn creature, but I could not convince her that I had spoken the truth. She even summoned other waitresses to back up her assertions. Naturally her friends took her side in the argument. This puzzled me. Although I would not take the words of ignorant working girls in preference to Mr. Barclay's interpretation of the case, my curiosity could not be appeased. My mind was riddled with questions that had no right to enter that holy ground. Doubtless I was at fault. Somewhere in my sly psyche was buried an untruth which I had not the courage to force out and boldly face.

If only Nature had endowed me with greater courage I should have purged myself by sharing known truths with the best of all confessors. Too timid to uproot the festering sores of buried doubt by laying my problems at the feet of Noble Barclay, I comforted myself with the excuse that a busy man occupied with problems of international import had no time for my petty concerns. This, however, was bare comfort. "Oft in the stilly night" have I wakened to wonder at the excessive discretion of my employer and his daughter. Was there not some hidden knowledge anent the connection between Mr. Wilson's death and the misdirected telephone message? Why was Mr. Barclay so stern in commanding my silence and rejecting Mr. Ansell's story?

Whatever the dark secret was, I knew it not to be mine. Nor did I cast the slightest shadow of suspicion upon Noble Barclay. With his unfathomable faith in humanity in general and his friends in particular, this paragon of honesty might readily have been victim of some cruel fraud. Tragedy is the inevitable result of deceitfulness. Out of the roots of falsehood evil flowers; that is the law of Nature and she is a stern taskmaster.

PART THREE

Whose Tartan?

by John Miles Ansell

"Cynics, alleged to possess lively and inquiring minds, are in reality the most incurious and rigid tribe in existence. Their minds are frozen streams, their hearts as hard as granite. In the time of Jesus, cynics jeered at the Christ. Because they were told in childhood that grass is green they believe this must always be so, and if the grass on their front lawns should turn cerise, they would gaze upon its ruddiness swearing they saw it verdant."

My Life Is Truth
NOBLE BARCLAY

"Look, my pretty," I said to the nurse who enjoyed the adjective with-out deserving it, "I admire you but I can't afford you. I can't afford this expensive layout. How the hell did I get here?"

"Don't worry, Mr. Ansell. If somebody couldn't afford these things, you wouldn't be in this room."

I lay back on the expensive bed and tried to figure it out. Since my knees had given way under me in the office and I had felt myself hurled through space on the cannonball express, I was not clear about anything. My adventures with rock cliffs and crack trains had been delusions, and here I was in a hospital room that was not white and narrow, but done in muted colors and with a big corner window through which expensive sunlight streamed.

They would feed me nothing but gruel. Along with the breakfast tray came Noble Barclay.

"How you feeling, lad?"

"I'm still trying to figure it out. Maybe I'm not bright. They tell me I lost consciousness and one of the scrubwomen found me on the floor. Didn't I hear the ambulance doctor say something about bichloride of mercury?"

"You must have been dreaming," Barclay said. "Too much imagination, lad. Comes from working on all those detective stories." He laughed. "I'm giving you a holiday from *Truth and Crime*."

"I was expecting it."

"Afraid you'd lose your job, eh? What kind of a heel do you think you're working for?" This pleased Barclay. He laughed jovially. "You're being promoted, son. As of this week you're editor of *Truth Digest*."

"*Truth Digest?*"

"The newest Barclay Truth Publication. Truth in tabloid. Fits into your vest pocket but contains the best that is being printed, not only in our own magazines, but in all popular periodicals. What do you think of the idea? Original, isn't it?"

The idea of a digest magazine was about as original as a Christmas greeting. "Won't you," I asked cautiously, "meet a lot of competition?"

Barclay considered. "It's true, there are other digests but this would be the first Truth digest. Get the idea? We've been selling reprint rights to other digests and even carrying their stuff, originated in their offices and written by their staff people. But what do we make on it? A few thousand a month. Think, lad, of the money we'd coin with our own digest. And what a medium for bringing our message to the public."

"What about your contracts with the other digests, Mr. Barclay?"

"Don't you worry about that, John. We've got the best attorneys in the country. You're to keep your mind on the editorial side. It's a cinch, boy, six magazines of our own to draw on, just as a start. Absolutely no cost for editorial matter, and anything we'd like to feature in *TD*, we can print first in one of the other magazines. Beautiful setup, isn't it?"

I agreed. The setup couldn't have been prettier. "But," I said, "*Truth and Crime* and *Truth and Love* can hardly be used as a source of digest stuff."

"Not as much as *Truth*," Barclay said. "The bulk of the digest material would be from it. We've got a gold mine to draw on, exposés, political stuff, war, human interest. And *Truth and Health*! Look at the other digests, filled with health stories, medical discoveries, reducing diets, the newest cures . . ."

"Mostly phonies," I put in.

"We can expose them," cried Barclay. "And once in a while we can throw in some *TC* or *TL*, nothing the public likes better than a good fact romance or a true crime. And *Truth and Beauty* gives us the woman's angle. What do you think of the new job, boy?"

"Sounds good."

"Good?" sniffed Barclay. "That's the best job you ever dreamed of. Boy, you don't know. It's going to thrill you so that you'll have to be dragged away from your desk nights. It might be hard work but not too hard for an intellectual like you. Look at the public you'll reach, the chance you'll get to tell them straight simple truth instead of the guff that's usually concealed under a welter of literary language. It's a man's job, lad. As of this week your salary is two hundred per."

Two hundred a week? Was I still unconscious? Wake up, Ansell, you're hearing voices. In a split second the cannon-ball express is going to crash head-on into solid fact. If the bichloride of mercury had been fantasy, what of the seventy-five dollars a week raise?

It was not a dream. There, solid as the hospital bed, was Noble Barclay, radiating health and good humor, and the nurse, who was not pretty, coquetting all over the place because she was attracted by his wealth or his virility. Aware of the admiration, Barclay exhibited more of his good humor. "You don't believe me, John? Sounds too good to be true, huh?" His enjoyment was so frank that I did not flinch at his making a show of it.

He strode across the room. He covered its length in seven steps and strode back to the bed. "Don't belittle yourself, lad. You know you're a damn good editor. Do you sit around like the rest of the highbrows, wisecracking, while the staff writers get the material?" He paused beside the bed, looking into my face. "When an organization like mine is lucky enough to find a man of your caliber, it's our job to hang onto you and to find work worthy of your talent. Why, if you weren't satisfied with us you'd be looking for another job. And some other publisher would grab you like that." He made a gesture intended to show how hungry publishers would grasp a smart young editor by the coat collar and swing him into a mahogany swivel chair. "Don't think you're not worth the price. I'm too canny a businessman to pay that salary to a lad who doesn't deserve it."

He turned to the nurse. "Could he have a cigarette, young lady? I don't smoke myself but when a smoker gets a piece of startling news he reaches for a cigarette. Will you get one for him?"

"He's not supposed to smoke."

"Get him a drink of water, will you?"

"Do you want one?" she asked.

"I don't mind if I do," I said.

She poured some water from a glass jug. I saw the look of disappointment in Barclay's face.

"Look, my pretty," I said to the nurse, "Mr. Barclay wants to talk to me privately. Would you mind stepping out for a few minutes?"

She went.

Barclay winked at me. "You're an astute person."

"I'd be a moron not to understand those elephantine tactics."

He laughed again. I stood in well with Noble Barclay; he liked me for being fresh. I finished drinking my water, and as I put the glass back on the bed table, I remembered something. "I've got it," I cried. "The water. Last night I took a drink of water . . ."

"I have a favor to ask of you," he interrupted. "I happen to be interested in the English Grille and I'd be grateful if nothing more was said about those shrimps you ate last night."

I looked around. There were no bars on the windows and the walls weren't padded. I tried to ask a couple of questions, but Barclay rode over my interruptions like a hopped-up jalopy. He was not so much concerned, Barclay said, with the financial returns from the Grille as with the fate of Smith, its proprietor. Smith was one of his followers, an ex-dipsomaniac reclaimed by Truth-Sharing.

"His story is remarkably like my own," Barclay assured me. "And since you've read the Introduction, you must realize how I feel about Smith's making good. Don't repeat what I've told you about him because it wouldn't help his morale if the story became common gossip. Smith's pulled himself out of the gutter, so to speak, and made a pretty good thing of the Grille. That's why I feel so strongly about this affair last night. If the story got out, it might ruin the restaurant. And God knows what would happen to Smith."

"Wouldn't his belief in Truth help him survive it?" I asked, not without malice.

"It was the belief that he was a failure that made him shun Truth and sent him on the downward path. A repetition of the experience might doom the man." He caught my eye and asked for understanding. "Keep it under your hat, won't you, Ansell?"

I leaned back upon the pillows, closed my eyes, tried to look sick. I needed time to think about Barclay's sudden generosity and his unctuous interest in Smith. A bribe had been offered, so that I should forget I had taken a drink of water from a blue carafe on the desk in my office.

Curiosity tore at my guts, made me sicker than the poison. I knew that I'd get nowhere by asking questions. There was only one way for me to find out what really had happened. As long as I worked at my job and kept quiet about the water in my carafe, I could do as much undercover investigation as I wanted. When I found the answer, I promised myself, I would spare no one. You can't poison an Ansell and get off without paying the price.

There was no danger. "You think I'm astute, Mr. Barclay. But what if I should happen to eat shrimps again?"

"You're too clever for that. From now on you'll be more careful."

There was a long silence. I looked at Barclay and he looked at his reflection in the mirror. The smooth son-of-a-bitch took it for granted that his bribe was enough to make me forget that drink of water.

The nurse knocked at the door, peered in and opened it wider to admit a bunch of yellow chrysanthemums. Behind them came Eleanor. When she saw me leaning weakly against the pillows she let out the prettiest little groan I ever heard.

"You're all right now, aren't you?" she whispered, her breath catching between the words.

I enjoyed her sympathy and kept up the fraud. Barclay beamed as if he dropped happiness into our outstretched hands.

"I'll leave you kids alone now," he said. "You've probably got a lot to say to each other." At the door he saluted me. "Anything you need, John, just say the word. And don't worry about the job. We'll get someone to pinch-hit until you're well again. Good-bye, kids."

He left. Eleanor took off her hat and gave the flowers to the nurse.

"Take a long time finding a vase," I said. "My weakened condition requires that I spend some time alone with this young lady."

After the nurse had gone Eleanor sat in the armchair halfway across the room. She had become prim. Her skirt crept up and she pulled it down over her knees. I broke the news about the new job.

"Isn't Father wonderful!" she said.

I was irked. When a man tells his girl about a raise and a big job, she ought to praise him. *I'm glad you clipped that coupon, John. Now you are a big executive and we can get married.* If she read the ads in the Barclay Truth magazines she'd know she ought to praise the man rather than her father.

"Why did you come here, Eleanor?"

"I . . . I . . ." she stumbled over the words. "I heard you were ill. I was worried."

"Worried about me? I didn't know you'd care enough to worry."

"I liked you from the very first day," Eleanor said. The sun shining through the big window turned her hair to gold. Her skin was pale ivory gilded by the sunshine.

"I didn't know it," I said. "You were so elusive."

"Elusive?"

"I thought you regretted having gone out with me that time," I said. "I thought you were angry because I'd asked too many personal questions. I had no idea you were so sensitive."

Her hands were folded in her lap. She looked down at them. When the cynics at the Editors' Table made fun of Noble Barclay, she tightened into a steely mold. "People are always asking questions. They think they can find out more about Father by being nice to me."

"Thanks," I said, "for your frank opinion. It's nice to know what someone really thinks of you."

She jumped up and came over to the bed. "You've got to understand, Johnnie. I'm not suspicious. It's only the way people have always acted toward me. Being *his* daughter isn't easy, you know."

"Evidently you've changed your opinion of me. That's something to be thankful for."

"I was sorry I got angry with you that day," she confessed. "Only I didn't know what to do about it. I never had the courage to admit it, but I hoped you'd forgive me." The shy color crept back into her face. "Honestly, you won't believe it, but I used to wait for you to come out of your office, so we could ride down together in the elevator, and I'd hope you were having dinner in the Village, so we could be together on the bus."

"Did you?" I cried. "That's why I went downtown so often. Don't you know I live uptown? I liked riding on the bus with you . . ."

"Once you said you were in a hurry and were taking a cab, and asked if you could give me a lift. Remember?"

"As soon as you got out, I told the driver to turn around and take me back uptown."

"Did you!" she cried.

"Let's not beat around the bush," I said. "I'm crazy about you and I didn't know whether you liked me or loathed me. Every time I tried to make a date, you'd pull that startled-faun stuff and . . ."

"I was afraid."

"Not afraid of me," I laughed. "Why, I thought you had written me off because I was kind of fresh about your old man. I was afraid you'd want a guy to believe in that stuff about purging your unconscious and secrets being festering sores. By me, that's a lot of . . ."

"Stop it," she said. "Please, let's not talk about it."

"If we're going on from here, we've got to talk about it."

"Please."

"How can we be friends, how can we ever mean anything to each other if we're afraid to talk about something as close to you as that? Besides," I couldn't help sounding facetious, "isn't that the basic tenet? Face the truth, uproot shame, confess . . ."

"I love my father."

She said it as if I had denied her that right. Her eyes looked dark because the pupils were dilated, and hard cords rose in her neck.

"Naturally," I said. "Naturally you do, he's your father. It's only natural for you to love him."

She crouched over the bed. Her voice was low and level, without inflection. "He believes every word of it. Everything he writes is completely sincere. The Introduction—it's his own story. He went through hell and he saved himself and he believes he can save other people."

"I wish you weren't so unhappy, kid." I reached for her hand.

Eleanor smiled, the radiance returned and her hand lay warm in mine. "What makes you think I'm unhappy? I want you to believe in my father. You don't have to believe in Truth-Sharing but believe in him, a good man, a sincere man."

My hand tightened around hers. "Okay, I believe he's sincere."

"Do you really?"

I was supposed to be a sick man but my strength was remarkable. I put my arms around Eleanor and pulled her down beside me on the bed. Unfortunately the nurse came in and we were forced to separate.

Eleanor stayed over an hour. We talked about my new job and she kept telling me how important it was. "There's one thing about Father that no one can deny. He's a brilliant businessman and he'd never have given you that wonderful job if you didn't deserve it."

I'd been able to stand up against Barclay's flattery, but Eleanor's praise sold me one hundred percent on that brilliant young editor, John Miles Ansell. Hard work, intelligence, tact and good sense—that's how I became a success at twenty-six.

After five days at the hospital, I was discharged. The doctor advised a few days' rest and Barclay said I could have a two-week vacation with pay. I went home to see my mother and to brag to the family and old friends about the new job. They were plenty impressed. After all, two hundred a week.

After a few days the adulation ceased to satisfy me. I wanted to get back to work and to Eleanor. Over the long-distance wire she had confided that she missed me.

On Thursday, December sixth, just two weeks after the excitement, I came back to work. My pockets were full of notes jotted on old envelopes and business cards. These were bright ideas for *Truth Digest*.

Everyone came into my new office to congratulate me. On the wall above my desk hung Noble Barclay's picture autographed to his dear friend, John Miles Ansell. Directly under it was a chromium tray with a Thermos jug and glass. They were made of green plastic to harmonize with the interior decoration, but otherwise they were exactly like the blue carafe and glass in the *Truth and Crime* office.

I made a vow. No matter how thirsty I might become, I'd never take a drink from that jug. For the past two weeks I'd been trying to figure out the movements and motives of the character who had tried to poison me. Any office stooge might have done the trick. The whole staff had known that I intended to work late that night. Miss Kaufman had been instructed to tell the night watchman that I would return at eleven. Instead, I had come back at seven-thirty. Whoever had slipped a dose of poison into the blue jug must have visited my office while I was eating lamb chops at the Grille.

Most of the office staff left at five-thirty. Those who stayed were concentrated on overtime work: finishing manuscripts, reading proof, checking copy, balancing accounts. Nine chances out of ten, no one would have noticed an intruder in my office. There were so many legitimate excuses he—or she—might have offered that such a visit would hardly have been counted an intrusion. Or even remembered.

Anyone who worked later than seven signed the book when he left. Therefore, I figured, it had probably been between five-thirty and seven that the bichloride had been dropped into the water in the blue carafe.

If I had died that night, there would certainly have been an autopsy followed by an investigation. But the police would have stumbled up a dozen blind alleys before they found a straight path. I was a new employee; I had no enemies in the office. My arguments with the boss and his aide had concerned editorial policy. No sane policeman would consider that motive for murder. It is much simpler to fire a troublesome employee than to have him killed.

No one in the office had the slightest suspicion of dirty work. To everyone except myself the link between my fight over the Wilson story and the alleged seafood poisoning was invisible. And sometimes I wondered whether I hadn't been delirious that night.

I wanted to hear office gossip. I questioned my stooge tactfully.

What worried Miss Kaufman was the fact that I had eaten seafood. "I thought you had an allergy. I remember distinctly one night when you worked late, Mr. Ansell, you asked me to have your dinner sent up and you said you ate everything but shellfish. You said you were allergic to lobster, crabs, clams, oysters and shrimps."

"Okay, Miss Kaufman, I'm allergic. But I was careless that night. I ordered lamb chops but they took so long to cook them that I told the waitress to bring me a shrimp cocktail. I can't digest shrimps and that's why I got sick. Are you satisfied?"

"It's none of my business." Miss Kaufman was rummaging in the bottom drawer of the desk. Her back was toward me and I studied the curves under her thin silk dress. "You'd better take this home with you."

"What is it?"

She handed me a manuscript envelope. "The Wilson story."

While I had been away, the February issue of *Truth and Crime* had gone to press. Munn had got one of the staff writers to finish the Dot King piece. All copies of the Wilson story were to have been destroyed.

"Mr. Munn asked me to bring them to his office," Miss Kaufman said. "He thought I'd only made the usual three carbons, but I always make an extra one for the author in case he ever wants to do a book. You'd better put this where no one will ever find it."

"Thanks, Miss Kaufman. And look, can you get me a large picture of a shrimp salad or a shrimp cocktail?"

"Shrimp salad or shrimp cocktail, Mr. Ansell!"

"Very large and preferably in color. I'd like it framed."

"What for?"

"To hang over my desk," I said. "So that I never forget why I'm here."

She stared at me and shook her head slowly. I have often seen the same look on my mother's face and the same bewildered movement of her head.

At half past twelve I washed my hands and combed my hair carefully. I intended to celebrate my promotion by taking Eleanor to an expensive restaurant.

Munn was in the washroom. "Congratulations, young fellow." The clown's mouth curved as if his smile had just been put on with grease paint.

I plunged my hands into the hot water. "Thanks, Mr. Munn."

"A great honor for a young man like you. Most fellows twice your age'd give their eye teeth for a chance like that."

"My eye teeth have been extracted. I gave them up for my dear old Alma Mater, the University of Hard Knocks."

He made an effort to laugh. "When Barclay asked me about promoting you, I gave him my frank opinion of your ability. Maybe you can guess what I said." He looked at me expectantly, waiting as if I were his partner in the minuet. "I've always admired your talents. Even when I was obliged to disagree with you on certain matters of policy, I respected your opinions."

I hoped my face showed contempt. If there is any creature lower than the snake it's the stooge. Now that I had become editor of Barclay's best magazine, Edward Everett Munn was on my side. He'd always respected my opinions.

"Let's have lunch someday," he said, looking at his wrist watch. "At my club. Sorry, I must run now. Got a date."

I took a lot of trouble with the part in my hair and worked over my tie. Then I strolled toward the *Truth and Love* office, making myself walk slowly so that I should not seem too anxious.

"What about lunch?" I asked, throwing open the door.

"What about it?" echoed Lola Manfred.

"Where's Eleanor?"

"Gone to lunch."

I was staggered. "Lunch! Alone?"

"She went with some of the girls, I think."

"But I . . ."

"Did you invite her?" Lola interrupted. "I think she was waiting all morning for an invitation. That's the trouble with you men. You always take us so for granted." Lola's voice, which usually was pitched so that deaf people three miles away could hear her without earphones, softened.

"Take her away from here, Johnnie. If you love the gal, get her out of this hell hole."

I stared. For the first time since I had known Lola I understood what people meant when they spoke of her faded beauty. Like everything else in the Barclay offices the legend of Lola Manfred had seemed false to me. In the 1920s Lola had been a slim poetess, the toast of Greenwich Village. She was supposed to have deserted a millionaire husband in Paris to live her own life, to write delicate verses about love and death, and to starve.

That was long ago. It was hard to associate the editor of *Truth and Love* with a slim girl who had written a slim book of sad little poems. Lola's legs were still lovely but the rest of her body was grossly fat, all bloat and alcohol. She had the eyes of a child, round and wide-set and blue as flowers.

"How long have you worked here, Lola?"

"Countless centuries. Only God's old enough to remember."

"Why do you call it a hell hole?"

She looked at me sadly, holding her head on one side and narrowing her blue eyes. "I'm tired, Ansell. A weary trollop."

"Have lunch with me?"

"Second fiddle? Time was when they asked me for my own sake. Ah, memory! 'Tis all the aged strumpet has left. Where do we eat?"

I felt gallant. I saw myself, one of those world-weary youths of 1925, drinking myself to death for love of Lola Manfred. "How about the Algonquin?"

She yawned. "As far as I'm concerned one saloon is like another." She ran her hands through her hair, pinned on the side of her head a pirate's hat with a dagger hanging over her right eye, tossed a mangy fur cape over her shoulders, rubbed the toes of her slippers against her stockings and started out. In the foyer, as we waited for the elevator, she looked at herself in the mirror.

"Would you say that face reminded you of old Gorgonzola? Very, very old Gorgonzola made from the milk of scrofulous goats."

The elevator stopped for us but Lola paid no attention. She was digging through the antiques in her pocketbook. At last she pulled out a tarnished lipstick. With tiny, caressing movements of her veined hand she painted a Cupid's bow. A new group of Barclay employees was gathering before the elevators.

"How the devil did you ever get that high-class job?" Lola asked. Her voice could have called the cattle home from far fields.

I jolted her elbow. In the group around us there were probably one or more of Munn's spies.

Relentless, she boomed, "Not that I'd begrudge it to an ambitious fellow, but how a clean-cut type like you ever got a break in this dump is what baffles me. Have you also discovered where the body's buried?"

We had let three cars go by. Suddenly Lola decided that the art work on her mouth was finished, and shoved me toward the elevator. Someone hurried in behind us. I smelled toilet water and peppermint. It was Munn, dressed like a clubman in a velvet-lapelled overcoat and derby hat.

"That's how I keep my job," Lola confided in her booming contralto. "I not only know where the body's buried, I've got maps. X marks the spot. I'm doing my autobiography and when it's published some juicy fruit is going to hang from the gallows tree."

The elevator bounced to a stop. Munn excused himself as he pushed past us. Lola thumbed her nose at his back.

We took a taxi to the Algonquin. The lobby was filled with people waiting hungrily to recognize celebrities or be recognized themselves. "In twenty years," Lola said, "nothing about this dump has changed except the costumes. When I started coming here skirts were so short that if a breeze blew your bra showed."

A crowd waited at the dining-room door. The head-waiter looked at me indifferently, but when he saw Lola, he was like a father whose wandering child has returned. Within seconds we were seated at one of the better tables.

"We don't see much of you anymore, Miss Manfred," the head-waiter said and bent over our table like Essex before Elizabeth.

"That's what you tell all the girls," Lola said.

"You used to come every day, Miss Manfred." The head-waiter's brown eyes were reproachful. "Don't you like us anymore?"

"I don't sleep with the better literary set now. Will you please have one of your nice waiters rush to this table with three old-fashioneds?"

"Three, Miss Manfred?"

"Two for me and one for my youthful paramour."

Unruffled, the head-waiter moved away.

"You're disgusting," I said. "Why do you always have to show off?"

"I'm too lazy to write poetry. And the self-expression offered by my duties on *Truth and Love* does not satisfy my exhibitionistic nature." She took off the pirate's hat, put it on the seat beside her, looked at her face in the mirror, cried, "What a Gorgonzola!" and blew a kiss to someone on the other side of the room. When the waiter brought our drinks Lola raised hers in a toast.

"To the painful death of Noble Barclay!"

"Can't you find some other way to earn your living?" I asked. "When it flavors your liquor, it's going too far."

She held up the glass and squinted at me through the ice and liquor. "I wish you'd stop talking about him all the time. I came here to forget."

"It was you who proposed the toast."

A waiter thrust menus into our hands. I asked Lola twice what she'd like for lunch. She shuddered delicately. I ordered Vichyssoise, liver and bacon and salad for both of us. A man waved across the restaurant at her and she threw him kisses with both hands. "Isn't he growing repulsive, though?" she inquired of me, and smiled at the man.

When she had finished the first drink she said, "You'd be surprised if I told you how long ago it was that I first read the Barclay Bible."

"I thought you didn't want to talk about it."

"I read it before six million suckers had paid him their good dough, before it was translated into sixteen languages. I said it was hogwash and anyone who plunked down a dollar for it would be carried off to the nut house. Prophetic, wasn't I?"

"You've been saying it ever since. At least since I've known you."

"My opinion. May it ever be right, but right or wrong, my opinion."

A fat man stood over our table. Lola raised her eyes to him slowly.

"Why haven't I seen you of late, beauty?" asked the fat man.

"Darling!" exclaimed Lola. "I've been thinking about you for weeks. We must get together. Do give me a ring soon." After he had gone she said, "I'd have introduced you but I don't remember his name. I think I had an affair with him. He's an oaf."

She settled down to her second drink. There was something childish about the way she held the glass in both hands and bent her head like a baby with a mug of milk. Looking at me over the glass, she asked, "Do you remember Coué?"

"Was he also one of your lovers?"

"Don't be silly. He was French."

"I didn't think you were prejudiced against any race, color or creed."

"I mean he was a Frenchman in France. He did come over here for a lecture tour, but I never heard him. What I'm trying to say is that I laughed at his book; I thought autosuggestion was pure hogwash. I go into hysterics over all those psychology and Unity and Rosicrucian Help-Yourself-to-Health-and-Wealth books. Once a boy friend took me to an Oxford Group meeting and I laughed myself into the nearest saloon. I'm just giving you my record." Her voice softened and she said to the middle of the room:

> Mock on, mock on, Voltaire, Rousseau,
> Mock on, 'tis all in vain!
> You throw the sand against the wind,
> And the wind blows it back again.

"When I write my autobiography I'm going to call it 'Sand Against the Wind.'"

"That's a nice poem. You haven't lost your touch."

"Kind of you, Ansell, too, too kind. I'll mention you in my book. The young man who paid me the ultimate compliment. Mixed me with Blake."

I frowned. Her chatter skipped ahead of my lame intelligence.

"Blake," she said emphatically. "Blake, William, English poet, 1757–1827. You heard of him probably at college."

I did not mind the sarcasm. The poet's name had rung a bell in my memory. The bell tolled but I could not remember whose funeral it marked.

Lola prattled on. She had said that she wanted to forget Barclay, but he had become her obsession. All roads led to Truth-Sharing. "They're not so different, you know, Buchman and Barclay. Buchman made the Oxford Movement a success because Moral Rearmament provides the exaltation of confession. Public confession, mind you. A few true believers get together and relieve themselves by telling each other what a hell of a time they had being immoral. Out in the Bible Belt when I was a kid I'd go to revival meetings and witness the same kind of orgasms under canvas."

"Are you defending Barclay?" I asked.

"Explaining him to myself. I've got to tell it to myself over and over, otherwise I'd commit suicide out of sheer disgust for the human race. The things people believe! Were you ever psyched?"

"I'm not inhibited, thank you."

"As an enlightened intellectual, you probably consider psychoanalysis the last word in spiritual pathology."

"Spiritual is an unscientific term. You ought to be more precise when you get into these discussions."

"You sound like a professor. What I mean is this: In psychoanalysis you not only get relief by naming your sins and lifting them out of the mysterious hell of the unconscious, but you also transfer your guilt to the doctor. Barclay uses something of the same technique. Look at the Introduction to his book. No matter how evil the poor suckers think they are, Barclay's worse. He's committed all the sins in the calendar and he's willing to take on the burdens of his followers. Truth-Sharing cleanses in a cheap, easy, popular way. You don't have to pay the doctor or fear the tortures of hell. It's the poor man's psychoanalysis. You find a bosom friend, get him excited about Truth-Sharing, and then confess your sins, your frailties, your secret thoughts, whip yourself into a hysteria, release the sense of guilt and whoops! my dear, deliverance."

"You make it sound too simple."

"All theories are simple to the people who believe them. When the tormented heart cries out for relief, it doesn't make much difference what method heals the pain. It doesn't matter what you believe as long as you *can* believe. 'Mock on, mock on, Voltaire.'"

The waiter brought iced soup. Lola ate two spoonfuls and asked for another drink.

"Do you think Barclay explains himself that way? Do you think he knows that he owes it all to the psychiatrists, the psychologists, the theologists, the theosophists, the faith healers, the priests, the witch doctors and ancient gods?"

"Why should Barclay figure it out?" Lola asked. "He doesn't have to. Why explain a miracle that brings you hundreds of thousands of dollars every year?"

"Just the same he strikes me as a sincere guy," I said. "He certainly doesn't spare himself when he talks or writes about his guilty past, and you can't deny that he practices what he preaches. Whether we mock at him or not, Lola, I feel that Barclay believes he's got the true formula for health and happiness, and he wants the world to share it."

"At one dollar the volume, three-fifty in morocco. And yearly subscriptions to his magazines."

"That makes him no less sincere. Most roads to happiness extract a higher toll. The modern Messiah can't walk barefoot."

"What price sincerity?" Lola tossed the phrase at a roomful of complacent celebrities. "What's sincerity worth except to the man who profits by it? We are surrounded by hordes of people who can believe in anything sincerely as long as it brings them a good living. Fascists believe in Fascism, don't they, especially the big ones whose attitudes pay a profit? There's nothing in the world, my friend, so sincere as self-interest."

The waiter stood beside our table listening to Lola's talk. She noticed him at last, pushed the soup cup toward him and said, "Lucky you. You can afford to be sincere about your work. It's not hard to believe in a good meal."

"Thank you, Madame," the waiter said.

"I'd like another drink."

"Not till you've eaten," I said.

"Strong-minded, aren't you?" Lola pouted. "A nice thing, plying me with liquor and asking a lot of impudent questions. Now that you've had your way with me, you get stingy."

"Eat your lunch. When your plate's clean, I'll buy you another drink."

Five more men came to the table. Each time it was a love reunion, followed either by a lapse of memory or the news that the ex-lover was *but* repulsive. When she had finished her salad I told the waiter to bring coffee for me and a double brandy for the lady.

"How you understand me! I shall put you in my memoirs. 'John Ansell, a talented and handsome youth.' How do you like that?"

"Splendid. Just so you don't say I was your lover."

"How ungallant!"

"I prefer my amours retail."

I let her finish her brandy before I asked anymore questions. As I lit her cigarette I said, "You must have known Barclay a long time."

She sighed. "Longer, darling, than I care to remember."

"Was he one of your lovers?"

"Take that back or I'll leave the table."

"Perhaps Wilson was," I said, still looking into her eyes. It was a shot in the dark but not too inaccurate. The bell that rang at the name of Blake had reminded me that Wilson's collection had included a number of valuable Blake items.

"Who, dear?"

"Warren G.Wilson."

There was no alteration in her posture or her expression. One blue-veined hand rested on the table. The other held the brandy glass. Her face did not change. No muscle tensed or contracted. I felt rather than saw the wincing and shrinking.

"Warren G. Wilson," I repeated.

"Never heard of him."

Lola finished her brandy, fished around on the banquette and accused a busboy of stealing her hat. The head-waiter hurried over to soothe her while the busboy and I crawled under the table. We did not find the hat until Lola got up. She had been sitting on it.

"This is a plot to discredit me." Her hands smoothed the hat as if they were comforting the old wreck for some cruel insult. Then she put her hat on at a crazy angle and forgot all about it. On the way out of the hotel she stopped to speak to another brace of ex-lovers. Both, she confided when we were in the taxi, were filthy bastards.

"And you're not much better. The lousiest detective I ever saw. Why don't you learn the tricks? You can get a course by correspondence, five dollars down, five a month."

Her voice was hard. She had tried to be funny and had not succeeded. For the rest of the way back to the Barclay Building she looked out the window.

Eleanor was reading proof in the *Truth and Love* office. She looked demure and beautiful in a dark dress with a stiff white collar and starched cuffs. The office smelled of fresh-cut flowers. On Lola's desk stood a glass vase filled with American Beauty roses. It had not been there when we left the office and I wondered, jealously, who had sent them to Eleanor.

"Did you have a good lunch?" Eleanor asked.

"Superb," Lola said. "He's a dream man, a gent of the old school. He buys you hundreds of drinks and expects nothing for it." Her voice was rough and I could tell that she was still smarting from the wound inflicted by my ignorance.

"I'm sorry if I said anything out of the way, Lola. I certainly didn't mean to hurt your feelings."

"I'm bloody but unbowed," Lola said. Then she noticed the flowers. She looked accusingly at Eleanor.

"It's so hot in here," Eleanor said apologetically. "I opened the box and put them in water. It always hurts me to see flowers die. There was no card again."

Lola tossed the pirate's hat into a corner. The fur cape lay in a heap on the floor. She kicked it with the toe of a shabby patent-leather slipper. Lola must have been close to fifty, but she put on a show like a spoiled three-year-old.

Eleanor picked up Lola's hat, dusted it and hung it up. She shook the dust out of the fur cape. "We needn't keep them in the office," she said. "I'll give them to the girls in the reception room. They're always so grateful. I'll be right back, Johnnie." And Eleanor carried the roses out of the office.

Lola swept out, too, turning back at the door to inform me that she had to pee. In a few minutes Eleanor came back.

"What's the matter with her?" I said. "Why'd she lose her temper all of a sudden?"

Eleanor shrugged. "She drank too much at lunch, I guess. She'll be all right in a little while."

"Must be pleasant for you, working with all that temperament."

"I feel sorry for her. She's been unhappy lately. She's such an unhappy woman." Eleanor looked at a water spot left on Lola's desk by the vase.

I was still uncertain about the flowers and I said cautiously, "Why did the roses make her angry?"

Eleanor wiped off the spot. "American Beauties always do. This has been going on for months. She probably loathes the person who sent them."

We dropped the subject. I was less interested in Lola's tantrums than in Eleanor's charms. The stiff collar and demure dress made her particularly seductive. I kissed her. She softened in my arms, snuggled against me, let me kiss her forehead, her neck, her mouth.

"You're wonderful, Eleanor. Any other girl would keep her eyes on the door and remind me that someone might come in."

"I don't care who knows I love you."

What could a man do about a girl like that, a girl who wore a chastity belt but handed him the key? Since she would not worry about our being caught in the office I was the one who had to remember conventions.

I straightened my tie and combed my hair. "I wanted you to have lunch with me glamorously in some costly dive, but you found a worthier escort. What about dinner?"

"It's cooking."

"What's cooking?"

"Dinner."

"Whose dinner?"

"Ours, foolish."

"I may be dull," I said, "but your persiflage perplexes me. I'm inviting you to dine with me."

"And I'm telling you that our dinner is being prepared by Brenda who works for me afternoons. You've been ill and you oughtn't go around eating in restaurants. Brenda is preparing a simple but nourishing meal."

I kissed her again. I was a happy fellow. The girl loved me. She worried about my health. She planned my meals. She let me kiss her as often as I liked and did not care who knew that she loved me. This would have been the best evening of my life if it hadn't been for Blake. The same Blake, William, English poet, 1787–1827.

In a city of seven million, it should be possible to find three people who know and like the same poet, quote him and collect his works. There was a logical connection between Eleanor's tastes and Lola's. They worked together and probably talked about authors and books. I figured it out that way when I saw the poet's name lettered on the backs of three volumes in Eleanor's apartment.

She had gone to the kitchen to mix a Martini. I wandered around the living room, looking at her things, noticing how cozy she had made the small apartment. When Eleanor had come to the hospital to see me she had told me something about herself and I knew what a struggle it had been for her to convince Noble Barclay that she would rather live alone in three rooms on East Tenth Street than to enjoy the luxury of his duplex on upper Fifth Avenue.

I had just started reading the titles on the second bookshelf when Eleanor returned with the Martinis. We drank to each other and started making love again. The mulatto maid kept coming in and out, setting the table and pretending she did not see us.

The Martinis were excellent. The olives had no pits and the glasses had been chilled. Eleanor's skin was as cool and smooth as a flower just out of the florist's icebox. She was in my arms and I was looking over her shoulder at the second bookshelf when my eye hit on the volume of Blake.

Eleanor felt the tension my body and pulled away. "What's the matter?"

"Nothing."

"Why did you recoil?"

"I didn't recoil."

"Excuse me. I'll go and wash," She left, walking stiffly. I did not call her back nor kiss her again, but went straight to the bookshelves.

The first Blake was a modern edition, published in 1937, illustrated with reproductions of the poet's drawings. A silver sticker inside the back cover showed that it had come from a Greenwich Village bookstore. The second was a biography of the poet. And there was an old volume, probably a collector's item and worth a lot of money. There was an inscription on the flyleaf. As I read it my heart stopped beating.

To that most genteel lady, Eleanor Barclay, from her humblest admirer, this Valentine.

W.G.W. February '45.

She called to me from the next room, telling me to have another cocktail and promising to be ready in three minutes. Three minutes were like three years. I remembered the look on Eleanor's face when she came out of the Ladies' Room after her session with Grace Eccles. I put the Blake back upon the shelf guiltily and started to poke at the fire. The logs had been treated with some salt preparation and the flames were liquid stripes, orange and blue, gold, purple, scarlet, with an occasional tongue of sulphurous green.

"Hello, Johnnie," Eleanor said.

She wore a long black velvet thing, a hostess gown, I think it is called, with a full skirt and low neck. She had on old-fashioned earrings set with dark red stones and a big red pin, shaped like a heart, on her shoulder. She was beautiful, she was a lady, a genteel lady to whom a humble admirer had given the poems of Blake as a Valentine.

Dinner was ready. Brenda lit the candles. I pulled out Eleanor's chair, became formal and bowed over it. The candlelight gave her face a different look. The wonder of this girl was that she could look like so many different people: an innocent youngster or a sorceress or what they called in our office, a business girl. Or a genteel lady. This should have made me love her more, love the variable qualities which would prevent boredom, but I was distressed by the variable qualities. I loved her, but I did not know what to expect of Barclay's daughter.

Just around the corner from Eleanor's apartment was the hotel where Warren G. Wilson had lived and died. You could walk there in two minutes. I thought of Eleanor hurrying along East Tenth Street, the plaid coat pulled tight around her, and her high heels tapping the pavement.

The dinner was good. Brenda took away the soup plates and served broiled chicken, broccoli and browned potatoes. There were hot biscuits, strawberry jam and a thin white wine. It was my first dinner at her place and I am sure Eleanor had thought about it and had a long conversation with the maid.

Conversation flowed along, but it had no meaning. A lady in black velvet entertained a guest. Have some more chicken, please. Do you like this wine? It's a Rhine wine. Rhine wines are my favorite. We talked about books and I asked if she liked poetry. I had not read much poetry since I left college, but I talked as if I gave three nights a week to the Browning Society. Finally I managed to say, casually, "I see you're fond of Blake."

"Not wildly. He's too mystic for my taste. The combination of naïveté and mysticism leaves me cold." There was no emotion in her answer. The Blakes might have been birthday presents from old school chums. "I had a friend," she went on, "who tried to make me appreciate Blake. That's where I got all the books." She nodded in the direction of the shelves. "In fact, I've known two fans in my life."

I could name both of her Blake fans, Lola Manfred and Warren G. Wilson. Instead I remarked with heavy humor, "Nice highbrow evenings you three must have had, getting together and reading his works."

"We never did. As a matter of fact, they didn't even know each other. Why aren't you eating, Johnnie? You ought to, you know. You've lost weight."

She was so sweet that I hoped her concern for me was honest and not an attempt to divert me from memories of the poetry lovers. Through the rest of the meal she talked rapidly and gaily. Everything I said, whether it was funny or not, made her laugh. In the circumstances her nervous vivacity made me restless.

Brenda left, and for the first time Eleanor and I were alone in a secluded place. I did not even try to sit next to Eleanor on the sofa, but chose a chair at the opposite side of the room. She seemed disappointed. Her movements were jerky. She changed seats frequently. For a while she stood with her back to the fireplace as if she were cold.

I went away early. My excuse was reasonable. I had not been out of the hospital for long, and the new job had taken a lot out of me. I needed sleep.

"Yes, of course, I understand perfectly," she said as she took me to the door. "Well, good night."

"I've had a swell time. The dinner was swell. Thanks."

She did not offer her hand nor ask me to come again.

I rode uptown on the top of the Fifth Avenue bus. My feet were cold and I remembered how cozy it had been at Eleanor's. I got angry, not only at myself, but at William Blake and Warren G. Wilson. A mystic poet and a correspondence-school tycoon, both dead, were ruining my love life.

As I unlocked the door of my one-room bachelor apartment I

heard the phone ring. I caught it just in time. It was Captain Riordan, my friend at Police Headquarters.

"Have you run the Wilson story yet?" he asked.

"What?"

"The murder of Wilson, the guy that took the name of the correspondence course. He was murdered last May. I thought you were going to write it up."

"Of course I remember. I was shocked at your calling me about it tonight."

"Shocked. Why?"

"Coincidence. I just happened to be thinking of that story.

Riordan was friendly, but he was still a cop. I knew nothing definite about the Wilson murder, and I was certainly not going to tell him that the girl I loved could look both blonde and brunette, that she wore a plaid coat and that Warren G. Wilson had sent her a Valentine.

"They've got the woman in the plaid coat," Riordan said.

"Go on."

"She got lit and staggered out of a Third Avenue bar and told the cop on the beat she was the girl who had taken the elevator up to the thirtieth floor of Wilson's hotel the night he was murdered."

I tried to sound cool about it. "Who is she?"

"Name's Arvah Lucille Kennedy. We found the name in her purse."

"Has she confessed?"

"She passed out. When she's slept it off we'll question her. I called you because you told me your story was going to press this month, and I thought there might be a new development."

"Thanks," I said. "I appreciate your thinking of me."

"I didn't want to put you on the spot by solving your Unsolved Mystery before the magazine came out."

"You think you've got it solved then?"

"Arvah knows something. Otherwise it wouldn't have taken six months and a bun to get it off her chest."

After Riordan had hung up I sat on the studio couch and thought about the Unsolved Mystery. Was my face red? Remorse broke out in beads on my forehead. I hated myself for having tolerated the suspicion that Eleanor knew something about the murder. My relief was so great that I conveniently forgot Grace Eccles and how Eleanor had looked when she hurried out of the Ladies' Room after that secret session. I even forgot the shrimps.

I dialed Eleanor's number.

"Hello," she said in the querulous voice of a woman who has been called out of a hot bath.

"Eleanor . . ."

"Oh, it's you."

"Eleanor, I suppose you're angry with me. You must think I'm an awful jerk. But there was a reason . . . maybe not such a good reason, Eleanor, but something . . . something . . ."

"What reason?"

I hesitated. What would she think if I told her suddenly over the phone that I had imagined her mixed up in a murder? I used the first excuse that popped into my head. "Look, Eleanor, I'm crazy about you. And I was afraid to make love to you, afraid you'd be angry . . ."

"Did I act that way?"

"I guess I'm shy."

"Why, Johnnie! And I was afraid I'd been too forward. I've acted like a brazen hussy. I thought you were disgusted with me."

"Eleanor, my sweet. You're wonderful. You're beautiful. Can I come back?"

"Now?"

"Right away."

"It's so late."

"I've got to come and tell you how sorry I am. I want to say good night properly. I want to thank you for that wonderful dinner. I've got to tell you how much I love you. Eleanor . . ."

"Hurry," she said.

I ran down the stairs carrying my hat and coat. On Madison Avenue I tried to leap into a cab parked for a stop light. In the cab a man was making love to his girl, and he shouted at me to get out. An empty cab finally came along and I told the driver to make it snappy. It seemed that we got caught in traffic at every intersection. When we got to Tenth Street I jumped out before the driver had pulled up at the curb. Eleanor must have waited at the window because the latch of the door started clicking before I rang the bell.

I leaped up the stairs. The door of Eleanor's apartment was open. She was waiting in the hall. Her hair hung loose over her shoulders and she had on a blue robe. I took her in my arms.

"My God, Ansell, you do look silly with that smirk on your face. What's up?" Tony Shaw asked.

We were sitting on stools at the counter of the Barclay Building drugstore. It was half past nine in the morning. I was so hungry that I had ordered a double orange juice, a bowl of oatmeal, two eggs, ham, toast, Danish pastry and coffee.

"I'm feeling healthy," I told Tony as I finished my oatmeal and started on the ham and eggs.

I had never felt better in my life. I had never seen such a beautiful morning. Alexander, having found new worlds to conquer, was a slouch in comparison with John Miles Ansell. I was in love with Eleanor and she with me. We had decided to get married. She hoped our children would have curly hair like mine, and I had put in a bid for a daughter who would look exactly like her mother. Eleanor had confessed that she had been annoyed the first time she met me, interested the second, and in love the third. I could not name dates, but my ardor made up for the deficiencies in the history of my passion. Eleanor and I were right for each other. We belonged. Nothing in the world could ever separate us.

Tony Shaw finished his coffee and left. The waitress brought my Danish pastry and second cup of coffee. Someone took Tony's deserted stool.

"'Morning, Ansell. How's the bright young editor?"

My coffee tasted bitter. The world had been so beautiful that I had forgotten the existence of snakes, lice, cockroaches and Edward Everett Munn.

"Good morning," I said, and ate a little faster.

"How about lunch tomorrow? Are you free? I'd like to take you to my club."

When Munn talked about his club there was a solemn, almost

reverent look on his face. He was not a man born to clubs; he had achieved one. Now that I had a good job and had shown myself a man of some importance in the office, I was to be patronized by a clubman.

"Thanks, but I don't believe in clubs. They promote class feeling. When it comes to clubs I'm a bit of a Communist."

The waitress set before him a cup of hot water and a tea bag. He took out his watch and set it beside the saucer while the bag dangled in his teacup.

"The Wilson case may be solved, after all," I said.

"Wilson case? Oh, the Unsolved Murder. Really?" he inquired politely.

"Yep, it may be solved. Warren G. Wilson's murderer is probably in the hands of the police at this very minute."

Without consulting his watch Munn yanked the tea bag out of the hot water. The clown's mouth formed several wordless syllables before he asked, "Who was it?"

"The lady in the plaid coat. She staggered into a policeman's arms last night and confessed that she'd gone up to the thirtieth floor the night he was shot."

"What's her name?"

"Kennedy. Arvah Lucille Kennedy."

He picked up the tea bag by the string, and dangled it in the hot water again. His eyes were fixed upon the cup as if there were nothing in the world so important as the strength of his morning tea. "Has she confessed?"

"She was so tight she passed out in the cop's arms. The last I heard she was sleeping it off. They expect to get the full story this morning."

"It's about time." Munn lay the soaked tea bag on his saucer, measured a level spoonful of sugar and squeezed some lemon into the cup. His lips moved and I thought he was counting the drops.

In the mirror behind the counter, between the signs—FRESH ORANGE JUICE 20¢ and BANANA ROYALE 35¢—I could see him blowing into his hot tea. He took out his cigarette case.

As he offered it, I said, "Every time you do that I tell you I don't smoke Turkish. Can't you remember?"

He grinned as if he thought this a remarkably funny joke. It occurred to me that he smoked Turkish because he was stingy and knew that few people would accept the cigarettes he offered. I changed my mind and took one.

"If I were you I wouldn't say anything about this to Mr. Barclay, Ansell. He won't be interested."

"What won't he be interested in?"

"This lady."

"Which lady?"

"The one in the plaid coat who rode up to Wilson's apartment that night. You seemed wrought up about her."

I put out the half-smoked cigarette and lighted one of my own. "Why do you think Barclay won't be interested? Everyone is interested in the solution of a mystery."

He crushed the light out of his cigarette and went through the regular routine of squeezing out the unsmoked tobacco and rolling the paper into a little ball. "I don't think you like me, Ansell."

"You're oversensitive," I said. "I'm sure I've never done anything to give you that impression."

"I've always tried to help you; I've given you a hand wherever I could and you've always laughed at me. Someday," he hinted in a whisper, "you may need help. I'm not without power in the organization."

"Thanks, but I don't believe in patronage. I'm the sort of fellow who fends for himself. Pulls himself up by the bootstraps, so to speak. Why is it, do you suppose, that my salary was raised to two hundred a week if it wasn't for my hard work and willing spirit?"

His mouth worked. "I've warned you, young man. If you're too smart to take a hint . . ." He slipped off the stool and, without finishing the sentence, left.

I was too smart to take the hint. Hating Munn and not wanting him or Barclay or anyone else to think I'd take a bribe, even temporarily, I did exactly what Munn had advised me not to do. Whether or not Barclay was interested in the lady in the plaid coat, he was going to hear about her. Even though the unknown Arvah might be proved Wilson's murderer, Barclay was involved in the case. When I had pursued my private investigations too far, someone had slipped a dose of poison into my water bottle. Then I had been bribed with a big raise and an important job. Probably other people had been bribed, too. What about the voice in the ambulance? Either I had been poisoned by shrimps I never ate or a few crisp bills had been slipped into the hand of an underpaid ambulance doctor.

Instead of dictating it to Miss Kaufman, I typed the memo myself. I did not want her to ask questions nor offer advice. The memo, I thought, was fat bait and would make the fish bite.

MEMORANDUM
From the office of: J. M. Ansell.
To: Mr. Barclay
Date: 12/7/45

Ref: Ms. 1028-TaC
Unsolved Mystery (Warren G. Wilson case)

According to information I have received privately from my contacts at Police Headquarters, this murder has been solved.

Inasmuch as we have gone to the expense of making layouts, illustrations, etc., I suggest we absorb this expense by having part of the story rewritten, eliminating the Unsolved Mystery angle, and run it in TaC. All objectionable matter, such as reference to spirituous liquor, irreverence toward correspondence schools, etc., can be eliminated.

Any personal objections you may have had to the use of this story are obviously eliminated by the solution of the mystery.

Copy to E. E. Munn.

I filed the third copy and sealed the other two in manila office envelopes, addressed them to Barclay and Munn, pasted red *Rush* stickers on them and put them in my Out-Basket.

Miss Kaufman came in, looked suspiciously at the Out-Basket, but did not ask why I typed my own memos. "You'd better step on it," she said. "Mr. Barclay won't like a new editor being late for a meeting."

I strutted out, the new editor bound for his first conference. On the way I passed the *Truth and Love* office. The door was open. Eleanor turned from the typewriter and blew me a kiss. At the risk of keeping her father waiting I stepped into her office and took her in my arms. She squealed.

"What's the matter? Don't you like it?"

"I love it, but the door's open."

"You weren't so cautious yesterday."

"It's your reputation I'm thinking of, Johnnie."

Lola Manfred had not come in. Eleanor was worried. "I've called three times but no one answers the phone. I can't imagine what's wrong. Lola always lets us know if she's going to be away from the office. Do you think anything could have happened?"

"She's probably sleeping off a hangover. How about dinner, Eleanor? We ought to celebrate. Think of some place expensive you'd like to go. Still love me? Then give me a kiss for luck and wish me well, I'm on my way to my first *Truth Digest* conference."

No one broke a bottle of champagne over the masthead of the new magazine. The boss was a teetotaler. We launched our ship on a dollar-fifty blue-plate sent upstairs by the Barclay Building Grille. The lunch conference was said to promote friendship and good feeling, which enabled Barclay to enter the expense as legitimate on his income-tax returns.

The conference table was covered with a damask cloth. Dishes and glassware were decorated with Barclay's monogram, surrounded by laurel wreaths. The forks were so heavy that the lightness of the food was barely noticeable.

Barclay sat at the head of the table. Opposite him was Gloria, his wife. He had found her in Beverly Hills, California, where her type is said to be indigenous. She was a long-legged, high-shouldered, full-breasted beauty. Every third month *Truth and Beauty* printed Gloria's picture to prove that healthy motherhood does not destroy the form divine. She had given Barclay twin sons.

At conferences Gloria represented the Woman's Angle. This custom had been instituted long ago when Barclay was married to his second wife, a Vassar graduate, said by office veterans to have been a highbrow. No one could accuse Gloria of anything like that.

I was the honored guest at the luncheon and sat at Barclay's right. At his left was Old Faithful, E. E. Munn. Next to Munn sat Loring Wince of the Advertising Department, then J. J. Javes of Legal, Burton English of Circulation, Henry Roe, Editor of *Truth Magazine,* and completing the group. Dr. Mason of the Board of Religious Coordination.

When we were all seated, a silence fell. It was like the moment before Opening Prayer. From the street rose the traffic noises, blurred and indistinct. Dr. Mason breathed through his mouth.

"Gentlemen," Barclay began, "and Mrs. Barclay. Our meeting today is a happy one. First of all we greet the new editor of a new magazine. From the day he entered our organization I recognized this young man's potentialities. Gentlemen and Mrs. Barclay, John Ansell."

It was like being singled out in the school assembly. Except for Gloria and Javes of the Legal Department, I had met them all before. I noticed Munn nodding as if he, as well as Barclay, had recognized my potentialities from the start.

Mrs. Barclay smiled graciously. "Why aren't you eating your cocktail, Mr. Ansell?"

"I don't eat shellfish. I have an allergy," I said.

"We don't believe in allergies." Gloria's smile condoned my ignorance. "We've proven they're part of the medical racket, another way of putting money in the doctors' pockets. Don't you just adore *Truth and Health*?"

"But shellfish doesn't agree with me," I argued. "I haven't touched it since my freshman year at college, when I'd eaten some . . ."

Barclay cleared his throat.

I remembered why I was the new editor, guest of honor at this luncheon. "Oh!" I said as if I'd been hit on the head with a steam roller. "I did eat shrimp last week and the next thing I knew I was in the hospital."

Barclay grinned.

Gloria's lovely brow puckered. "You must have had some humiliating or terrifying experience in early youth. In your unconscious mind it's probably associated with shrimps. Do you remember ever having been hurt or punished at the same time as . . ."

"My dear," Barclay interrupted, "your intentions are admirable, but we haven't time now. These are busy men."

She accepted the rebuke with a modest smile.

"The purpose of this meeting is to discuss our new magazine," Barclay said.

They all stopped chewing and nodded.

"This new magazine is going to be terrific. Brief, punchy, succinct, timely and," Barclay paused for emphasis, "courageous!"

They all nodded again and Munn repeated, reverently, "Courageous."

"Not that we've lacked courage in the past," Barclay continued. "In all modesty I say that no braver trumpet has heralded the truth to the reading public than the Truth group. We've bared the truth about subjects which no other publication would have looked at through a microscope or touched with antiseptic gloves."

"How true!" muttered Dr. Mason, scraping up cocktail sauce with a soda cracker.

"When I first told Ansell my idea for the new magazine, do you know what he said? He said I'd have to face stiff competition in the digest field. As if I didn't know! As if this were the first time the Barclay-Truth Publications have had to face competition."

An office boy came in, dropped mail into Barclay's In-Basket, looked over his shoulder at the lunch table and went out contemptuously. Among the mail in Barclay's basket I saw a manila office envelope decorated with a red *Rush* sticker.

" . . . and we're going to fight competition just the way we fought it in our other publications. How? By cutting the price. Just as we've done before. Remember, Wince, when we started *Truth and Love*? *True Story* and *True Confessions* were on top of the market at twenty-five cents a copy. We beat them by a dime. Was MacFadden furious? And when I brought out *Truth and Health* to compete with his beloved *Physical Culture*, and undersold him by a dime, he was ready to have me drawn and quartered." Barclay enjoyed the recollection. We were his guests and his employees and could not interrupt as he launched into a lengthy account of his prowess as a magazine publisher.

He did not, I noticed, bother to mention those magazines which had failed. *Truth in Pictures* could not compete with *Life*, nor even with its imitators. The younger generation had spurned his *Truth and Youth*, and while *Truth and Beauty* managed to stay alive, she limped far behind her competitors in what is known as "the woman's field." His motion-picture magazine had died ingloriously. Although Barclay had poured a mint of money into the project, *Truth in Hollywood* could not endure.

While Barclay entertained us with a detailed history of his triumphs, two waitresses entered, took away our empty cocktail cups and placed before each of us a plate containing creamed chicken, mashed potatoes, string beans and a few limp beets.

"In our new publication," Barclay thundered, "we shall be courageous as no other digest is courageous. As of this day, boys, the brakes are off. *Truth Digest* is going to make magazine history. And more than that, it's going to leave an indelible mark on modern civilization."

"What about advertising?" asked Loring Wince.

Barclay shook his head. "We're going to make more money without it. What do you think of that, boys, a magazine without advertising?"

"What's so new about that?" asked Burton English. "None of the digests carry advertising."

Munn looked hurt. He had no power over the insolent fellows in the Advertising and Circulation Departments. They brought in the money and could be as impudent as they liked.

"In considering the contents of our first issue," Barclay said, "I've made a survey of our magazines for the past ten years and found some great stuff. Dr. Mason . . ."

The Head of the Board of Religious Co-ordination looked up guiltily, as if it were a sin to enjoy creamed chicken.

"That campaign you and your associates prepared, Doctor, to run spiritualist fakes and other faith-parasites out of the country, that's as fresh as the day it was written. We might have to bring it up to date by including a few timely items, but very little work is required. And Henry," Barclay aimed his charm at Roe, "I want to reprint that remarkable series you did for us in '38 . . ."

"Not that stuff on unmasking dictators of the WPA?" Burton English cut in.

"Why not?" demanded Barclay.

"It's dated, and besides, many of our readers don't like it. Plenty of them have been on the projects."

Barclay shook his fork at the dissenter. "Truth Publications will never quit fighting until we're rid of dictatorship in our country, whether the dictatorship of a Stalin, a Roosevelt, or a Philip Murray. We may endanger ourselves in the battle, we may lose our worldly goods, our lives, even our liberty, but let us not falter in our duty."

"Hear! Hear!" That, of course, was E. E. Munn.

Burton English winked. Loring Wince smiled to himself. These cynics were less concerned with principles than with profits.

"What about the woman's angle?" asked Gloria brightly.

Barclay thanked her with a gracious smile.

It was the chance Munn had been waiting for. "I suggest illegitimacy."

"Good old illegitimacy, it never fails," said Wince of Circulation.

"Got to be careful," warned Javes of Legal.

Dr. Mason agreed.

"Do you gentlemen, and Mrs. Barclay, remember that confession in last April's *Truth and Love*?" asked Munn, "about the woman who refused marriage?"

"I do," cried Gloria. "'I Spurned a Wedding Ring.' She had six daughters."

"Perhaps she should have settled for the ring," I said.

Wince and English laughed. Munn looked pained.

The waitresses were in again. One was removing our plates while the other served ice cream and a square inch of pound cake.

"Syphilis is better," Dr. Mason said.

"I agree." Burton English was now quite serious. "We always go to town with syphilis."

The waitress dropped a plate of ice cream.

Barclay frowned slightly at the interruption of the conference. "I vote no on syphilis," he said, "particularly for the first issue. Syphilis has been overdone lately. The most conservative magazines are taking it up. I've got a better medical piece. 'Consider Your Glands, Medicine's Biggest Racket.'"

We considered our glands. In the corner the waitresses conferred in whispers. A critical situation had been caused by the ice-cream accident. One order was missing. All but Dr. Mason had been served. He looked anxious.

"Just a couple of minutes, dearie," the waitress said to him soothingly, and skipped off.

Javes of Legal asked, "When was it printed? I don't remember any gland pieces recently."

"I'm having it written now," Barclay said.

"Don't digest magazines use reprints?" asked the literal-minded legal member.

"This will be a reprint. *Truth and Health* will be on the stands a few days ahead of the *Digest*. That will give it timely quality. Shaw's doing the piece. I told him to give it the same guts and punch as 'Perversion in Our Colleges.'"

The waitress came back with a double order of ice cream for Dr. Mason. He took it like a Sunday-school treat.

"I've got an idea," Munn said eagerly. "If we want lively material, what about a condensation of the Podolsky articles?"

Henry Roe put down his spoon. "Are you crazy?"

"I believe they increased *Truth* circulation," Munn said coldly. "Isn't that true, Mr. English?"

"Increased cancellations."

Munn started to protest, but Barclay silenced him with a wave of his ice-cream spoon. He addressed himself to the Circulation and Advertising Departments. "Was it our fault that Russia didn't seize Manchuria as soon as the Jap war ended? Podolsky thought she would. So did I. So did a great many people who are wiser than we are, politically speaking. Let's say that Podolsky made an error."

"It wouldn't be the first time," I said.

"Are you questioning the integrity of one of our contributors?" Munn asked. "A rather important contributor, by the way. After all, he's a well-known authority on world affairs."

"A well-known fake," I added.

The silence was uneasy.

Gloria smiled brightly. "But General Podolsky's so charming. He has such old-world manners."

"He isn't a general," I told her. "He was never an officer in the Czar's Army. He's not even a Russian. His adventures never happened and most of his facts have been proved false."

Munn let out a hollow laugh. "Ansell must have been reading those Red newspapers."

"Like the *New York Times* and the *Herald Tribune*, Mr. Munn?"

"Ansell's right. You're right, lad," Barclay assured me. "Like everyone else in the world, Podolsky's made mistakes. But he's always been ready to acknowledge them. As a matter of fact, my faith in Podolsky is so great that I've asked him to join our staff."

Gloria beamed.

"In what capacity, may I ask?" queried Munn.

"As sort of roving reporter," Barclay said. "Later I may give him an editorial title. Right now I want him to travel around the country, take the national pulse, so to speak. I expect a sensational series for the new digest."

"Couldn't we use his articles in *Truth* first? Save a little money," suggested Munn as solemnly as if he were proposing a world-shaking idea.

"That's what I'd planned," Barclay said.

Munn wilted. Henry Roe winked at Gloria. She suppressed a giggle. The waitresses brought coffee for Javes, Wince, English, Henry Roe and me. Munn and Dr. Mason had tea, and Barclay and Gloria drank milk.

The contemptuous office boy brought in the afternoon papers. The conference table was in use, so he put the papers on the metal cover of the radiator just behind my chair.

I looked over my shoulder and read the headlines. Then I turned my back to the table and read a front-page column:

PLAID-COAT SUSPECT FOUND
Mystery Woman Confesses Ride in
Death Elevator

"The woman in plaid, sought in connection with the death last May of Warren G. Wilson, bachelor recluse, confessed this morning to Captain A. C. Riordan of the Detective Bureau that she rode in the elevator to Wilson's floor the night he was shot in the back. She is Arvah Lucille Kennedy, divorcee, of Bayside, L. I. Suffering pangs of . . . turn to Page 21."

I turned to Page 21. Barclay went on talking about policy, truth and the new digest. Arvah Lucille Kennedy had not killed Warren G. Wilson. She had never met the late tenant of Suite 3002-4. On the night of May eleventh, wearing a plaid coat, she rode to the thirtieth floor of the exclusive apartment hotel because her *friend* did not want her to be seen getting off at the twenty-eighth. She had walked down two flights for the sake of her friend's reputation.

Her friend was Frederick Semple, morning-coated manager of the hotel. He could not set a bad example to guests nor let employees discover that he had relations with the Bayside divorcee. It was for Mr. Semple's sake that Arvah had kept silent for six months.

"What are you reading, Ansell?"

Everyone at the table stared. I could see that Dr. Mason and E. E. Munn were shocked by my bad manners. "You'll be interested, Mr. Barclay," I said, and handed him the paper.

He was about to refuse it when I pointed to the plaid-coat headline.

"Excuse me, boys," muttered Barclay and began to read the Kennedy story.

Loring Wince and Burton English lit cigarettes. J. J. Javes of Legal asked Gloria if she minded a pipe. Munn told her that he admired her chapeau. I watched Barclay.

In the wire basket on his desk was the envelope with my memo. The basket was less than ten feet from where I sat, but I could not, in the sight of the boss, the boss's wife and six other employees, snatch mail from the boss's desk.

"Very interesting," Barclay said as he handed me back the paper.

We went on with the meeting. I contributed nothing. It was my first important conference and I was a two-hundred-dollar flop. English, Wince, Mason, Javes and Roe offered bright ideas or criticized unprofitable ones. All I thought about was the memo in Barclay's basket.

It was after three when the meeting broke up. English, Roe, Wince and Javes left. Dr. Mason stayed for a private word with Barclay. Gloria was talking to Munn. I had no excuse for hanging around. I walked to the door slowly.

Barclay had gone to his desk. Dr. Mason leaned over it, whispering some confidential question or opinion. Barclay was not listening. He had taken the mail from his basket.

As I left he was opening the envelope with the red sticker.

The phone rang.

I looked at my watch. It was twenty minutes to four.

"Yes, he is," Miss Kaufman said. She put down the phone and turned to me, saying, "He wants you in his office. Right away."

I was glad. The agony was about to start, but the suspense was over. Barclay had promoted me, raised my salary, made me his new favorite in order to keep me quiet. I had accepted the bribe and he thought he had me where he wanted me. And how he had discovered that I was not content to stay quiet in my niche.

Munn passed me in the hall. "Great meeting, wasn't it?" Evidently he had not seen my memo.

Miss Eccles smiled, too. "Go right in. He's waiting for you, Mr. Ansell."

Gloria was still in Barclay's office. She greeted me brightly. "I'm so glad to know you at last, Mr. Ansell. Daddy's told me so much about you. You must dine with us some night. I'll arrange it with Eleanor."

News traveled fast in the Barclay office. I did not mind their knowing about Eleanor. What puzzled me was the air of approval. Barclay nodded over Gloria's invitation. On his desk, at the center of the blotter, my memo lay.

"Lover," Barclay said to his wife, "I've got to speak to this young man about business. I'm sure it wouldn't interest you."

"Yes, dear." She kissed her husband, wrapped herself in sables, waved a farewell, and was gone.

Barclay picked up the memo. "What's the meaning of this, lad? Trying to be funny, eh?" The approach was mild. He had probably planned his strategy.

"No, Mr. Barclay."

"What are you trying to get at?"

"Don't you know?"

Barclay knew the power of silence. In the outside offices typewriters were clicking, people talking on telephones, office boys slamming doors, but Barclay's quarters were soundproof. There was only the muted hum of traffic, twenty-five stories below.

"Look, Mr. Barclay," I began nervously, "I heard the lady in plaid had been found and I naturally thought the murder'd been solved." I spoke in the clear monotonous voice of a schoolboy reciting the multiplication tables. "As I told you in my memo, I thought we could use the cuts instead of junking them. Save the organization some money."

It was a neat excuse. Showed that I had the interests of the firm at heart, rather than a single magazine. It should have convinced Barclay of my good will.

He shook his head. Strong, tanned hands clenched and unclenched. He seemed older. There was not so much arrogance in his carriage.

"Tell me, Mr. Barclay, why do you want to suppress that story?"

He crossed the office. The thick carpet muffled his footsteps. He came close to me and we stood side by side, Barclay six foot three and Ansell, a pint-sized runt. But Barclay could not answer my question.

I went on bravely. "What have I got to be afraid of? I don't eat shrimps. I can't take seafood. I could get the waitress to say that I ate lamb chops that night."

"You're a cocky little guy, aren't you?"

"I don't like being pushed around. Why the hell are you afraid to run the Wilson story?"

Barclay walked back to his desk, head high. "All right, I'm going to lay my cards on the table. After you know, you may change your tune. Sit down."

I sat down.

The door opened. Munn rushed in, the carbon copy of my memo in his hand. "Did you see this?" he said.

"I know all about it, Ed. John and I are talking it over now." Barclay had recovered his poise. Edward Everett Munn was the dirt under his feet.

Munn looked at me as if he could not believe that I was there, sitting in a comfortable chair, peacefully talking to the boss about that infamous memo.

"I shan't need you, Ed."

"I'd better stay." Munn stood firm.

"I told you I didn't need you," Barclay snapped. "Get the hell out."

There was neither devotion nor obedience in the look Munn gave Barclay. I expected a retort, even a quarrel. But Barclay had caught the look of rebellion in Munn's face, and had turned to stone. The silent trick was evidently one of his strongest weapons. Munn shrugged one shoulder and went away.

"What's this all about, Mr. Barclay?"

"Why are you so keen on this Wilson story, John?"

"I'm a writer, Mr. Barclay. I wrote a story. You said it was a good story and then you refused to publish it. That's all that concerns me."

Barclay rolled my memo into a cone and swept its point back and forth across his desk blotter. It was the first time I had seen him make a nervous or unnecessary movement. "Do you know that Eleanor was a friend of Wilson's?"

There was a long silence. He looked at the paper cone, at the desk blotter, at his hands, while he waited. I showed no surprise. I wasn't shocked because I had had this information already—from Wilson himself. Back on St. Valentine's Day he had inscribed a volume of poetry to a genteel lady.

"Was she?" I had decided to play dumb, to wait and learn.

"Do you know she had a date with him the night he was killed?"

That hit me harder. It took effort for me to answer in the same dry monotone. "Did she?"

A light burned green in the box on Barclay's desk. He spoke into a grilled panel. "I'm busy now. I'm not taking any calls." The room was getting dark. Twilight had entered like fog. The big man sat quietly at his desk, shoulders bowed, arms extended, hands limp beside the bronze nudes that held a cauldron of ink.

In a voice so cold and distant that I barely recognized it as my own, I said, "She had a date with Wilson the night he was killed, you say. What happened? Do you know the facts, Mr. Barclay?"

He crushed the pink memo and tossed it into the waste basket. "You know how I feel about secrets." His voice was warmer. Barclay had decided to take me into his confidence. "I don't believe in secrets.

Buried truths are festering sores. Dig them out, cleanse the wounds, tell the truth no matter how painful. That's my creed and I try to live by it. But when someone else is involved," he drew in his breath, "and that person has never confided in you, it plays the very devil with your conscience."

"Wait a minute. If she hadn't confided them, how did you know Eleanor's secrets, Mr. Barclay?"

"Eleanor had a date with Wilson; they were to have dined together the night of his death. I learned about it by mistake. The switchboard girl thought his message was meant for me instead of Eleanor. Mr. Barclay, not Miss Barclay, you understand. As soon as I learned about it I sent for Eleanor and demanded an explanation."

"Why?"

"Eleanor had never told me she knew Wilson."

"Should she have?"

He swallowed twice, nodded and said, "A father is a father."

"So I've been told. Do you always demand an explanation when you discover that she's dining with a man? Or was there something special about Wilson?" My voice was low, my manner objective. I might have been asking his opinion of an unimportant editorial detail.

"If you knew the facts you wouldn't be quite so flippant, young man. Eleanor had a gun on her when she came into my office. She was hysterical . . ." His voice trailed off, and he looked beyond me into the window which the room's lights and the sky's darkness had turned into a mirror. It gave back a hard, glazed portrait of Noble Barclay.

"A gun. Why?"

"She'd been in the Studio, directing pictures for *Truth and Love*. When she came up here, the gun was in her hand."

"What the hell's that got to do with Wilson?" I shouted. Barclay's facts had not got under my skin. They were too tenuous and irrelevant. What irritated me was his assumption that I ought to be frightened off by scattered hints. "Are you trying to scare me off by hinting that Eleanor shot him with one of the Studio guns?"

Barclay winced. "You love her, John. You and I, we both love that kid. I was glad when I saw that she was falling for you. A clean, intelligent and ambitious young man. Why do you suppose I've been trying to build you up? You've got a great future, you know."

"Shrimps, Mr. Barclay. I do not eat shrimps."

"Eleanor needs you. You can help her, take care of her . . ."

I saw then that Barclay wasn't merely playing a game. Veins bulged on his forehead. The sweat stood out in giant dewdrops. His eyes clouded.

"Look, Mr. Barclay, let's get at the facts. You found out that Eleanor had a date with Wilson, and you sent for her to come up here. She had a gun in her hand, one of the property guns from the Studio. It wasn't loaded; those guns never are. Granted that she could have got shells if she had wanted them, why should she? What possible reason could she have had for wanting to kill Wilson?"

"She was very angry when I sent for her. Irrationally angry."

"Why irrationally? She's a grown woman and even though a father is a father, must she be interrogated whenever she dines with a man? What was there about Wilson? You must have known something, Mr. Barclay, to have sent for her."

"Did she ever mention Wilson to you, John?"

I had begun to sweat, too.

"That's what I thought," Barclay said. "She's kept it from you, too. It's that secretive strain in them. Her mother was the same way. You could never tell what she was thinking." He passed his hand over his eyes as if he had caught a glimpse of some hideous shape lurking in the shadows. "Eleanor's mother killed herself, you know."

I did know. The Introduction to *My Life Is Truth* is Barclay's autobiography.

"Her family," he went on huskily, "overbred aristocrats. Sensitive. Secretive. She's been growing more and more like them. John, I've been worried." He wiped the sweat from his forehead. His voice, more than his words, confessed hidden fear. I thought of the creed by which he lived. Buried truths are festering sores . . .

"Are you trying to tell me, Mr. Barclay, that you believe Eleanor killed Wilson?"

Scorn twisted his mouth. His dark eyes hardened. Noble Barclay shuddered with contempt at John Miles Ansell, an insensitive dolt who asked stupid questions. Everything that Barclay had tried subtly to convey I had cried aloud. Why, unless sternest truth demanded, should a father accuse his daughter of murder?

Barclay walked off. At the end of the room, he squared his shoulders, turned and came back to me. The mood had lightened. He was no longer contemptuous, but sympathetic, my ally in sorrow. His hand fell upon my shoulder and his eyes sought understanding.

"She needs love, John." His voice tightened. "If I'd been able to help her mother, she'd have been all right, too. We've got to take care of that girl, you and I . . ."

I shrugged away from the heavy hand. "Your facts haven't convinced me. They're irrelevant. They don't prove anything. I care too much for her to believe she'd be capable of anything like that." It was a noble speech, but unconvincing. I did not even succeed in fooling myself.

"Fine!" Barclay boomed. "Splendid, my lad. Good for you. That's what she needs, love, devotion, unswerving loyalty."

"I'd have to have proof," I blustered, "damn good proof before I'd believe anything."

"Then you'll never do anything to harm her." Barclay offered his most magnanimous smile. "You'll do everything in your power to protect her. I can trust you to look out for my little girl."

He swung out his hand. I took it. The clasp was strong, hard and dry. To Barclay that handclasp meant he had won me, and we were united now in our determination to protect Eleanor. To me it was phony, like the oaths and handclasps and drawn blood of schoolboy vows. I jerked my hand away. Barclay let his drop and stood quiet for a moment. There was a pinched look about him. He seemed afraid to turn around. I listened, too. There was no sound in the office except his heavy breathing.

It had grown very dark. The room smelled of sweat.

There was a sheet of yellow paper stuck into my typewriter. On it Eleanor had typed:

Johnnie darling:

I can't go to dinner with you in an old hat. Loving you as I do, it is imperative that I have a new one. I shan't be back at the office, so stop by for me around seven. I do love you.

E.

A silly note, but I liked it. The switch from melodrama to millinery lightened my mood. How could I suspect a girl who had to buy a new hat because she loved me? Notice that word, *suspect.* I tried again and again to reassure myself by arguing that Barclay had dragged Eleanor's name into the case merely to throw me off the scent, but I could not achieve one hundred per cent conviction. I did not believe Eleanor had killed Wilson but I was sure she knew something about the murder.

Why, for instance, had she never told me of her friendship with Wilson? Why had she kept it from her father until the switchboard gave *Mr.* Barclay's secretary the message intended for *Miss* Barclay? Was it merely coincidence that this happened on the day of Wilson's death, or had there been some connection? Why had Barclay summoned his daughter from the Studio when he heard that she was dining with Warren G. Wilson?

It was half past seven when I arrived at Eleanor's. I was late deliberately. My idea was to get her out of the apartment, into some public place where we would both have to be careful of our words and our voices. I had no definite plan, but I knew myself well enough to distrust any vows of discretion.

She greeted me sweetly. We kissed.

"What's the matter?" she said. "Why are you like that?"

"Like what?"

Without answering she went off to fetch her wraps. I looked at the Blake again, studied Wilson's inscription. When I heard her coming, I put the volume back on the shelf. She was wearing a fur coat that smelled faintly of camphor. Her hair hung loose. It was tied on the side with a brown bow.

"Where's the new hat?"

"I didn't get one."

"Why not?"

"I couldn't find one I liked."

"In all that time? You were gone two hours."

"I don't like the hats this season. They look like deformities."

On Fifth Avenue we turned. Eleanor went on talking about hats. She was trying to be funny. The season's hats were all designed by men who hated women, she said, or by hideous women who wanted to destroy other women's looks.

"You've certainly given a lot of thought to the psychology of modern millinery," I said. "Why don't you do a piece for *Truth and Love* about it?"

"I'm sorry if I bore you."

"Where were you this afternoon?"

"I went to buy a hat."

"Why didn't you buy one?"

We had started across Fifth Avenue. A bus came along. I jerked Eleanor toward the curb.

"What's the matter, Johnnie? Why are you acting like that?"

"If I'm acting any differently than I usually act I'm not aware of it. Why are you so sensitive?"

I had hold of her arm. She pulled it away. "You kissed me as if I had halitosis. Then you got mad because I talked about hats. In fact you accused me of lying because I couldn't find a hat I liked. Then you practically yanked my arm out of its socket."

"I'm sorry. I was trying to save your life."

"Maybe you're sorry about last night. Perhaps you regret it now, saying you love me and," she hesitated, shy of words, "making plans."

I did not try to comfort her. We walked at opposite edges of the sidewalk. I led her past five restaurants to the door of Jean Pierre's.

"How about this place?"

"No." Before I had a chance to argue, she had turned around and was walking downtown again.

"Want to go to the Brevoort?"

"I don't care."

"Why don't you like Jean Pierre's? The food is wonderful."

"I don't want to eat there."

"Does it remind you of Wilson?"

The attack was not planned. Impatience had shoved me off balance. I was too restless to fence around any longer, too undisciplined to follow a pattern.

Eleanor said, "Is that why you took me there?"

"Why didn't you tell me you knew him?"

We were again at a crossing. Eleanor darted into the street so that I'd have no chance to take her arm. At the other side she waited. Falling into step beside me, she remarked coolly, "I've known lots of people I've never told you about. Have I ever told you how Lindbergh kissed me? I'll show you the photographs if you're interested."

"You knew I was writing the Wilson story."

"No, I didn't. Not until you were ill at the hospital. Alfie Witzel was doing a *Truth and Love* yarn about Tommy Manville and I had to finish it, because he was rushed over to *Truth and Crime* to finish your Unsolved Mystery." She spoke as if there had been no more to it than a switch in office routine.

"Just the same I should think you'd have told me about him."

"Why?"

"It isn't everyone who's been intimate with a murder victim."

"I was never intimate with Mr. Wilson."

"I don't mean intimate. I mean you knew him and he was murdered. It seems strange you never mentioned him. When I was free-lancing I knew a woman who came from the same part of Chicago as Loeb and Leopold and she made a career for herself of it."

"I didn't know him so awfully well." She glanced down Fifth Avenue toward the hotel where Wilson had lived and died, and then looked away as if it had been no more important to her than Grant's Tomb. Her defiance had melted into a strange sick indifference.

"Were you in love with him?"

"Don't be a fool, Johnnie. He was forty-eight. Let's not go to dinner right away. Are you hungry?"

"Aren't you?"

"I couldn't look at food. Let's sit in Washington Square."

The night was cold. We must have looked like a pair of idiots to the cop who watched over his shoulder as we chose a bench. Idiots, or lovers who had no place for privacy. We did not sit like lovers. There were six or seven inches between us.

"How long did you know him?"

"Mr. Wilson?" From where we sat we had only to raise our eyes and we could see the terrace of Wilson's apartment. "I met him last year. In September. September thirtieth."

"And you say you didn't know him very well."

"I didn't."

"You seem to be pretty accurate about the day you met him. It must have been sort of important to you if you remember it that well."

She laughed. "I remember the day because it happened to be important to me. It was the day I broke my engagement."

That knocked the breath out of me. "There seems to be a lot of things you've never told me."

"I wanted to forget about it."

"Who was the man?"

She jerked her dress down over her knees and pulled her fur coat over the hem of her dress. A man and woman passed, pushing against the west wind. It was a raw night and we were a couple of fools to be fighting on a bench in Washington Square.

"Who was he?"

Eleanor laughed again, mirthlessly, and the woman looked back at us. After a while she said, "I hated him."

"And you were engaged to him?"

She nodded.

"Why?"

"I oughtn't to get emotional, ought I, now that it's all over?" Her voice sounded like one of the smaller brass instruments. "It was just after my father married Gloria. Not that I dislike Gloria . . ." she grimaced and went on quickly, "Gloria's very nice. She adores my father. This man was older; he seemed kind and he was a good friend of my father's, too . . ."

"But you didn't love him?"

"Oh, God!" She began suddenly to laugh. There was no gaiety in it. It was like the laughter of someone who had not laughed for years, a deaf mute finding a voice and using it in mockery. The tones were all metal. They hit me in the pit of the stomach.

"Shut up," I snapped.

The policeman was standing under an arc light Her laughter floated out to him.

"Control yourself," I said.

The laughter ended as abruptly as it had started.

"Sorry," whispered Eleanor in a meek little voice.

"You needn't talk about it if it affects you that way. Would you like a drink?"

"No, thanks. I'd like to tell you about it, Johnnie. You see, I once thought that I could learn to love a man. I tried," her voice was humble, "but I couldn't bear it if he kissed me or touched me. I thought I was frigid. A frigid woman. I was reading for *Truth and Love* and there was all that stuff about failing to respond to normal love, and I was afraid I wasn't normal. I thought I hated men." She looked at the apartment building standing tall among the old four-story houses. "I've never said this aloud before."

"There's nothing for you to be worried about. You're perfectly okay, honey. You're wonderful." I reached across the bench for her hand. The memory of last night's love sent the blood rushing through my body.

She slid toward me on the bench. I put my arm around her. To hell with Warren G. Wilson! The scene in Barclay's office had begun to fade. Her hair blew across my face.

"Believe me, Johnnie, you're the first man I've ever loved."

"I believe you," I said.

"Mr. Wilson was nothing but a friend." She pressed my hand. "I've got to tell you about him, or what will you think? I have nothing to hide." Her face was close to mine, and in the lamplight I could see the contrasts. No wonder Gustav and Jean Pierre had not been able to name the exact color of her hair and eyes. With every variation of light and mood she was different.

"I'd been engaged for almost a year," she said. "And then I decided I couldn't stand it anymore. That was September thirtieth. So I went into my father's office and told him about it. I was scared to death. This man, you see, was my father's friend."

"How'd your father take it?"

"He was wonderful, just as kind as could be. Lots of people don't understand Father; they think he pretends to believe in Truth-Sharing because it's made such a lot of money, but he is sincere, Johnnie. That I know with my heart; Father is the most sincere man in the world." There had crept into her manner the defiance with which she always met her father's critics. "Father said I was sensible to face the truth; he was glad he'd educated me to be honest with myself; and I certainly need not marry a man I couldn't love. Father was wonderful . . ."

She would have gone on talking about Barclay, defending him against unspoken criticism, if I had not interrupted. "What had this to do with Wilson? You met him that night, you say. Where?"

"At Jean Pierre's. I picked him up. Have you a cigarette, Johnnie?"

I lighted one for her. She pushed closer toward me on the bench, fitted her shoulder under my armpit.

A new tenant had moved into Wilson's apartment. I saw the lights go on in the room beyond the topmost terrace.

"How did you happen to pick him up? What were you doing in Jean Pierre's? Dining alone?"

"I'd gone to dinner with Lola. In a way it was a sort of celebration. Lola'd never approved of this man I was engaged to . . ."

"Oh! She knew?" I said and felt angry about it, cheated because neither Eleanor nor Lola had ever spoken to me about the engagement.

"I'd never told her in so many words that we were engaged. I never told anyone," Eleanor shivered delicately. "No one knew except Father and Gloria. But Lola guessed. She watched me when I talked to him; even on the phone, she said, I showed it. So naturally, when I broke it, I asked Lola to have dinner with me. Or maybe it was Lola who suggested it. I don't remember. I do remember that she suggested Jean Pierre's because I'd never eaten there. Lola insisted on buying the dinner, and we ordered wonderful food, petite marmite and sweetbreads en cloche and a green salad and profiteroles and coffee . . ."

"Considering that you'd just discarded your fiancé, your appetite wasn't at all bad."

"That's just what Mr. Wilson said."

"Oh, you told him your life story."

"I told him why I was eating alone, and how an emotional crisis always affects my appetite." "Eating alone! I thought Lola was with you." "Right in the middle she remembered that she'd stood up a lovelorn young man at the Lafayette. So she had to excuse herself. She paid the bill though and told me to finish my dinner."

Wilson's apartment was dark again. The curtains had been drawn. I had seen pictures of the living room and I wondered how it had been when Wilson lived there and Eleanor came to visit him. "So the minute Lola left you alone, you picked up a man?" "That's not kind of you, Johnnie. You make me sound like a trollop. Anyway he picked me up. He was sitting at the next table and he kept watching me . . ." "Through the soup, sweetbreads, salad, dessert and coffee?" "He was very courteous about it. He sent the headwaiter over to ask if I'd accept a liqueur. Then he came over to my table and said I looked awfully familiar . . ." "Couldn't he have thought of a more original line?" "It was true. He'd seen my picture in the magazines. After all, Johnnie, I've been the Truth Girl since I was twelve years old. When you've had as much publicity as I've had, you can't be fresh to people . . ." "Not when they come to your table and offer you liqueurs." "Mr. Wilson wasn't like that. He was one of the most interesting men I've ever met. He knew such a lot about poetry, for instance, and the life of marine animals and the Russian novelists and desert vegetation." She took a last puff at the cigarette and threw the stub on the gravel walk.

"You used to go up to his apartment," I said.

"Why shouldn't I? Mr. Wilson wasn't fresh. And besides I'm independent. I earn my own living. If a girl supports herself why shouldn't she go to a man's apartment?"

"Look, dear, I'm not trying to put you on the spot. I know Wilson wasn't fresh; he talked about marine life and the Russian novelists and desert vegetation. He had seven hundred phonograph records and always gave you the best brandy. Why shouldn't you have gone to his apartment?"

"You're talking like my father," she said coldly.

"Oh! He didn't approve, I take it."

"He was furious when he found out."

"Apparently he doesn't approve of the same conduct for his daughter as for the heroines of his true-love tales."

"That's just what I told him," Eleanor said. "I told him I was shocked at finding him so hypocritical."

"Was that on the day he discovered that you knew Wilson?"

"What do you know about that day, Johnnie?"

"I know the switchboard operator made a mistake and sent a message intended for Miss Barclay to Mr. Barclay's office. I know that when your father sent for you, you were down in the Studio . . ."

"Who told you? My father?" Her voice had grown brassy.

"Let's try to keep our heads," I said. I wanted to sound strong and dependable. I hoped that Eleanor would feel that she had at last found someone in whom she could safely confide. "For some reason or other, everyone seems to get hysterical when Wilson's name is mentioned. Please, please try to keep calm . . ."

My words had the wrong effect. She was starting to laugh again. I took her hand and twisted the wrist so that it hurt. Her laughter ended abruptly.

"I'm sorry," I said, "but I didn't want you to go hysterical on me again. I can't stand it."

"You're right," she whispered. She fished in her bag for a handkerchief and wiped her eyes. I lit her another cigarette.

"Look," I said, "we're going to hold hands. If you feel that you're going to start laughing, just squeeze. Although I don't see why you get so worked up every time we mention something that happened six months ago."

She squeezed my hand. "You're sweet, Johnnie."

"Now, take it easy. I'm going to ask you some questions. Why did your father get so upset at discovering that you had a date with Wilson?"

Her hand lay quiet in mine. "I don't know," she said. "It seemed ridiculous. After Father got that message from the switchboard operator, he phoned Mr. Wilson to see what it was about."

"Then your father knew Wilson?"

Her hand tightened. "Obviously, if he phoned him. He must have known where Mr. Wilson lived. And I guess Mr. Wilson must have told him the message was for me . . ."

"What did the message say?"

"It was only to remind me of our dinner date. That we were meeting at half past seven. It wasn't a very revealing message."

"Obviously your father had some reason for sending for you and asking about Wilson. Or does he do that whenever you have a date?"

Eleanor began to push at the gravel with her foot. "We had a ghastly fight, the first fight I'd ever had with Father. What right had he to forbid me to see Mr. Wilson?"

"Your father evidently knew Wilson and had something against him."

"He said Mr. Wilson wanted to destroy him. He said the only thing Mr. Wilson lived for was to hurt him."

"Sounds pretty melodramatic," I said.

"That's what I told Father. But he wasn't as bad as Ed. Ed was all excited. Father got angry and told him to keep his mouth shut. He kept snapping the lid of his cigarette case until I nearly went crazy."

"So Munn was there, too?"

"What do you think?" she asked scornfully. "Father had him telephone Mr. Wilson and say I couldn't have dinner with him. I was furious."

"Naturally. But didn't you find out what it was that Wilson had against your father?"

"He told me Mr. Wilson had done him a bad turn."

"Sounds as if your father ought to be the one who wanted revenge."

She shook her head. "I said that, too, but Father thinks it's more human to hate people we've injured than those who have hurt us. I think that's sound psychology, don't you?"

I thought of Lola Manfred and how she had once said that Noble Barclay had put the word, psychology, into the one-syllable class.

"Johnnie . . ." Eleanor looked at me intently, her eyes straining in the dim light to catch my expression.

"What is it?"

"When my father talked to you, did he mention a book?"

"Book? What kind of book."

"Then it doesn't matter, I guess. It must only have been my imagination." Eleanor sighed. "I looked in the newspapers after he died, but there was never any mention of a manuscript."

"You mean Wilson was writing a book?"

"He was writing a book," she said in a slightly irritable way as though I should have got this information from some psychic source. "I told them about it that night when my father said Wilson was only living to hurt him. I said Mr. Wilson was only living to finish his book. Ed Munn got awfully excited, but my father said Mr. Wilson was a fraud and nobody'd believe his book anyway."

"Do you know what the book was about?"

"I know the title."

"What was it?"

"*The Autobiography of Homer Peck.*"

My fingers tightened on hers. This was not consciously an exorcism of hysteria; it was my impulsive reaction to the title of Wilson's book.

"Are you shocked, too? What does it mean?"

I drew a deep breath. "I don't know. When I was working on the Wilson story I came across a reference to this Peck guy. I don't know anything about him, but it rings a bell. Do you remember what they said about Mr. Peck's autobiography?"

"They didn't say anything at first. They seemed to hold their breath. You know what I mean, Johnnie, when the silence becomes louder than sound. It embarrassed me and I began to chatter. I said . . ."

"What?"

"It was silly. About the title of Mr. Wilson's book. I had told him I didn't like it. Why should he call a book an autobiography unless it was about himself? Or fiction, of course, written in the first person. But he said it wasn't fiction. He said it was the truth about fiction, that's why it was stranger than fiction."

"Is that what you told your father?"

"Uh-huh."

"What'd he say?"

"I don't remember." She pondered. "Ed wanted to say something, but Father sent him away. Father said he wanted to talk to me privately."

"What'd he tell you?"

She uttered a half-note of laughter. "His life story. About how he used to be drunk all the time and full of passion and how his dear mother had died of a broken heart and it was his fault that my mother killed herself, and all the rest of it."

"Then it wasn't the first time he'd talked like that to you?"

"I've been hearing it since I was six." She laughed again, ruefully. "But there's something about my father when he tells that story; he's so sincere and powerful that when he used to lecture, people thronged to the platform to confess their secret desires and their hidden sins."

"Did you confess?"

"I had nothing to confess. But he broke me down; he can always do that. Makes me feel that I've been stubborn and willful, that there's something weak and inferior that I have to compensate for by trying to express my own will. And then he shows me that I'm not alone in these unworthy feelings and that he understands and forgives, and I'm all right. Perhaps you don't believe me."

"It's happened to me, too. When your father uses his charm the beasts of field and forest lie down together."

"But when it's over and you're away from him, it stops. You fall with a thud. I've been falling a lot lately. People like Gloria and Grace Eccles can read a chapter from the book and become uplifted again. Not me though, not lately." She laughed again, but this time her laughter was free. "I've never talked like this before in my life, Johnnie."

"That night," I said slowly, "you fell with a thud, huh? How long after?"

"Later in the evening. Father took me to dinner and made a terrific fuss over me. It was like old times before he met Gloria. He made me feel so wonderful and important I felt disloyal for having questioned him. And then," she ran her hand through her hair, "then he had to broadcast; it was Friday, *Voice of Truth* night, so he put me in a taxi and sent me home. I suddenly realized that I'd been a sucker and he hadn't given me a single reason why I shouldn't go on seeing Mr. Wilson. So I phoned him . . ."

"What time was it?"

"Half past nine, ten, I don't remember. I tried calling him again Saturday, but there was no answer. So I thought maybe he'd gone away for the week-end."

"When did you find out he was dead?"

"Sunday. It came over the radio." Her face in that uncertain light was like a mask made of some brittle material like clay or china, and her eyes were like hard stones set into the mask.

"What did your father say about it?"

"I never mentioned it to him."

"The hell you didn't!" I let go of Eleanor's hand and stood up. I couldn't believe her. It was incredible. On Friday evening she and her father had quarreled about Wilson; on Sunday morning Wilson's murdered body was discovered and Friday night named as the time of his death. "You must have talked about it. It's not possible."

"No." Her voice had gone flat. "Father and Gloria had gone away Saturday morning, to spend the week-end in Washington with the Senator. I didn't see him until late Monday afternoon in the office."

"And you didn't mention Wilson?"

The flat voice continued, "Father didn't bring it up; so I never mentioned it either. I'm always afraid to face things that I know will be unpleasant. I guess you don't believe me."

"For a couple of Truth-sharers you Barclays are about the most secretive people I've ever met. Why were you so afraid to talk to him about it?"

She had grown rigid. I had seen Eleanor like this before, protecting herself in the same steely way against the gibes and criticisms of the cynics at the Editors' Table. Tonight, for the first time, I had heard her question her father's sincerity. She had given a fine exhibition of resentment. Until now I had thought it was her love for Noble Barclay that made her so contemptuous of all scoffers. She had told me, defiantly, "I love my father." I saw now that it was not love, and not pride that she had been protecting, but doubt.

That clinched it for me. I said, "He thinks you did it."

"My father?"

"He thinks you killed Wilson."

"Did he tell you that?" Her voice was low and polite. She might have been asking whether I thought it would snow or if I liked two pieces of sugar in my coffee.

Night classes at NYU had let out. Bareheaded girls and spectacled youths rushed across Washington Square. Their voices were young and carefree, but typical of New York, nasal and arrogant.

"He told you that, Johnnie?"

"This afternoon your father warned me against trying to find out anymore about this case. He's been protecting you and what he tried to say is that if I love you, I ought to . . ."

"Do you believe it?"

"No, I don't," I said, "but I think you know more than you pretend."

Her hands lay in her lap. She looked up at me, straining to see my face. Her lips moved but she did not immediately speak. The city, too, had become quiet. A curious kind of silence surrounded us as if we had suddenly entered a soundproof room.

She hugged the fur coat tighter about her. "You don't love me," she said bitterly. "You're like the rest of them, wanting to find out something. You wanted to know about us. You wanted to talk and write articles and show off. You made me think you loved me . . ."

An ambulance shrieked down Fifth Avenue. Its siren roused me. The circle was broken; I heard every living sound: the taxi horns, the tires, the brakes, the clatter of heels on the pavement, the shrill young voices. The NYU students were still passing, talking of their class work, probably, of French and trigonometry, of economics, of UN, the Russian drives, of Benny Goodman, Jack Benny and Benay Venuta.

Eleanor had gone. She had hurried off, clattering along like the others on her high heels. Bareheaded, fur coat open, one of the crowd, like the girls she envied, the college girls with unimportant fathers. I hurried after her. NYU students swarmed the path. Three girls walked arm in arm, whispering. I cut through their secrets. "Where's the fire?" they shouted after me.

At Fifth Avenue and Eighth Street, Eleanor jumped into a cab. I rushed across the street after her but a horn warned me and I leaped back to the curb. The lights had turned green. Eleanor's cab moved off. Before I could find an empty taxi, hers was nothing but a red tail-light among a lot of other red tail-lights.

I walked up Fifth Avenue. At Twenty-third Street I remembered that I had not eaten dinner. I decided to go into Childs. On the way I bought a newspaper. I did not read it right away, for I was too concerned with my own affairs to care about the rest of the world. When the waitress brought my steak and French fries, I opened the paper.

It was a conservative paper, not a tabloid, so that I did not see Lola's picture until I turned to Page 3. It was a one-column cut made from an old photograph taken when Lola had been slim and young and dark-haired. The headline ran across two columns. It read:

POETESS FOUND DEAD

Lola Manfred's Body Found in
Greenwich Village Apartment
Suicide, Police Theory

I pushed my plate away. The odor of the fried potatoes sickened me. The waitress hurried across the tiled floor, but I had already grabbed my hat and overcoat. I motioned toward the table where I had left two dollar bills beside the plate. The waitress stared after me through the plate-glass window.

I started walking north, thinking of Lola and what she had said about her autobiography. *Sand Against the Wind* was to have the title because Lola had mocked at everything. She had to be an exhibition-ist, she explained, because she had become too lazy to write poetry. There had been more to it than that, I thought. Something besides laziness had paralyzed her talent.

At Thirty-fourth Street I went into a cigar store and waited in line until the phone booth was empty. Fortunately Riordan's home phone number was in the little book I carry in my pocket.

"This is Ansell," I said and waited for the name to register. "Ansell of *Truth and Crime* Magazine."

"I know. In trouble, Ansell?"

"Lola Manfred didn't commit suicide. I'd bet my last dollar on it."

"Who's Lola Manfred?"

"Haven't you seen the papers? Poetess discovered in Greenwich Village studio apartment. They say it's suicide, but I have a hunch. Lola Manfred knew who killed Warren G. Wilson . . ."

"Just a minute," Riordan said. He must have put his hand over the mouthpiece and talked to someone else. Then he said, "Meet me at Headquarters. It'll take me about twenty minutes. I've got to get dressed."

As I hung up I thought I heard a woman's voice protesting.

PART FOUR

The Serpent's Tooth

by Eleanor Barclay

"Look deep into your unremembered past. Let your thoughts drift aimlessly. Awful images may float into your mind, images too terrifying to be recognized by your conscious personality. Do not repress them; do not let shame defeat you. If you are ever to conquer Self, to become whole, free and unafraid, you must dig hidden, obliterated, censored memories out of your consciousness. Be not afraid. Wander freely and nakedly in the deepest, darkest, most forbidding jungles of memory."

My Life Is Truth
NOBLE BARCLAY

As I stretched my hand toward the doorbell my heart began to pound so that its throbbing seemed to fill the foyer. Such a chic little foyer all done up in black-and-white squares by a decorator who secretly loathed the rich and hoped they would suffer claustrophobia waiting for elevators. There had been, three years earlier when Gloria rented the apartment, a wan philodendron in a white pot on the black marble table. In my vague and sentimental way I had felt sorry for a living plant imprisoned by Fifth Avenue elegance, and had watched it as a mother with a puny child. At my father's door the philodendron flourished like the green bay tree.

My hand fell away from the doorbell and I held it over my heart, believing the pressure could mute that noisy throbbing. It was like me to be thinking about the philodendron when I had to face my father and ask him a question which for months I had been afraid to whisper to myself. All of my life I have turned from unpleasantness to study the frost patterns on a window pane or the play of light and shadow under a tree, to listen to the buzzing of a fly or the steam hissing in the radiator.

There were actually two questions, the one I had been afraid to ask my father, and the other newly born out of my conversation on a park bench with Johnnie. When Johnnie told me that ugly tale I had not turned away. Every fiber of me listened. I had heard not only voice and words, but I had tuned my ears to catch the undertones, the significance, the meaning of the meaning.

Your father warned me against trying to find out anymore about this case. He's been protecting you and what he tried to say is that if I love you . . .

While I rode uptown in a taxicab and as I stood in the black-and-white foyer, looking at the philodendron and attempting to quiet the tumult within me, these words were like a far-off echo. I was determined to greet my father boldly, to question him courageously, and not to let him charm me into docility and agreement.

The door was opened by Hardy, Gloria's butler. I hurried past him through the Empire drawing room which had been decorated for Gloria by a pale young man who made a religion of interior decorating and gave every room a name. Father's study, which was called Contradiction, was down the hall toward the rear of the first floor. I hoped that I would not find him there, for then I should have been obliged to ask my questions immediately, and my courage was faltering.

Except for the chatter of servants in the kitchen the first floor was quiet. In the second-floor sitting room I found Gloria. She lay on a fur rug before the fire, wearing leopard-skin pajamas and studying her French grammar. The room was filled with an expensive scent, one of those synthetics called *Fierce* or *Flagrant* or *Fearless*.

"Hello, Eleanor. I hope you know you stood us up for dinner. What's the idea? Don't you know what night this is?"

"Where's Father?"

"Are you out of your mind?" Gloria rolled over on her back with a liquid movement acquired by years of ballet training. "It's Friday."

"Friday?" I must have sounded like a cretin. In the Barclay family calendar Friday was more sacred than the Sabbath.

"Isn't it awful about Lola?"

"What about Lola?"

"Don't you know?" Gloria sat up, embraced her knees and drew in her breath. "She's committed suicide."

I walked unsteadily to a wing chair close to the fire. It seemed, as I eased myself into the chair, that I had always known that Lola would be found on the India print cover of the studio couch with an empty glass on her wormy walnut table.

"Why do you think she did it?" Gloria asked, her bosom rising and falling in excitement. "Drunk, I suppose."

Hardy knocked on the open door, arranged his handsome face in proper solemnity, announced, "It is one minute before nine, Mrs. Barclay." He then made a ritual of tuning in WBOR.

Downstairs the servants were grouped around the kitchen radio and in the nursery the English Nannie listened in snobbish loneliness. From every part of the house rolled the *Battle Hymn of the Republic*, and a baritone sang one line, "His truth goes marching on." The music faded, an announcer said, "This is the *Voice of Truth*," and after a heart beat's pause, my father began: "Good evening, friends. This is Noble Barclay."

Before I knew Lola Manfred, my mind had never admitted doubt. Faith was rooted in my worship of my father, not in his philosophy. I had gone through periods of rebelliousness—once when I refused to pose for anymore Truth-Girl photographs and once, for seven weeks, when I wanted so much to go to college—but in the end I was always sorry because I had been willful and disloyal.

Until I was six years old I had lived with my mother's people and heard my father's name whispered like a naughty word. When he came to fetch me I was as terrorized as though the Devil had come to lead me off to Hell; I kicked and fought and bit until the movement of the train had lulled me and I fell asleep in his arms.

In my father's house adoration had been the prevailing mood. There were devoted servants and doting secretaries, all Barclay followers, ex-invalids or reformed sinners restored to health and respectability by his teachings. I became chief drum-thumper in the procession of converts. Governesses read to me from my father's book as though it were the Bible.

One word struck terror in my heart. Disloyalty. The word cast its shadow upon the memory of departed servants and secretaries. And when I was twelve, his worshipful wife, Janet, became overnight as hateful as a disloyal upstairs maid. The next morning my father had my things packed and off I was whisked with a governess and a plump, red-haired secretary to Florida. Father joined us. The redhead remained loyal for almost a year, and then she left us, too, and there was a happy interval when his daughter, the Truth Girl, had no rivals.

When I was seventeen, Father took me to California. When he was not too busy he wooed me as though I were as blonde and breasty as his favorite starlet, and had flowers sent to my room every day. Father became busier and busier with tasks involved in launching his magazine, *Truth in Hollywood*, and on the way home Gloria had a drawing room on the same train.

In New York Ed Munn waited at the station to take me home in a taxi while Father drove Gloria to her hotel in the limousine. It was my loneliest year. We had a big hotel suite but Father seldom used his rooms. I had no friends. I had never gone to school and it was better to dine and go to a show with Ed than to spend my evenings alone. That was during one of the periods of rebellion, when I wanted so desperately to go to college. I thought that if I had a tutor and crammed hard enough I could slide through the examinations.

My education had been haphazard. Whatever I had learned I owed to Janet Ordmann Barclay who thought intelligence and knowledge more important in a governess than the pretty legs and large breasts which were my father's standards. He did not approve of formal education. In his unregenerate days he had been thrown out of four colleges, and felt it his duty afterwards to expose the weaknesses of modern education. *Truth* Magazine writers proved that college weakened moral fiber, bred perversion, encouraged drunkenness, spread degeneracy. Charts with little cartoon men mounted on ladders showed that the percentage of failure was higher among college graduates than among the untaught.

Noble Barclay's daughter was educated in the offices of Truth Publications. I was young then and believed what I read. *Truth and Love* editorials preached on the curse of the frigid woman, and I thought there must be some congenital cause for my apathy and disgust when my fiancé tried to hold my hand.

No one in the office was told about our engagement. I cringed

when Ed's dry cautious fingers touched me, and shrank from the rubbery feel of his lips. Fortunately the man was not hot-blooded. He
"respected womanly delicacy" and avoided any real conflict between
us. My education was progressing. I looked at other men, measured
him against the clever young cynics who wisecracked at the Editors'
Table and lost their jobs through disloyalty; I compared him with the
sleek young advertising solicitors in double-breasted suits and bright
neckties. Presently I began to play an elaborate game of hide-and-seek,
became coy, capricious, frail, and finally deceitful in my excuses to
avoid a dinner or an evening with him.

One day in the office Lola Manfred whirled around in her swivel
chair and said, "There's no law, kid. You can say no to the jerk."

I was working on a manuscript called *That Braun Woman, The
Truth About Hitler's Love Life.* The pages littered the floor and I stooped
to pick them up, glad for an excuse to hide my scarlet countenance.
"What are you talking about?" I demanded, choking over the question.

"I'm neither deaf nor blind. I can always tell who's on the phone
when you answer, and when he corners you here in the office, I sicken
at the sight of your innocent agony. You loathe him, Eleanor. Why do
you let him pursue you?"

I tried to be loyal. I told her my fiancé was kind-hearted, understanding, my father's dear friend. Lola snorted. I had to defend myself
because I was engaged to him, and I lashed out at Lola, accusing her of
prejudice and intolerance.

"Do you believe in Truth-Sharing, Eleanor?"

"Yes, of course."

"Why are you blushing?"

"I love my father."

After that, in my presence, Lola was less critical of Father. But I
knew just the same that she continued to broadcast scorn particularly
if Ed Munn or some other "loyal" employee was within earshot. That
was typical of Lola. The posturing, the dirty words, the hard-boiled
attitudes were veneer over a tender and tremulous heart. She was
unendingly generous and patient with poor and simple people; bitterly cruel to the pompous and arrogant.

I learned to love Lola, but in self-defense I was sometimes arrogant and always too proud to let her see that I agreed with her about Ed Munn. But when I finally had the courage to tell Father that I wanted to break the engagement (he told Ed for me), then I celebrated by going to dinner with Lola.

It was that night, deserted by her between the entrée and the salad, that I met Mr. Wilson. It was an innocent pickup and a virtuous friendship. I often talked to Lola about him and planned a meeting for them over my congenial dinner table. I thought Lola and Mr. Wilson would like each other. There seemed coincidence in their common passion for Blake who is not a popular poet, and I felt certain that we would become a warm trio. Both of them seemed to understand me in the way older people who have not forgotten youth can understand the young.

I told each about the other, tried to arrange dinner parties, but never succeeded. Although Lola seemed to grow more and more petulant when I chattered about Mr. Wilson, I found nothing strange in her behavior. Lola was an unhappy woman, often irritable. So I quit talking about things that disturbed her. And when Mr. Wilson died, the circumstances were so bewildering that I brooded but could not talk about it, and I never told Lola that the man whose murder was reported in the newspapers had been *my* Mr. Wilson.

"Now that Lola's passed away, you'll probably be editor of *Truth and Love*," Gloria observed, looking up from the French grammar. The broadcast was over and she had returned to her schoolgirl pose, so that when my father came in, he would chuckle and smack her buttocks.

"Shut up!"

"What elegant manners you have, Miss Barclay."

"I don't care. It's positively ghoulish of you to think about her job when she's . . ."

"Not cold in her grave?" Gloria looked at me sharply. "What a mess you are, Eleanor! Why do you go about without hats all the time? You'd better comb your hair and put on some powder before your father comes home."

When, brushed and docile, I came out of Gloria's dressing room.

Father was sitting in one of the wing chairs with Gloria on the floor at his feet, her tilted chin supported by both hands.

"Ed's handling it for me," my father was saying. "'Spare no expense,' I told him, 'give her a decent funeral, I'm paying for it.' She didn't leave a sou, poor soul, hadn't even provided for a decent burial. But I want to do the right thing; she was a loyal employee . . ."

Lola was dead and could not resent the remark. "She wasn't loyal. She hated you and you knew it," I told my father.

Gloria looked as if I had said something indecent. The room was hot and sickening with the scent of *Fearless or Fierce* or *Flagrant*.

"Now that she's dead," my father said reprovingly, "it doesn't behoove us to speak ill of her. Poor Lola had faults, but who that is human hasn't? Young people, Eleanor, are likely to be intolerant. You misjudge Lola. She had a bitter tongue. It probably amused her to poke fun at me, but she was never disloyal."

Gloria's voice rose and fell in enjoyment of the morbid situation. "What did you find out? Drunk, I bet."

"There'll be an inquest. You may be asked to testify, Eleanor."

"What do I know?"

"That she was emotionally unstable. That she drank too much. That she indulged a tendency toward melancholia. You were with her yesterday. What sort of mood was she in?"

I did not answer Father's question, for I was thinking of Lola as I had last seen her. She had stamped on her fur coat and gone off to the Ladies' Room, but when she had returned, remorseful and over-rouged, she had been contrite and eager to please me. I had been too self-centered to pay much attention to Lola; I was annoyed at her childishness and concerned with trifles, for Johnnie was coming to my house for dinner. Five phone calls to Brenda, all finicking and worthless, about the chilling of cocktail glasses and heating dinner plates and being sure the flowers were properly arranged. It was too late now for apology or contrition, and useless to wonder if my selfishness was not in part to blame for her despair.

"The tragedy of waste. Waste of life and waste of talent. All because of alcohol." Against the fire my father's profile was dark and strong and sad.

"No," I retorted. "You oughtn't to say that. It was worse than just alcohol . . ."

"Worse?" shrilled Gloria, stroking the leopard skin pajamas so that her hands would call attention to the curves beneath the stiff fur. "What's worse than drunkenness and suicide?"

"Unhappiness," I said. "Whatever it was that made Lola drink. You ought to know that, Father. Look at your own experience. It wasn't until you discovered what made you a drunken bum . . ."

"That's entirely different," interrupted Gloria irritably. As the wife of Noble Barclay she had to believe in absolute honesty, but she preferred not to think about the more sordid chapters in my father's history.

"You found out about yourself and learned to overcome your weakness and were able to give up drinking," I continued, speaking to my father and ignoring Gloria's disapproval. "Lola's trouble was worse than. yours because she felt more deeply."

"Nonsense," sniffed Gloria.

"Her capacity for feeling," I stumbled on, "was too much for her. She couldn't bear the way the world is, the way people are fooled and tricked and misled when they try so humbly to be honest and happy."

"How ridiculous!" snapped the wife of Noble Barclay. "If she felt sorry for people why didn't she try to help them, like your father, instead of wallowing in liquor and licentiousness. Isn't that so, Daddy?"

My father sighed.

The glass-enclosed clock tinkled and there was Hardy, as if on signal, with a tray. "Pineapple, grape or apple juice?" he asked, offering the tray.

"No, thanks," I said.

"Drink some; it's good for you."

The obedient daughter drank her apple juice, and gazing, innocent-eyed, at her dearly beloved parent, pondered his reason for accusing her of murder.

Weak-kneed, pale-lipped, quaking, I said, "Father, I must talk to you."

Gloria's blue eyes gleamed expectantly.

"Privately," I added. "It's very important."

My father was not unaccustomed to such requests. An audience with the creator of Truth-Sharing was a privilege granted only to members of the family, close friends and the very rich and influential. He rose and extended his hand, and after he had apologized to Gloria, we went down the stairs to his study.

This was the room the religious young decorator had called Contradiction. It was a crazy mixture of old alabaster, a marble desk supported on the backs of three wrought-iron blackamoors, modern bookcases of wood bleached to the whiteness of bone and black plush curtains held in place by white plaster hands. Above the fireplace hung a pink nude with bloated haunches and on the opposite wall there was a skilful but morbid painting of the pelvic bones of some large animal.

"What is it you want to tell me?" my father said gently.

I closed my eyes. This was no time for me to be looking at nudes and skeletons. In our calendar the blackest sin was disloyalty, a danger which, I used to think, could never threaten Noble Barclay's daughter. In our office, where skepticism was endemic, I had thought I was immune. My defense had been shrillness whose vehemence failed to conceal my weakening. I caught the disease from the people I liked best, those who were frankest in derision.

Disloyalty came to me, I think, in the Ladies' Room. Stenographers and file clerks, more than the clever critics, caused my final disillusionment. These girls would never confide in the boss's daughter, but when you have to hide in the toilet to enjoy a cigarette, you can't help overhearing confidences not intended for your ears. I heard the girls talk; I knew that two of them worked a week for the price of one of Gloria's hats; I grew hot with indignation at the injustices of petty fines and deductions. My father, who advertised his love for mankind in five magazines and a weekly broadcast, told me that I did not understand business when I asked why he paid the girls such miserable wages.

Mr. Wilson also contributed to my education in disloyalty. He had not been so noisily arrogant as the group at the Editors' Table, but he had asked his share of questions about my father's practice of his creed, about our home life with Janet in the old days, and father's marriage to Gloria, and about my early days in my father's house in Great Neck. Mr. Wilson had not been outwardly critical; he had discussed my father's philosophy with the amused detachment of a cultivated bishop inquiring into the antics of a sawdust-trail evangelist.

After Mr. Wilson died I closed my eyes and my mind to clues that might have solved the mystery. I was sick with terror, but my terror had no substance, for I knew nothing except that my father and Ed Munn had talked in a dark and evil way about Mr. Wilson's hatred and his aching need for revenge. In the office that afternoon I had tried to laugh at their melodramatic phrases, to hide my bewilderment in humor and bravado, but I had been horrified by the suggestion of conspiracy that their silences and secret glances concealed.

Buried truths, my father's book says, are festering sores; they poison the mind and corrupt the spirit. The sore had suppurated; it was green with pus, gangrenous and putrid. I was guilty, too, guilty of the willful error to which my father attributed so much of human suffering. And like the rest of the fools and invalids, I blinded myself deliberately, donned a mask to shield my squeamish eyes from the furious light.

For a short time the blinders had been off. The sudden light was more than I could stand. I became ill, physically ill, hurried home with a splitting headache, deserted Johnnie the day Grace Eccles insisted on five minutes of Truth-Sharing in the Ladies' Room. It was not so much what Grace revealed as what I imagined as background for the sum of her small odd facts. Why had my father forbidden her ever to mention the name of the murdered man? Why was his anger so fierce when Grace asked him about the gun which I had absent-mindedly carried out of the Studio when I had been summoned so peremptorily to his office?

"What is it you want to tell me?" my father asked again.

I had been off in a trance. Startled, I stared up into his face. He seemed a stranger beside me on the hard gray couch. He was smooth, tanned, exercised, massaged, handsome and healthy, but his face still showed the ravages of his dissipated youth. I looked at the insolent jaw and thought of that swaggering young drunk my mother had loved so extravagantly that the failure of their marriage was death to her.

He caught my scrutiny and, sure of his charm, smiled. "What do you think of that thing, Eleanor? You've got good taste." He nodded toward the painting of the animal's pelvis.

"It's repulsive."

His pleasure was ingenuous. "My taste isn't so crude, is it? I'd have thrown it in the ashcan long ago, only Gloria tells me it's art. The Lord knows I've got enough horses' asses around me in the office without having to hang one up in my home." This was Noble Barclay, a robust, jolly man, entertaining his daughter with a small, not unkind joke against his wife.

My voice was smooth, creamy, the Sunday-afternoon voice of a good child as I asked, "Why did you tell John Ansell what you told him this afternoon?"

"So he came to you and blabbed. Chivalrous, isn't he?"

"That's not the point. I want to know why you said it."

"Why did you bring the gun up to my office that day?"

I looked away, at the white plaster hands clasping the black plush curtain. "The gun had nothing to do with it. It was a mistake; you know that, Father. I was told to rush up to your office; I'd just signed for the gun; I picked it up instead of my pocketbook. That isn't the point . . ."

My wrist was locked in my father's strong hand. "Tell me the truth, child."

"I'm waiting for you to tell me the truth, Father. Why do you pretend that you think I killed Mr. Wilson? Why were you so furious when you found out I knew him? Why did you say all those ridiculous things about his hating you and wanting to destroy us?"

My wrist throbbed under the cruel fingers. I was ashamed to tell my father that he was hurting me.

He sighed. "Must we go over all of this again? I explained it to you then. I . . ."

"You explained nothing," I said, forgetting that it was considered disloyal to contradict Noble Barclay. "You played the heavy father; you shouted and ordered me around and reminded me that I ought to respect you. But you never told me why; you never explained your insane fury and your unreasonable hints about *my* being in danger because I knew Mr. Wilson."

"He had deceived me. It was part of a plot. He wanted to use my own daughter against me."

"Why?"

Father looked at the bones of the horse and sighed again.

"You told me that Mr. Wilson hated you and lived only to revenge himself upon you," I reminded him. "Then you said he'd injured you and because he wasn't strong enough to acknowledge the truth about his own weakness, he turned against you. But you never told me what he did and how he . . ."

"Sh-sh, you're shouting!"

"I've got to know."

"You're getting hysterical. Calm down. Sit quiet for five minutes and say nothing." His dark bright eyes shifted toward the black marble clock on the mantel. "Five quiet minutes and then we can share the truth, bitter as it is, about this unfortunate incident."

"I'm not hysterical, I . . ."

"Quiet!"

I sat rigid, watching the hands of the clock moving so slowly that they seemed to know my anxiety and to wish to thwart it. Scenes of this sort were not new to me. My father had often made me sit for five minutes without moving a muscle. In his book this was suggested as a preface to confession. The effect was supposed to be soothing, but I had always grown more nervous during the enforced silence that preceded the hearing or telling of something unpleasant.

The door opened silently and Ed Munn was there. He had not bothered to knock. Ed stood tall in the doorway, looking down at us, his eyes bland, his grin rubbery.

"I've made all the arrangements. The inquest's on Monday, and we'll have her buried the next morning. Funeral's strictly private."

Wrapped securely in the cotton wool of my own concerns, I had forgotten Lola. Recollection stabbed painfully. "Why did she do it?" I cried. "Has anything been discovered, Ed? Do you know anything?"

Ed sucked at his lips. "Drunk, of course. There were empty bottles all over the place."

"Why? She'd been drunk before. There were always empty bottles. Something must have hurt her frightfully . . ."

One insolent shoulder was lifted. He did not even bother to shrug properly. "Probably discovered that one of her lovers had betrayed her."

I shivered. Ed's unctuous voice sickened me. He considered Lola a bad woman; her virtue was beyond his understanding. Lola had been capable of compassion and indignation; Ed was all oily self-righteousness.

"I didn't expect to find you here, Eleanor. It's an unexpected pleasure."

"Thanks."

"Why are you sarcastic? I'm trying to pay you a compliment."

"Am I sarcastic? You said it was a pleasure to see me and I thanked you. Nothing sarcastic about that."

"You're always sarcastic with me. You act as if I wasn't—weren't—good enough for you. Maybe I'm not a college graduate, but I'm no pint-sized runt . . ."

"Please, Ed." My voice was querulous, too. Nothing made me more uncomfortable than the sound of a grown man's whining.

"Cut it, Ed. That's all finished," my father snapped.

"Is it?"

"I told you over a year ago she'd never have you. And I made it clear that I wouldn't force her into it. She's a grown woman; her life's her own. I'm sick of arguing with you about it . . ."

"Once you needed something," Ed interrupted. "And you gave me your promise that if I helped you, you'd use your influence . . ."

My father's eyes glittered and in the light shed by the lamp behind him his white hair shone like a crown. Ed leaned forward, shoulders drooping, long arms hanging loose. The lamplight illumined their hatred. I saw then that Ed Munn held some secret power which my father feared and resented.

"Please, Ed," I said quietly, "please leave us. I want to talk to my father."

Ed Munn was aware of his power, proud, showing my father how far he could go. A weak man had discovered and armed his arrow at the Achilles' heel of his superior. Slowly, turning his distorted smile upon me, Ed gloated, "About Wilson's death, huh? You want to know why your father blamed you for it, don't you? You want to know . . ."

"You've been spying," I said.

"That's my job." Ed's voice was all syrup and complacence. "Your father's made it my business for years to spy for him. The habit's developed. How can I help it if I spy on him for a change?" The speech sounded as though it had been written and memorized.

"Okay, Ed, but get the hell out now, will you?" Father said.

"I don't want to."

"Get out."

The elastic grin widened as Ed turned to me again. "That boy friend of yours is too inquisitive. We thought he'd keep his mouth shut if he thought you'd done it."

"Was that your bright idea?" I asked coldly. "I can see the Machiavellian touch."

"Get out," my father said again.

Ed seated himself in one of the metal chairs and held fast to the arms with his white, thin-skinned hands. There was swagger in his movements, defiance in his voice. "I'm sick of being kicked around. I'm tired of broken promises. You're going to keep your word to me or . . ." The pause was heavily significant.

"I must say, Ed, your threats worry me a lot," my father said with mock joviality. "Honestly, I'm shaking in my boots, I'm so afraid of you."

"Please tell me," I begged, "what's this all about? Why all the mystery? Why do you want Johnnie to quit asking questions about Mr. Wilson?"

No one spoke. I looked up at my father's gleaming dark eyes and the white crown of his hair. My father, I whispered, my own father who used to walk with his hand around my forefinger and kiss my bruises. I had not forgotten the security of his arms and the strong tenderness of his caresses. These were sentimental things, but memory is all slyness and deceit, and I knew that I was lost unless I rejected it. I thought about Mr. Wilson who had been murdered and I said in a clear, bold voice:

"Was it you, Father?"

He did not answer, and I said, "Was it you who killed Mr. Wilson? Tell me the truth, please."

It struck me as curious, even then, that I should demand the truth of Noble Barclay. I had been taught, nearly all of my life, that truth was his nature, that a camel might pass through a needle's eye more comfortably than a word of deceit fall from his lips.

He raised his head. "I've done much wrong in my life, Daughter. I'm responsible for the death of my beloved mother and of your mother, my sweet wife. It was my stubborn pride and my weakness that broke their hearts. I have sinned but I have not committed murder. I have not aimed a gun at a man's heart."

"Someone shot Mr. Wilson in the back," I said.

My father shook his head as though he were denying accusation, and his fists clenched and unclenched in nervous challenge. Behind him were the black curtains and the white amputated hands. "Have you believed all these months that I was guilty of murder? Why didn't you come to me openly and talk to me about it?"

"You haven't answered my question, Father."

"You were suspicious, child. You locked suspicion in your heart and were unwilling to admit the cleansing light of truth."

"I was frightened," I admitted. "You acted so strange that night, and then I found that Mr. Wilson was dead. I was afraid, Father . . ."

"If you'd only had the courage to speak to me," he interrupted. "Believe me, child, I had nothing to do with the murder. As a matter of plain fact, it wasn't until the following Monday morning, on the train from Washington, that I found out Wilson was dead."

"The news must have been a blow," observed Ed Munn who had been enjoying our argument.

"Are you still here?" Father said.

Ed stood up. He was smiling and his thin red mouth curved and coiled like a snake. He and my father hated each other so violently that the stench of their malice filled the room.

From the floor above came the enraged sobs of a child awakened by a nightmare. The other twin was disturbed by the sobs, and started shrieking, too. When this had ended we heard Gloria's silvery treble:

"Coming up soon, Daddy?"

"I'm busy, Lover. Go to sleep."

"Don't be long. Daddy. I'm lonesome."

The house became quiet again. Ed shifted, turning toward me with a smirk that suggested evil victory. "One thing I've always wondered, Eleanor. Why did you bring that gun up from the Studio? Did your father tell you to bring it?"

"Damn you, Ed, it was a mistake," I shouted. "Father sent for me in such a rush that I was upset and absent-minded. I picked up the gun instead of my pocketbook. You know that . . ."

"Sh-sh!" my father said. "You're screaming. Of course it was just a coincidence. Ed's just trying one of his tricks again." To Ed, he added, "You make her nervous. If you've got anything to say, say it to me."

Once more Gloria's soprano floated down the stairs. "I'm lonely. Please hurry. Daddy."

"For God's sakes!" I shouted up at her. "He's not your Daddy; he's your husband. You're a grown woman and you've borne him two children. Can't you call him by his name?"

"Poor Eleanor." Father led me toward the couch. "The poor kid, her nerves are shot. Let her rest, Ed, let her recover from the shock." Father arranged the pillows, and waited solicitously, as though I were an invalid, until I had stretched on the couch. "I'll go up and tell Gloria that you didn't mean it, dear. I'm afraid you've hurt her feelings. She's a sensitive girl, Gloria. Come on, Ed. Time you were going home."

"I'm staying," Ed answered. He sat as if he had been molded into the chair.

Father left. I closed my eyes, played the shocked and weary role, hoping with idiotic optimism that Ed would respect my fatigue. A few strained seconds passed. I turned to the wall. The modern chair did not creak when Ed got up and the thick rug silenced his footsteps, but every nerve in my body knew that he had come close to the couch. I turned my head, opened my eyes and Ed, taking this as a gesture of grace, sat beside me. He reached for my hand. I snatched it away.

"Why must you do that, Eleanor? Are you afraid of me?"

His hand encircled my arm and slid down slyly until his clammy fingers were locked about my wrist. I tried again to pull away, but his hand tightened and he moved on the couch until his leg touched mine.

"Please let me go."

His fingers relaxed slightly, but he still held my wrist. "Why can't you be nice to me? I'm tired of being treated like a dog." His face was close to mine and I smelled the peppermints he had been munching. He always smelled of synthetics, of mouth wash or *Russian Leather* or peppermint or shaving lotion. These scents revolted me; they were more offensive than an honest human smell; they were odors designed to hide the scent of living.

"What's wrong with me, Eleanor? I was good enough for you once. What's wrong with me now?"

He was good enough once; he was the only man I knew, my only friend, my dinner date, Ersatz for a sweetheart. I had been a lonely kid in a big hotel suite without friends or school routines to give form to my days. There were books from a Madison Avenue lending library and the movies and Ed Munn to take me out, like a grown woman, to dinner. He was adult if not charming, a suitor, and he sent beautiful boxes of French chocolates with tiny sugar violets decorating the top layer.

"I was always nice to you. Why did you turn me down?"

"Look, Ed," I began.

"Look. Look," he interrupted. "Is that the only verb you know? Are you asking me to look with my eyes, or do you wish me to listen to what you have to say? I know where you acquired that habit. From Ansell. You've been seeing him, he's your . . ."

I slid off the couch. I stalked with my back up toward the door. My hand on the knob, my shoulders high, my chin in the air, I said coldly, "Please go now."

"Eleanor, Eleanor, little girl," his voice was meant to be tender, but it was off key and it whined through his nose. "Why don't you like me? What can he give you that I can't? Who's he, anyway? Little runt of a writer, he wouldn't even have a job if . . ."

"Get out."

"I was always crazy about you," he whimpered, his voice becoming more and more soprano. "You were a cute little thing when I first knew you, in a red raincoat with a little hood. I knew then you were the girl I wanted. I made up my mind to study and improve myself so I'd be worthy. You were like a princess to me . . ."

It was hideous and ironic, after what I had learned about him that

night, to hear him whine like a small boy about red hoods and prin-
cesses. When he had first come to the Great Neck house Ed Munn had
been my father's secretary, a lank white worm of a man who abased
himself and flattened against walls when a member of the family
passed. His hands had trembled when he sat down to dinner with us;
he had barely eaten, taken small careful bites and wiped his mouth too
often. I had heard my father growl at Ed, laugh at him sarcastically,
give orders in a high-handed imperious way. Father had never wasted
his charm on the male secretary because Ed was as faithful when he
was kicked as when he was treated kindly.

"It's a good match," he said, looking at me with abject eyes, "you
and I, heirs to the business. Who else could take Noble Barclay's place?
The twins? It'll be eighteen or twenty years before they're old enough
and the way Madame's spoiling them they'll be polo players instead of
executives. By the time they're old enough to come into the business,
you and I will be in control . . ."

"Really," I said, laughing at his false righteousness and his trans-
parent affections, "you ought to take a course in love-making. The red
raincape was one thing and father's business another. I may be a princess to you, but you've planned a morganatic marriage for me with
you as the lucky commoner. If you had an ounce of intelligence in
that place where you hatch your filthy schemes, you'd have had sense
enough to keep quiet about the business."

"What's Ansell got that I haven't? Why do you let him make love to
you? You were the cold type. You couldn't bear having your hand held,
but you let him stay all night . . ."

"You dirty sneak, you've been spying on me."

He made a show of laughter, but his mirth had no foundation. It
was smirking empty revenge and he expected me to cry or cringe or
beg him not to tell my father. "I thought I'd catch you," he cried and got
hold of me again, pulling me toward him and pinning me against his
chest with the thin strong cords of his arms.

My hands ached with the need to slap and scratch, but his arms
were a jail, and all my kicking and shoving were like the writhing of a
creature caught in a trap. "I loathe you. I can't bear it when you touch
me. You're repulsive; you make me sick. Even when I was engaged to

you, when I was so young and stupid I didn't know what I was doing, I was ashamed to wear your ring or let anyone know about it."

He quivered with hurt rage. His pallid cheeks had become colored by a faint girlish flush and his eyeballs protruded.

"You're vulgar," I cried in ecstasy, for the pleasure of hurting Ed Munn had filled me with cruel energy. "You're a vulgar, revolting man; everybody laughs at you; nobody takes you seriously. Why, if you were a leper," I went on rapturously, "people wouldn't be more anxious to shun you. All those lotions you use, the hair tonic, mouth wash, the peppermints, they can't start to conceal the stink."

"I'm vulgar, am I? You loathe me?" His mouth twisted in such a way that I could not tell whether it moved in anguish or perverse delight. His hand had moved toward his pocket and for a moment I thought he was reaching for a gun.

He pulled out a manuscript, folded lengthwise. "When you've read this, Miss Barclay, you may change your tune."

"What is it?"

"Read it."

There was no signature on the manuscript. I recognized the paper as the yellow second sheets we used in the office for the first drafts of our stories. The tide was typed six spaces above the opening sentence just as we were instructed to type manuscripts in the office: *A Short History of Homer Peck.*

"Homer Peck!" I said. "That's the name Mr. Wilson used in the title of his book. *Autobiography of Homer Peck.* Who was he?"

"You'll find out." Ed laughed. It was so false and off key that my nerves quivered at the dissonance.

I began to read. "*Twenty-three years ago in a poor sanitarium in Arizona . . .*" It was hard for me to concentrate. Twenty-three years was too long ago, Arizona too far away. "*. . . a young man lay dying.*" I read a few more sentences, and looked up from the pages at the white plaster hands grasping the folds of the black drapes. Black and white, steel tubes and hard cords gave the room the feel of a torture chamber, and the vari-colored walls affected me like the pitching of a ship. "*. . . had enjoyed his thirty years of living and viewed with unconcealed apprehension the approach of death.*"

The door opened and there was my father. I was pleased. My father was strong and kind. When I was a little girl he had lifted me high above his head and I had rejoiced in his size and the strength of his hands under my armpits.

"You seem to be quieter," Father said. "Feel better now?" Then he noticed the manuscript and came closer. "What's that?"

Ed bowed over my chair. "May I?" He took the manuscript and handed it, bowing again, to Father. The mock gallantry was awkward. Derision and rebelliousness did not become him. It was more natural for Ed Munn to cringe.

Father was far-sighted but he would not wear glasses and he held the manuscript at arm's length. Ed Munn watched, his eyes swollen with spite.

"Where'd you get it?" Father asked.

"Aren't you grateful? Aren't you going to thank me for getting hold of it for you?" Defiant, Ed Munn lit a cigarette. He had never before smoked in my father's presence, but he seemed not to care anymore whether or not Noble Barclay disapproved. "I expect my reward, you know."

Father's shoulders drooped. His eyes were reproachful, but the reproach was not directed at his disloyal aide. On the wall opposite him hung an unframed mirror. Reflected in. it was the drooping, beaten figure of Noble Barclay. Ed reached for the manuscript and Father let him have it without protest.

"What is it?" I asked. "Why are you so frightened? Who was Homer Peck?"

"How about that promise?" asked Ed, holding the yellow pages before him like a shield. The manuscript seemed to give him courage. With it in his hand he was Noble Barclay's equal. "Give me what I want and I'll give you this to burn, too."

"Why do you want it burned?" I asked. "What is it?"

I might have been tossing my questions at the wind. My father's color was robust, his hair a silver brush against the black drapes, but he was like a vividly colored model, a wax man in a shop window.

"She thinks I'm vulgar." Ed moved the hand that held the manuscript. The pages rustled. "She says I smell bad; she says people shun me like a leper. Make her change her mind, or . . ."

"What have I got to do with it?" I walked past my father and looked up into Ed's swollen, bloodshot eyes. "If you think you're going to blackmail my father into making me marry you because you know some old secret . . ."

My father pushed me aside. "Let me take care of this." He addressed Ed in a gentle, placating manner. "Let's not kid ourselves, Ed. You and I, lad, we're playing for big stakes. Who would it help if the business was ruined? Who else is going to pay you twenty-five thousand a year?"

Ed's tongue crept around his lips slowly. "I have my plans."

My father nodded toward the yellow pages. "You're right, son, I made a promise. And I'm a man of my word."

Ed came toward me. The smells of peppermint and hair lotion made me ill. Between my eyes and the lamp Ed's silhouette had become malignant and unsubstantial, shadowy as the future, a prophecy of my tomorrows.

"No," I cried. "Tell him no, Father."

My father shook his head in warning. I was not to deny Ed Munn, not to laugh nor insult him. Ed was dangerous, he knew something, he knew the secret that Mr. Wilson had known, the shocking truth that threatened the security of Noble Barclay. That much I saw clearly. That fine confession that introduced his philosophy in *My Life Is Truth* was not then the entire story of my father's old sins. There was still mystery in his life, buried scandal, guarded shame that the apostle of Truth-Sharing could not confide to his loyal followers. A buried truth, a festering sore, a wound that had not been cleansed with the sharp, clean antiseptic of confession. My father was slave to a secret and I was to be made prisoner, too, bound and shackled to his ancient guilt.

Gently my father urged me toward him, raised my chin with his hand and looked down into my eyes. His voice was aggrieved as though his stubborn child had defied him. "My little girl, my own dear daughter won't forsake her father."

"I'll do nothing," I said, "until I know what this is all about."

The telephone rang. Its muted alarm shocked us out of the spell of self-absorption. That gentle, mocking tinkle told us that we were not alone, that a real world existed outside of this black-and-white fantasy of a room, and that we had responsibility toward that outside world.

Father answered. "Yes," he said, "she's here."

"Is it for me?" I started toward the phone.

Ed blocked my way. "Ansell, I suppose."

I was hot, angry, passionate and resentful. There had been too much frustration that night. I could bear no more of it. My hand swung out. I heard the smack, felt swift pain flash through my hand, saw the red, irregular mark on Ed's cheek.

"You . . . you . . ." he spluttered. The rest of the epithet was lost in his throat. His jaw trembled and he stretched his tense, gaunt arms toward me.

Father stepped between us. "It was Ansell," he said. "He wanted you to know, Eleanor, that the police are on their way to Ed's place in Jackson Heights. He's wanted in connection with the murder of Lola Manfred."

"You'll have to get out of town," my father said. He had taken down the painting of the bloated nude and from the wall safe behind it removed an enormous roll of bills.

"Ten thousand," my father said and handed Ed the money.

He took it apathetically. His lack of greed surprised me. In the few minutes since Johnnie had called, Ed had grown smaller, thinner, older. Within the undistinguished blue serge suit his body had shriveled. He moved jerkily, like a puppet whose strings have gone slack.

"I didn't do it, so help me," he moaned.

These protestations went unheeded. Father did not seem to care whether Ed was innocent or guilty; he was interested only in getting Ed out of the state. Ed was to leave the building by the service exit, take the car which was parked outside, cross the George Washington Bridge into Jersey, drive to Philadelphia, leave the car, and take the first plane that was leaving for St. Louis, Memphis or New Orleans. He was to take the name James B. Thorpe. Father had a driver's license, State of California, all ready in James B. Thorpe's name. As Mr. Thorpe, Ed was to get transportation and a tourist card for travel in Mexico.

Father gave Ed the license, the car keys and the ten thousand.

"You'll have about nine of it left by the time you get to Mexico. You can live like a king on it down there. In six months you get the tourist card renewed, and in a year I'll send you some more money in the name of Thorpe, General Delivery."

Father had changed, too. He was on top again, the boss, wielder of power. Excitement heightened his color; his dark eyes glowed, and he worked out the details of Ed's escape with great enthusiasm.

"I don't know but what I envy you. No work, no responsibilities. Pretty señoritas, plenty of sunshine, plenty of dough. Life will be sweet for Mr. James B. Thorpe, the mysterious Gringo."

"I don't want to go."

"Perhaps you'd prefer the electric chair," Father teased. His enjoyment of the situation was cruel. It was payment and revenge; it was compensation for years of forbearance and smothered hatred.

"But I didn't do it." Ed was six feet of self-pity.

"You must take me for a fool!" Father cried contemptuously.

Ed grimaced. "Whatever I did. Noble, I did for you." He was injured righteousness; he was the victim of injustice; he was Sydney Carton declaring it a far, far better thing.

"You went too far," Father said icily. "No one ever suggested violence. I asked you to get me something. Your methods were your own idea and your own responsibility."

Ed moved forward. "Then why was a gun on your desk that day? Tell me why."

I sat far away, across the room. Father and Ed were no longer real to me; they had no color; they were like flat figures on a screen. Nothing was solid; reality had become celluloid fantasy; I was a spectator in a chair made of black cords and steel tubing.

My father left the room. When he came back he was carrying Ed's hat and overcoat. With his pocket knife he ripped all the labels out of the coat and sliced three letters, E E M, out of the hat's sweatband.

Ed put on the overcoat slowly and slowly walked to the mirror. He tipped the hat over his right eye. The effect did not please him and he changed the angle, grimacing at his pallid reflection. My father watched impatiently while this man, a fugitive and murderer, took time to adjust his hat.

By this time the police must have searched Ed's apartment in Jackson Heights. They would presently come here to look for him, for Edward Everett Munn was not only Noble Barclay's assistant but his best friend, a frequent guest in his home.

"Make it snappy, Ed. You haven't all night."

"Why are you treating me like this?" Ed implored, like a woman begging affection of a cold lover. "I'm doing this for you, giving up everything, my position, my place in the publishing world, everything I've worked for. The least you could do is show a little gratitude . . ."

I turned away. It was disgusting to witness such slavish fawning and cringing. My father was no more affected by the spectacle of human degradation than by Ed's woebegone pleas. He stood firm before the door, his right hand outstretched.

"Empty your pockets. Give me all your papers," he commanded.

"Why?"

"Don't be a damn fool. Suppose the police stop and search you. Come on, make it snappy."

As though he were yielding a treasure Ed handed Father a leather wallet, a pocket address book, a few letters with dog-eared corners. This did not satisfy my father. He searched Ed's pockets, removed a key case, the monogrammed cigarette box and a card that entitled the bearer to four more half-hour sessions at a Coney Island massage parlor.

"Where's the manuscript?"

"Manuscript?" Ed pointed vaguely toward the ebony table.

"Come on, don't stall, give it to me."

"I haven't got it."

"Don't lie to me. I'm not going to let you get away with it. Suppose you were caught with it on you!" Father snapped.

Ed looked around blankly. "I put it down. It was there . . ."

"Hand it over, Ed. No monkey business."

Ed seemed dazed. Father lost patience and swung out at him. Astonished, Ed whimpered and backed away. My father struck again.

I pushed back in the steel chair, grasped the black cords of the seat. It was the only time in my life that I have ever watched men fight. Ordinarily I shrink from the sight of assault and cruelty. But this time I watched avidly; my eyes followed every movement; I gloated as my father's blows rained harder and faster. Some perverse and brutal instinct came alive in me and my heart beat swiftly as I relished the heated ecstasy of revenge. My pleasure in watching the fight was no less than my father's in feeling his fists beat against Ed's soft flesh.

He deserved punishment, I thought. He had killed two people, my friends, and he had hurt others, defenseless typists and clerks and office boys, for the pleasure of showing his power. If, as I believe, humiliating people is killing them in small ways, Ed Munn's list of victims did not start with Warren G. Wilson. But who was I to judge the man? He had been the sycophant, the overseer, the servant who devoted his life and sacrificed his humanity to our welfare. If my father had reaped the profits and enjoyed the power, I had also accepted the benefits of his servile cruelty.

Servility was a deeply ingrained habit. Ed showed little spirit in defending himself and struck out feebly against his master. When he crumpled and fell, it was like the collapse of a dummy.

The doorbell rang.

Father paid no attention. He knelt beside Ed, searching the lining of his coat, feeling for the manuscript under Ed's shirt. Ed lay on the carpet, limp and spineless, his face the color of putty.

The bell rang again.

"Better answer it, Eleanor. Stall them as long as you can," Father said.

Evidently the servants had awakened. I heard voices and footsteps in the kitchen. Gloria called down the stairs. I opened the door and saw Johnnie. I do not remember what I felt when I saw him nor if I spoke a word of greeting before I fainted. All I remember is darkness and the sudden pain of light, Johnnie's arm tight about me and his anxious voice.

"You all right, kid?"

I was all right then, secure in a world of solid people. Johnnie was there; he stood for the solidity and rightness of the world. Gloria had come down a few steps and was asking, petulantly, why no one had answered the bell. Hardy, the butler, in a black dressing-gown and white silk scarf, hurried out of the dining room.

Father came out of the study. "Sorry you were disturbed," he said to Hardy. "Go back to bed."

To Gloria he called, "It's Eleanor's impetuous suitor, coming after her at this hour. Go back to bed, Lover."

"Come in, lad." Father led us to the study. This surprised me. In the circumstances I thought he would not want Johnnie to find Ed there.

The study was empty.

"Sit down, make yourself comfortable." Father fussed over Johnnie as though he were honored by this midnight visit.

"I'm sorry if I disturbed everyone," Johnnie said, "but I thought Eleanor might be shocked at the news, so I came to call for her. Mind if I smoke?"

"Go right ahead. Make yourself at home. Why did you think Eleanor might be overcome at the news? She broke her engagement to him more than a year ago."

"Oh," said Johnnie.

In that evening of shocking revelation, nothing had shamed me more than Johnnie's startled glance when he learned that Ed Munn was the man I had once promised to marry.

Johnnie took a long time with his cigarette. "Just the same," he said evenly, "it must have been a shock to discover that someone so close to her father killed one of her friends. Did he kill Wilson, too?"

With his fine, swinging stride Father went to the desk. He pulled out the chair and seated himself, looking at us as if we had come to beg for jobs or a raise in pay. "What gives you that idea, lad?"

"I have my reasons."

"Reasons or suspicions?" Father looked like an executive in one of those advertisements in the slick magazines. "I imagine you've confided those suspicions to your friends at the Detective Bureau, your old pals who gave you all those fine stories for *Truth and Crime.*"

Johnnie had started to flick the ash off his cigarette. He stopped, stared at the crystal ashtray and flicked the ash on the carpet. "Not at all, Mr. Barclay. I haven't had enough proof."

"What did you tell them?" asked Father as nonchalantly as if he had been asking the address of Johnnie's tailor.

Johnnie smiled. "When I learned that Lola Manfred had been murdered . . ."

"Wasn't it suicide?" Father interrupted.

"There was a man with her last night. Neighbors heard them quarreling."

Father raised his eyebrows. "That happened rather frequently, I suspect. Miss Manfred wasn't known as a celibate." It was disquieting to remember that this suave, immaculate, white-haired executive had a few minutes earlier beaten a man and called him a murderer.

Heedless of father's arguments, Johnnie went on, "I thought it was murder and called Captain Riordan to tell him he ought to investigate."

"Why did you do that? Had you some personal reason for getting involved in this case?"

Ignoring the question, Johnnie said, "Captain Riordan not only found evidence that Miss Manfred had a visitor last night, but certain identification."

"Of Ed?" I asked.

Father scowled at me.

Johnnie said, "It was lucky I went with Riordan to Lola's apartment, although I'd have been able to name the guy later when I read about it in the papers. Still, we got the jump on him that way . . ."

"What evidence, Ansell?"

Johnnie picked up the ashtray and carried it to the desk. I came and looked at it, too. There were two of my rouge-stained stubs in it.

"You don't mean to get Eleanor mixed up in this, do you?" Father said.

"Eleanor's mixed up in it already, and it's not my fault. Look into that ashtray, Mr. Barclay."

In the ashtray, beside my rouge-stained stubs, there was loose ash, a residue of unsmoked tobacco and two minute balls of crumpled cigarette paper.

"One of your best friends doesn't believe that cigarette stubs should be left around. He thinks they taint the air, that it's not good for the health," Johnnie said. He picked up a couple of grains of tobacco and smelled it. "Turkish. Just like the Turkish tobacco found in the ashtrays at Lola's. As soon as I saw those little balls of cigarette paper I was able to tell Riordan the name of Lola's visitor. Apparently he's been here, too, this evening."

A sudden gust of wind blew open the door of the terrace. A chill entered the room. On Fifth Avenue a siren wailed. Father got up and closed the terrace door.

"I told Captain Riordan that when he picks up this cautious connoisseur of Turkish tobacco not to use the verb 'look' if he means 'listen.'"

The siren's echo died and I wondered whether I had actually heard it, or whether it was a whim of my strained imagination. By this time I was certain of nothing; I wondered whether Ed Munn had ever been in this room, whether I had heard him whine his unconvincing denial of the murder. Out of the mists clouding my mind, I heard Johnnie's voice.

" . . . and I keep wondering what connection there was between Munn and Lola Manfred, and between Lola and Warren G. Wilson. Do you know, Mr. Barclay?"

My father shook his head. The movement was weary and without conviction.

"Why did you refuse to let me print the Wilson story in *Truth and Crime*, Mr. Barclay?"

The doorbell rang.

"Probably the police," Johnnie said. "Looking for Munn. Was he here when I phoned the news? Damn it, I didn't think of that until afterward."

Father stood up. "Take her home, John. Get her out of here. We don't want her involved."

"The police may want to question her."

"I'll take care of that. I'll take all responsibility. Take her home, son, she's all in."

Johnnie wheeled around. "Well, Eleanor?"

"I'm tired. Please take me home. I couldn't talk to them now, not now."

Father was pleased. "Use the service elevator. It's self-operated. Go straight to the basement. There's a corridor that will take you to Madison Avenue."

"Is that how Munn left?" Johnnie asked.

The bell rang again.

My father went to fetch my coat, but I rushed ahead, pushed past him in the hall and jerked my coat out of his hands. Father tried to hold it for me, but I pulled away from him and from Johnnie, too. I would not let either of them near me until I had my coat on; and on the drive home I held my coat tight around me, hugging myself with both arms, because I did not want anyone, not even Johnnie, to know I had the manuscript hidden in the inside pocket.

I put it in the locked box in a locked cupboard of my closet. Janet Barclay had given me the box on my thirteenth birthday. It was made of inlaid wood and had silver clasps and a silver lock. The box had been filled with old keepsakes, and when I cleaned it out I found a stale sugar violet. The lock was of soft silver and anyone could pry it open with a hairpin, but the cupboard door had a Yale lock, for I kept my jewelry there, my grandmother's gold bracelets and garnets, and the pearls Father had given me when I was eighteen.

In those first terrified moments after Johnnie had telephoned to tell me that Ed was wanted by the police, while my father made preparations for Ed's escape, and Ed clung with bloodless hands to the arm of the couch, I had taken the manuscript from the low ebony table. While they fought, while my father struck blow after blow, while Ed crumpled and whimpered on the carpet, I had the manuscript tucked behind me in the armchair. And when the doorbell rang and I hurried to answer it, I stopped to hide the manuscript in the pocket of my coat lining.

I did not know at this time what the manuscript revealed but I heard and saw enough to realize that it was dangerous. I had learned that night of murder and treachery; I had been shocked, hurt and disillusioned, but I followed an instinct that urged the protection of my father. It was the old habit, loyalty. He might be a fraud, a hypocrite, partner in murder, but he was still my father and his secret guilt, like the publishing business, the Barclay Building, the royalties, the country estate and all the stocks and bonds, was family property.

"He brought her roses," Johnnie said when we were in the taxi, the sirens and police cars and detectives far behind.

My thoughts had been on other things, and I must have seemed very stupid when I asked, "Who brought roses? Where?"

"Lola. There was an unopened box in her living room. Twelve American Beauties. Just like the flowers that sent her into a tantrum yesterday."

"No, Johnnie, it's impossible. She loathed him and he detested her. Of all the men in the world! Lola had a lot of lovers. It could've been one of them."

"Do you remember the name of the florist on the boxes that came to the office?"

They were always the same, American Beauties, a round, dozen, long-stemmed, unimaginative and expensive. G. Botticelli, the Personal Florist. But Ed Munn! In my wildest dreams I could never conceive of such a romance. Hadn't it been Lola who persuaded me, with subtle indirect argument and sly hints, to break the engagement?

Johnnie wanted to talk. I told him that I was too weary to think about the murder. This was not completely a lie. Fatigue was a pleasant drug that kept me from feeling or thinking. There had been too many discoveries that evening, too much emotion, a surplus of disillusionment. And if Johnnie asked certain questions, I should have been obliged to lie to him.

I disliked lying to Johnnie.

When we reached the apartment I gave my pocketbook to him and he found the key. He opened the door, turned on the lights and tried to help me with my coat. I pulled away sulkily and sat down, holding my coat tight about me.

"What a peevish wench! I guess it's because you're worn out."

"Please don't be angry, Johnnie. Please."

"Did you ask your father why he told me he believed you were mixed up in Wilson's murder?"

"Not tonight, please. I'm exhausted. Will you fix me a drink, a double triple highball with lots of ice and practically no soda?"

The drink was an excuse to get him into the kitchen. When I heard him running water over the ice trays I stole into my bedroom, hid the manuscript between the box spring and the mattress and hung up my coat.

Johnnie spent the night. He thought someone ought to be with me in case the police came. After he had tucked me in and kissed me he made up an uncomfortable bed for himself on the living-room couch. As soon as I heard his steady breathing and decided that he was sleeping, I closed the door between our rooms, wrapped myself in an Angora shawl and, smoking cigarette after cigarette, I read the manuscript.

When I had finished I put it away carefully in the inlaid box, locked it with the silver key, restored the box to the cupboard in the linen closet and hid both keys in the pocket of my plaid coat. There was no sane reason for these precautions as I did not think the police would search the house, but, until I had decided what to do about it, I wanted the manuscript hidden.

I opened the window wide to get the smell of tobacco out of my room, turned out the light and crept into bed. Under two wool blankets and a quilted comforter I shivered. A chill had settled in my bones. If Mr. Wilson were still alive, I should have doubted the history of Homer Peck.

I woke with a start. The blackness around me was broken suddenly by brightness as searing as pain. Johnnie stood beside the bed, naked except for the blanket wrapped around him, Indian-fashion.

"What is it, Eleanor? What's wrong, honey?"

I was crying and trembling. The comforter and two blankets had slipped to the floor and I was stiff with cold.

Johnnie covered me again, sat on the edge of the bed, took me in his arms. "Why are you so frightened? A nightmare?"

I spoke weakly. "There was a man, he was carrying me, it must have been a mountain pass. It was worse than that, it was . . ." But the anguish had faded. I could not remember clearly. "He carried me to the edge and threw me over." For a split second the dream's exquisite terror returned. I shuddered out of Johnnie's embrace.

He warmed milk for me, brought a hot-water bag. When I was soothed and comfortable, he returned to his couch. Again I waited until I was sure he slept, and again I turned on the lights. I had become afraid of sleep and of darkness because sleep is lonely and in the dark you are deserted by all of mankind.

When Johnnie woke in the morning he found me bathed, brushed and combed, rouge on my lips, a yellow ribbon in my hair and a starched apron over my best housecoat. The kitchen smelled of bacon and coffee. Bread was sliced and ready for the toaster; eggs and the beater waited beside a pottery bowl.

Johnnie kissed the back of my neck. "You look a lot better. Sleep well?"

I broke the eggs into the bowl. "Would you go downstairs, please, and see if the milkman's left any cream? I could scramble them with milk but cream's better. And you'll want some for your coffee."

"I want to ask you a couple of questions."

"After breakfast, darling. I never like to talk about serious things before I've had my coffee."

I was a happy, healthy little housewife. My coffee was strong, my toast and eggs ready at the same moment, my grapefruit cold and cut deftly out of the rind.

We were having second cups of coffee when the bell rang. Johnnie set his cup down hard upon the saucer. "I wish we'd had a chance to talk," he said, "but you were so nervous last night"

"I'm all right now. I can take it."

He pushed the button that opened the safety latch downstairs. "Look, kid, tell the whole truth, no matter what. Half the truth isn't any good; half the truth's the same as a lie." Then he opened the door.

Tall and straight, self-possessed, handsome, bringing the fresh air of December morning into my overheated room, Father marched past Johnnie, kissed me and said, "Good morning" as casually as if an early call were part of the daily program.

"Good morning, Father. We're just having breakfast. Would you like a cup of coffee?"

"My dear girl!" His anguish suggested that I had made some immoral proposal.

"Milk?"

He nodded, shook hands with Johnnie, took off his overcoat, looked the room over and chose the love-seat. I gave him milk in a tall highball glass and he drank it at one swallow. To Johnnie he said,

"Captain Riordan wanted to talk to her last night, but I told him she'd collapsed. He'll see her today."

I lit a cigarette. My hand trembled.

"I wish you wouldn't smoke so much. It makes you nervous," Father said. "They want to talk to you too, John. They want to find out if you knew, when you phoned last night, that Munn was with us. I told them I didn't know."

Father's eyes roved, took in the table set for two and the couch with the blankets and sheets.

"I stayed last night. Eleanor was nervous," Johnnie explained.

Father nodded. "He's a good lad, Eleanor. There's nothing that makes a woman so happy as a thoughtful man. You're a lucky girl. But I wish you wouldn't let her smoke so much, John. You see how nervous it makes her."

"It's not smoking that makes me nervous."

"You're very irritable," Father said. "I don't like that shrill note in your voice. It reminds me of your mother before she . . ."

"Please," my voice became shriller. "You didn't come here to talk about my smoking. Why did you come?"

Father's glance was reproachful. "Comes and sit beside me, Eleanor. I want to talk to you." He pulled me down to the love-seat beside him. His hands were cold and dry.

"I'd like a word or two alone with her, lad."

"Okay." Johnnie picked up his coat and hat. "I'll get the papers. Want me to come back, Eleanor?"

"Please come back."

"A fine lad," my father said as the door closed behind Johnnie. "A decent, honest boy, I could want nothing better for you, child."

"Why have you come here?"

"To see my little girl. Why are you so resentful? Afraid I'll disapprove?" He nodded toward the sheets and blankets on the couch. "You ought to know your father better than that, my dear. After all, I'm pretty broadminded—for a parent." He offered an engaging grin.

I moved away, pushed myself into a small space at the end of the love-seat. My cozy living room looked cramped now; the furniture seemed swollen and oversized. On the table in the window stood a lustre bowl filled with freesia which I had bought centuries before, on the night that Johnnie came to dinner.

"What happened to Ed, Father? Did he get away?"

Father was no longer handsome, no longer radiant nor young. The lines deepened along his mouth; the cheekbones protruded like rocky knobs below sunken eyes. I saw again the cruel peaks, the tormented paths, the endless precipice and the face of the man in my nightmare.

"What did you tell the police? You must have told them that Ed was there if they asked about Johnnie's knowing it. I suppose you had to tell them. Too many people knew—Gloria and Hardy and the elevator men."

"Eleanor . . ."

"What did you tell them?"

"My own daughter, my eldest, my favorite."

"How did he get away?" I persisted. "When I left the study to answer the doorbell, he was almost unconscious. Did he also go by the service elevator or was he hiding on the terrace? I noticed the door . . . I was afraid . . ."

Father sighed. The room seemed still to be shrinking, the walls closing in. The freesia petals were brown at the edges and shriveled. My father, too, seemed to be shrinking, closing in on himself.

"They're going to ask me what happened, Father. What shall I tell them?"

"You know nothing," he said, articulating carefully like a man who has been ill and is just recovering the power of speech. "You left the study. Ed was there with me. You went to the front hall, opened the door, greeted John, stopped to chat, probably to kiss him or let him kiss you . . ."

"I fainted."

"No need to bring that up. They'd ask a lot of fool questions. I told them you'd stopped for a little conversation or love-making, about five minutes, I said. I went out to see what was taking you so long and Ed disappeared. That's what I told them."

In my dream the night had been darker than death. I had tried to call for help, but I had no voice. He had carried me to the edge of the precipice and I had known his intentions, but I could not cry out for help because the man had been my father.

After a little while I said, "You didn't find the manuscript, did you?"

"How do you know?"

"I know." My voice was light, my eyes cold, my smile mocking.

"You, Eleanor . . . You've got it?"

I laughed.

"Where is it?" He waited but I did not answer. He caught hold of my wrists, jerked me toward him. "Eleanor . . . daughter . . ."

I tried to escape, but his hands tightened and they seemed so large, so tense and strong that I felt my bones crack beneath them. I tried again to pull free, but the pressure increased and I was afraid that his hands would break my wrists. Closing my eyes, shutting out the cruel brilliance of his glance, I saw again the jutting rocks, the nightmare road, the precipice.

PART FIVE
To A Genteel Lady

by John Miles Ansell

"I will know myself. I will recognize and admit the truth about myself no matter how shameful and guilty it may seem, for I know there can be no shame in me, no guilt, no weakness if I face the Truth and freely name aloud my shame, my guilt, my weaknesses."

My Life Is Truth
NOBLE BARCLAY

It was Saturday morning. In the tabloids and Hearst papers Lola Manfred had become headline news. *Greenwich Village Poetess Believed Slain.* That she was old, fat, weary and alcoholic seemed not to matter. No reporter bothered to mention the fact that she had not written a poem for years. Murder had restored her dignity.

The respectable papers were less rhapsodic. The word "alleged" was used frequently.

I read about it in a drugstore on Eighth Street and University Place. I drank two cups of alleged coffee and learned that the police were seeking a man believed to have been with Miss Manfred the night of her death. No paper named Edward Everett Munn. I ordered a third cup of coffee, so that I could stay at the counter and read the newspapers.

Eleanor had wanted me out of the way while she talked to her father. I hadn't needed any special lenses nor an improved hearing device to perceive that she was hiding something from me. Before she went to bed she had been nervous and later the nightmare had almost paralyzed her. She thought she had fooled me, but I knew she kept her light on and rattled papers for an hour after she pretended to be asleep.

In the morning I was supposed to have found her the cheerful little woman, a ribbon in her hair and her apron strings tied in a coy bow. That's what she thought. I wondered if she knew she had sugared my eggs.

I made up my mind to play it her way, just to see how far she would carry the ball. The arrival of Noble Barclay saved me from the sweetened eggs. After he had shed his paternal light upon us, there was no need to continue the pretense of appetite. I cleared the table for Eleanor and threw the eggs into the garbage pail.

For twenty minutes I dallied in the drugstore. My intensive study of alarm clocks, stuffed animals and la grippe cures must have convinced the manager that I was opening a rival pharmacy. Finally I bought three packs of cigarettes and started back. As I turned the corner on East Tenth Street, I saw a long black sedan stop in front of the remodeled brick house on whose second floor dwelt Miss Eleanor Barclay, the original Truth Girl.

It was a police car. Riordan got out. "Just the man I want to see," he said, clapping me on the shoulder.

The vestibule was three steps down. On one wall were mail boxes and brass-bordered cards printed with the tenants' names. Riordan gave the cards the once-over, but did not immediately ring Eleanor's bell.

"When you called Barclay last night, did you know Munn was there?" he asked.

"I didn't call Barclay. I was trying to locate Miss Barclay."

"You weren't sure you'd find her at her father's?"

"No. I called here first, but she wasn't at home. So I took a chance and called her father."

"He says you didn't talk to her."

"I asked for her, but he seemed unwilling to call her to the phone. So I let him have it."

"What do you mean, let him have it?"

"The news that his assistant, his supervising editor, his best friend had committed murder."

"We're not sure of that," Riordan said.

"What the hell!"

"All the evidence we have is some tobacco and a couple of wads of cigarette paper."

"What about the flowers? Did G. Botticelli know Munn? Had he bought her flowers there before?"

"Doesn't prove Munn killed her," Riordan said.

"Have you picked him up yet?"

"He's scrammed."

"No!"

Riordan nodded.

"Doesn't that prove something?" I asked. "He knew you were after him and he skipped. Must have had a guilty conscience."

"Did you know he was at Barclay's when you phoned?"

"Hell," I said. "If I'd wanted to cover up for the guy, would I have shown you the evidence in the ashtrays? You could spend forty years, Riordan, looking for a man who gets rid of his stubs that way. If I hadn't given you his name, would you have guessed that E. E. Munn, editor of Truth Publications had called on Lola that night?"

"Botticelli might have told us. We might have had a chance to pick up Munn before he was warned," Riordan said.

I was sore. When he sat with me in bars, drank rye at my expense and gave me stories for *Truth and Crime*, Riordan had seemed a friend. I saw now that he was less friend and more cop.

"You haven't answered my question," he said. "When you called Barclay's place, did you know Munn was there?"

"Hell, if I'd known, do you think I'd have phoned? Be yourself, Riordan, I'm the guy who tipped you off to Munn."

"Miss Barclay's your girl friend, isn't she?"

"We're going to be married," I answered.

"Maybe that's why you were so anxious to let her know that the other guy, the ex-boy friend, was mixed up with the Manfred dame?"

"Are you suggesting that I gave you the dope on Munn because I was jealous? Because I wanted him out of the way?"

"Could be."

"Nuts to that."

"When you got to Barclay's place last night, who opened the door?"

"Miss Barclay."

The answer must have checked with Barclay's story. Riordan nodded. "How long did you two stay out in the hall together?"

"Three or four minutes. When she saw me she fainted."

"Fainted? Barclay didn't mention it."

"It's the sort of thing Barclay wouldn't mention: He wouldn't want to get out that his daughter, brought up by the *Truth and Health* method, could be so frail and human."

Riordan grimaced. I could see that he did not believe all of my answers. This made me feel as if I were on the spot and had to defend myself. I felt guilty.

"Why do you ask me that? Was Munn supposed to have made his getaway while I was in the hall with Eleanor?"

"That's Barclay's story. Munn was supposed to have been in that room, the loony one that looks like the reception room of an asylum, with Barclay and the girl. You rang the bell. She went to open the door and was gone quite a while, so Barclay went to see why. While he was gone, Munn took a powder . . ."

"The hell you say!"

"Barclay thinks he slipped down the back way. There's a self-operated service elevator and a corridor in the basement that goes clear to Madison Avenue."

"I know. That's how Eleanor and I left."

"You did, huh? Why?"

I wondered. Barclay had been so urgent and Eleanor so eager that I had not stopped to ask questions. To Riordan I said, "It was when you came. Eleanor was exhausted and her father thought she'd better rest before she talked to you. He suggested the service elevator."

Riordan pushed the button beside the slot with Eleanor's calling card. A buzzer sounded. The latch of the inner door clicked open. I ran ahead.

Barring Riordan's way, I asked, "Did you mention Warren G. Wilson when you talked to Barclay last night? What did he say?"

Riordan pushed past me and started up the stairs. On the landing above we heard a door open.

Barclay swung out his hand to Riordan, wished him a good morning. "Back again, lad?" he said jovially to me.

There was no. sign of Eleanor. The couch had been cleared of sheets and blankets; dishes and cups had been removed from the breakfast table.

"Sit down, Captain. Take his coat, John. I suppose you'd like to see my daughter." It seemed Barclay's home, rather than Eleanor's.

I took a position like a St. Bernard before the bedroom door. Riordan chose a stiff chair and Barclay seated himself comfortably on the couch.

"Any trace of the fugitive?" Barclay asked.

Riordan said, "Why didn't you report the theft of your car, Mr. Barclay?"

Barclay scratched his head. "One of my cars stolen? I didn't know. My chauffeur hasn't reported any theft."

"At three-fifteen this morning a man named James B. Thorpe was picked up in Philadelphia."

"In my car?" Barclay asked.

"Black Chrysler coupe, registered in New York as the property of Noble Barclay."

"I have a black coupe," Barclay said. "Used it yesterday." His fist crashed against the table. "Damn it, I must have left it out again. Yes, I did. I'm afraid," his voice showed remorse, "the keys were in it. I sometimes leave it for the chauffeur to pick up."

"What about this Thorpe?" I asked. "Who was he?"

"Never heard of him," said Barclay.

"He carried a California driver's license. According to the description in it, this Thorpe was six foot three, weighed around two hundred and twenty. Doesn't weigh that much now. Skinny guy and just about six foot, the report says."

"Why was he picked up?" I said.

"Drunken driving."

"Drunk." Barclay whispered it like a dirty word. Clearing his throat, he asked, "Has he been questioned? Did he confess to stealing my car?"

"Wouldn't talk without his lawyer."

"Oh!" was all that Barclay said.

We all waited.

"Then he said he wanted the best lawyer in Philadelphia. The best, he kept on insisting. Said he was a man of importance, that they'd be surprised if they knew who he really was. He had ten grand in his wallet."

Barclay raised his eyebrows. "Has he talked to his lawyer yet?"

"They'll let us know when anything new turns up." Riordan appeared nonchalant, but he was watching Barclay's reactions out of the corner of his eye.

Eleanor came out of the bedroom. She had changed from her robe to a blue skirt and white sweater. She looked beautiful but unhappy. Dilated pupils made her eyes seem dark.

Her father beckoned but Eleanor would not sit beside him. She went to the far end of the room. "This is Captain Riordan, Eleanor. Captain, my daughter."

Riordan asked her about Lola. He wanted to know how friendly Eleanor and Lola had been, how many personal secrets Lola had confided, and if on the day of her death she had shown signs of despondency.

"Yes, she did," Eleanor answered emphatically. "She'd been all right in the morning, but in the afternoon she was strange. She lost her temper and threw her fur coat on the floor and stayed in the Ladies' Room for a long time. It was either because she'd had too much to drink at lunch or because someone had sent her some roses. Someone she disliked, I imagine."

"Roses," said Riordan. But no more on that subject. "Was that the last you saw of her?"

Eleanor looked up. She had been rubbing her wrists. "Yes, it was. I left about an hour later. I had some shopping to do. I wanted to buy a new hat." She tossed the phrase, defiantly, in my direction.

"What do you know of her relations with Munn?"

"She loathed and despised him."

"Are you sure?"

Eleanor went on massaging her wrists. "Positive."

Riordan turned to Barclay. "That's not what you told me."

"My daughter believed what Miss Manfred wanted her to believe. What the rest of the office believed." Barclay looked wise and secretive. "Miss Manfred told everyone she despised Ed Munn. It was a ruse to keep them from knowing the truth."

Eleanor jumped up. "I don't believe it! I worked with Lola. I saw her every day. I knew her better than anyone in the office."

"You knew exactly what Lola chose to have you know," said Barclay in a voice as smooth as castor oil. "Miss Manfred—though I don't like speaking ill of the dead—was sly. She didn't want anyone in the office, and particularly Eleanor, to learn about her relations with Ed because . . ." Barclay smiled and shook his head, "Eleanor had been engaged to him."

"No one in the office knew." Eleanor returned to the couch. She leaned against the cushions wearily as if, at this hour of the morning, she was already exhausted. "I can't believe Lola'd ever have looked at him. She'd have laughed if Ed had even tried . . ."

"Your voice is getting shrill, child. Remember what I told you this morning," Barclay interrupted.

Eleanor groped in her belt, found a handkerchief, covered her mouth. She was on the verge of hysterical laughter.

Riordan looked to me for help. The switch from the *Truth and Crime* angle to a *Truth and Love* scene disconcerted the detective. But I was no tower of strength. Barclay had once taken me in with that smooth manner. Experience made me wary. On the other hand, there was a certain amount of credibility in his story. Lola had been drunk and wanton; she might also have been sly. When she abused or insulted Munn, or regaled us at the Editors' Table with stories of his stupidity, she might have been laughing secretly at our naïveté.

"Did you know about this affair before Lola died?" I said to Barclay.

"For quite a while," he answered.

"Had Munn confided in you?"

"Don't like to be caught napping, do you, John?" Barclay laughed. To Riordan he commented, "Our young friend is typical of the skeptic who doubts whatever his own eyes have failed to see. What's your opinion, Captain? Do you think I'm fabricating?"

Riordan hesitated. He was, after all, a cop. And Barclay a big shot, a millionaire, author and publisher, owner of property, a boss. Why should Barclay *fabricate*? Had the boss anything to gain by making up a story about a love affair between his assistant and a loose woman?

"What reason would you have to make up the story?" Riordan asked.

Barclay turned his charm full upon Riordan. "I admit," he confessed ingenuously, "that I was deceived. I certainly misjudged Ed Munn. I knew this woman taunted him, tortured him, flaunted her lovers before him, but I never thought he'd go so far as to kill her. Frankly, I didn't think," the pause was effective, "that Ed had it in him. I've seldom met a less violent man."

Riordan fingered his ear. "I'd like to ask Miss Barclay a question. I asked you last night, but I want to hear her answer." This was police subtlety calculated to inform Miss Barclay that her story had better check with her father's, or else. "When your father answered John Ansell's call and told you we were after Munn in connection with Miss Manfred's death, what did he do?"

"He denied it."

"Denied what?"

"Killing Lola."

"And we believed him, didn't we, Eleanor?" Without giving her an opportunity to answer, Barclay went on, "That was natural, don't you think. Captain? After all, when you've been associated with a man for years, it's hard to believe he's committed a murder. And I'll tell you something else, Captain." Barclay was rueful. "I don't think I'd believe now that Ed had done it if he hadn't run off like that."

Eleanor had started rubbing her wrists again. I tried to catch her eye, but she avoided my glance. She was very nervous.

"I'm a man who prides himself on being a judge of human nature," Barclay said. "It just goes to show how your pride can deceive you. And how little one man knows of what's in another's heart."

We took it silently. Eleanor reached across the table for a china cigarette box. She offered it to Riordan and to me.

Riordan shook his head. "I don't indulge."

"Great!" shouted Barclay. "I congratulate you. Look at him, kids. A man of action and achievement, he doesn't think he has to prove his manliness by smoking and drinking. I wish you'd tell these youngsters, Riordan, why you eschew tobacco."

Riordan acknowledged the tribute with a jerk of his head. "I used to smoke two packs regularly every day of my life, but I wanted to see if I could get along without 'em. That was a year ago St. Patrick's Day." He did not mention his capacity for rye whiskey. Neither did I. It would be unbecoming for a host to remind his guest of the cost of entertainment.

"Before we go a step further, Captain, I want you to know something." Barclay moved toward Riordan. He must have counted ten before he spoke. His timing was perfect. We were all on the edge of our seats.

"I like the way you've handled this case. I must confess I'm deeply impressed by your honesty and your straightforward methods, Captain. I wonder if you'd mind if I mentioned it to the Commissioner. I'd like to congratulate him on the efficiency of his staff, particularly a certain officer . . ."

Riordan had turned as pink as a newborn baby. "Just as you like, Mr. Barclay. Glad you feel that way."

"That about finishes it, doesn't it, Captain? If you want us, you know where we can be found." Barclay had picked up Riordan's overcoat.

Riordan stood up, brushed wrinkles from blue serge. "You'll all be asked to appear at the inquest."

"We know that."

Riordan smirked. This was his big moment, one he could brag about to his in-laws. "Thanks for everything, Mr. Barclay. It's a privilege to know a man like you." Riordan shook hands with Barclay, nodded at Eleanor and me.

I was burning. Efficiency. Straightforward methods. The same old Barclay guff and Riordan eating it up like a turkey dinner. Once I had fallen for Barclay's line; I had let him call me a pint-sized runt and had wrung his hand in gratitude. But that was different. That was appeasement for a story he did not want printed in a magazine. This was murder.

"Wait a minute. Haven't you forgotten something," my voice echoed sarcastically Barclay's flattering use of Riordan's title, "Captain?"

"Forgotten something?" Riordan looked around.

"Warren G. Wilson. Remember him? The man who was murdered last May. When I called you last night and told you I suspected Lola hadn't committed suicide, I said there might be a connection between her death and Wilson's. You know now that it wasn't suicide, but what about Wilson? That was your case and I thought it was why you asked to be put on the Manfred investigation. Or am I wrong?"

Eleanor slid forward on the couch. Riordan transferred his hat from his right to his left hand, and shifted his weight. Barclay frowned in my direction. It was a warning.

Undaunted, I plunged into the gale. "When you talked to Mr. Barclay last night, Captain, did you mention Wilson?"

"The lad's tenacious," Barclay said, winking at Riordan. "Once he gets a notion in his head he sticks to it. Some people might call him stubborn, but I admire his tenacity. It's a sign of character."

A sign of character, is it? Okay, Barclay, I'll show you the quantity and quality of character in John Miles Ansell. "Was Mr. Barclay able to tell you anything about Wilson?"

Eleanor coughed. On Valentine's Day Warren G. Wilson had given her a book inscribed to a genteel lady. Until I forced it out of her, she had not mentioned her friendship with a murder victim. I tried to catch her eye, but she was looking down into the china box as if she expected to find a pearl among the cigarettes.

"Mr. Barclay didn't know Wilson," Riordan told me.

"You asked him?"

"Last night." Riordan swung around on his heels and glowered at me. "What gives you the idea that these people knew Wilson?"

"I told you."

"What did you tell me? That you had a hunch Miss Manfred was connected with the Wilson case. You had no proof."

"Look," I said, trying to give him a straight answer while I let Eleanor know that I had not mentioned her name, "I told you I had a hunch Miss Manfred had known Wilson. I told you what happened when I asked her if she'd known him . . ."

"What happened?" Barclay asked.

"She denied it," Riordan said.

"Denied it!" Barclay shouted.

"Yes, she denied it," I said, "but the way she denied it made me suspect that she was lying. She was too defiant, too emotional . . ."

"Had she been drinking?" asked Barclay.

"Uh-huh."

"Wasn't it characteristic of Miss Manfred to be defiant and emotional, particularly when she'd been drinking?" Again Barclay answered without giving anyone else a chance. "You see, lad, I know the tendencies of alcoholics better than you. My own unfortunate history gives me particular insight into their emotional responses. You say she was defiant in denying she'd known Wilson. Typical. Typical."

A door slammed. Eleanor had gone into the bedroom. I did not know whether she was irritated because I had divulged a family secret or because her father was an oily hypocrite. I did not much care.

Barclay appeared not to have noticed Eleanor's retreat. He was too intent upon his argument. "You see, Captain, the boy's got no proof that Lola knew Wilson. She was drunk, she was defiant, and he wants to make something of it. What's your opinion?"

"I can't see it," Riordan said. "Last night, when he told me about it, I was willing to take a chance. When you want to clean up a case, you'll follow any lead. But now that I've heard everything, Mr. Barclay, I'm inclined to agree with you. It doesn't make sense."

"Okay, it was just a hunch," I said. "But a valuable hunch, wasn't it, Riordan? How about Munn's having been with Lola? Would you have known that without my hunch?"

"Doesn't prove that either of them knew Wilson," Barclay laid his hand consolingly on my shoulder. "I know it'll hurt you to hear me say this, lad, but you never could take that turn-down, on the Wilson story. You thought you'd written a masterpiece, and ever since then you've had some cockeyed notion that I had a personal reason for rejecting it. You . . ."

"Look, Mr. Barclay . . ."

"You've got to learn to take it, son. You're not perfect; you're only human like the rest of the race. Everyone makes a mistake some time in his life. You may be a hell of a writer, but even Shakespeare turned out a few duds. It's going pretty far, don't you think, Captain," Barclay's hand fell from my shoulder as he turned toward Riordan, "when a fellow has to accuse others of intrigue just because they turn down his literary efforts?"

"Hell," I said, "I've had stories turned down before. Better stories and by better magazines than *Truth and Crime*. If you're trying to say that's the reason I think you . . ."

"What other reason could you have? What proof have you that Munn or I—since you insist upon involving me in this fallacious theory—had any connection with Wilson except that we didn't like your story of his death?"

I looked around for something to throw. There was only Eleanor's old china and antique furniture.

"Look, Mr. Barclay, was I or was I not poisoned the night after I started asking questions about the Wilson story?"

"Poisoned?" Barclay did not seem to understand.

"I don't eat shrimps, Mr. Barclay. I'm allergic to shellfish."

"Come now, John." That was the old Barclay, the smoothie, the professional confidant. "You're not going to deny facts. Everyone, Smith of the Grille, the waiters, the doctor, your nurse, they all knew you had ptomaine from eating contaminated seafood. Look up the hospital records—they'll show you. To say you were poisoned is not only absurd, boy; it's dangerous. Shows you to be suffering from a persecution complex."

"I didn't eat shrimps. I never do. Look, Riordan, he might have bribed them to say I did; I've suspected that all along, but it's not true. I'm telling you . . ."

Barclay smiled. He was so damn tolerant that I wanted to smack his sleek puss. Against that calm self-confidence my raging sounded like the anger of a three-year-old.

"I was poisoned!" I beat my heels against the floor and pounded my fist on the table. Mahogany shivered and china rattled.

Barclay smiled sadly. From the way he took it, an outsider would think I had only just made up the poisoning story and was trying to uphold my fiction with a display of temper.

"Why didn't you report it?" Riordan asked.

Barclay almost purred.

"I was bribed," I said. "By a raise of seventy-five smackers per week."

"Yeah?" Riordan looked at Barclay for confirmation.

"I wasn't aware, John, that you felt that way about your promotion.

At the time your gratitude seemed sincere." Barclay turned the full light of his countenance upon me. His voice dripped sympathy. "What did you have on your conscience, lad, that you couldn't accept a promotion and a raise without explaining it to yourself in that distorted fashion? What secrets are you hiding? What truth about yourself are you afraid to face?"

"For Christ's sake!" I said.

"He probably believes he was poisoned," Barclay told Riordan. He spoke in the voice of a high-priced specialist who has been called in to advise the family doctor. "It's remarkable how easy it is for some people to believe what they *wish to believe*. It proves what I said in my book and what I keep on saying in the magazine: anyone can believe anything if the urge is strong enough. You know what it proves?" His voice dropped. The confidence was directed at Riordan, but he was careful to see that I did not miss a syllable. "It proves that there's something deep in this lad that he can't face. You'll never find a healthy man, a happy man, a strong and confident man who can't dig down into the depths of himself and acknowledge the bitter truth. When a man has to go as far as this young man has gone to show that others are trying to harm him, there's something unhealthy inside. Don't you agree, Captain?"

"You're not kidding," Riordan said solemnly. "In my line I've met plenty of crooks who blame their troubles on the other fellow."

Barclay nodded his approval of this sagacity. "The human mind," he continued, "is the greatest natural phenomenon of all time, the eighth wonder of the world. Science has studied it for centuries, and what has it discovered? No more than I can tell you now in a single sentence. A man can will himself to believe that anything is the truth, and if he believes hard enough, it *is* the truth."

Riordan pondered and moved toward the cigarette box.

Barclay went on with the lecture. "It's as true in religion as in science. Faith, self-confidence, belief can work miracles. Have you read my book, Captain?"

"Sorry," muttered Riordan.

"Oh, I don't mind." Barclay was forgiving. "Lot of people haven't read it yet. I'll send you a copy. Read it. You'll find the case of this young man clearly explained, Captain."

"You'll find Mr. Barclay, too. His life story is told in the most intimate detail. Don't skip the Introduction. It's the greatest human document ever written on human despair."

The lid of the cigarette box banged shut. Riordan turned, putting temptation behind him. He held his hat in both hands, revolving it slowly.

"We've come a long way from murder," I said. "A long way from the Wilson case and Lola's death and Munn's escape. Barclay's philosophy is fascinating, don't you think, Captain? Probably you've heard some of the ideas before. Barclay's borrowed a lot from Christian and pagan, from medicine men and scientists, from theosophists, theologists, psychoanalysts, and the crank religions of the twentieth century. It's remarkable what men can believe, particularly when you know how many of them have swallowed Truth-Sharing."

Riordan's hat whirled faster. He was a detective, not an arbiter of philosophies.

Barclay sensed the delicate balance. Winningly, as if he and Riordan were allies of long standing, he said, "Haven't you noticed, Captain, that cynics are all the same? What difference is there between those who scoff at the old religions or those who scorn the revelations of a modern philosophy? What is it in their souls that makes these men so inflexible? Why do they hate themselves and despise the rest of humanity? Can it be envy? Must they sneer at Belief because they are incapable of Belief?"

Barclay bent forward, peering first into Riordan's face, then into mine. He looked and spoke as if he were addressing an audience of fifty thousand. All of his tremendous energy was concentrated in his ardent voice.

"Don't be distressed, John. It's been tough, but you haven't failed yet, lad. It's just that stubborn will of yours, that determination to beat the bigger fellow. Face yourself, boy, accept your shortcomings. You'll be bigger than any man on earth."

Riordan smirked. I knew what he was thinking. Just what Barclay wanted him to think: that I was a frustrated, envious, bitter, five-foot-five runt who used cynicism and sarcasm as a weapon against the six-footers. It was not a new tactic. Barclay had once done it with a mirror, but this time he put on a better show; he didn't need mirrors. He had me where he wanted, helpless and squirming. If I had argued, he would have twisted my arguments against me. If I had stated fact he would have proved that my facts were conceived out of frustration and envy. Barclay was the big man and he had more than inches to prove his stature. He had faith. That made him secure. I possessed no weapon strong enough to pierce that armor, no shield to protect me from his blows.

Therefore, ergo and *q. e. d.* I had not been poisoned. I had eaten shrimps.

The phone rang. I welcomed the interruption. Sweat rolled down my face. The act of wiping it off embarrassed me. I hoped the argument was over.

Eleanor hurried out of the bedroom. But Riordan had already answered the phone. It was his office reporting information just received from the Philadelphia cops. The man who had stolen Barclay's black coupe had been found dead in his cell. An empty glass vial lay on the floor beside the body. The police had not discovered it when they originally frisked him.

I watched Eleanor. She had not been present when Riordan told Barclay about the theft of the car and the arrest, in Philadelphia, of the drunken driver. The news meant nothing to her until James B. Thorpe's name was mentioned.

Her body stiffened. She stared at her father. "So it wasn't the terrace?" She had barely breath enough for the words.

"Terrace?" Riordan was puzzled.

"I thought he jumped off or had . . ." She caught Barclay staring at her and turned away. "It must have been a dream, but it seemed so real. It couldn't have, could it? There'd have been a body on the street. It seemed . . ."

"Stop chattering," Barclay commanded. To Riordan he said, "He was dead, you say, when they found him."

Riordan nodded.

With a fine monogrammed handkerchief Barclay wiped sweat from his forehead. "Then he didn't say anything? Didn't reveal his identity?"

"Know who he was?"

Barclay's head was bowed. The handkerchief hid the expression on his face. "Poor Ed," he said and blew his nose. "Poor fellow, he must have known the game was up."

The inquest was apathetic. Lola Manfred was declared dead. A few grains of tobacco, several minute balls of crumpled cigarette paper, an unopened box of American Beauties might have proved that Edward Everett Munn had been her final visitor, but they did not prove that he had mixed bichloride of mercury with her last whiskey and soda.

Riordan thanked me publicly for my assistance in the Manfred case, but he did not mention Wilson nor my hunch that there was a connection between the two murders. Probably Barclay had won him to the belief that I wanted revenge because my Wilson story had been rejected. In his own way, Riordan was right. Not a shred of evidence linked Lola Manfred's death to the murder of Warren G. Wilson. Time and the taxpayers' money could not be wasted on theories offered by a guy with a chip on his shoulder.

There was a surprise Witness. His name was Botticelli. He looked and acted like Chico Marx. Every week his boy had delivered flowers to Miss Lola Manfred. When Botticelli testified, the Coroner and the jury rocked with laughter. In spite of the comedy, the florist's testimony clinched Barclay's theory. With American Beauties at eighteen dollars a dozen, it had to be love.

Eleanor testified briefly. She had come in late, walking between her father and his attorney. She wore her black suit and a black sweater and a string of small pearls. She looked severe, like an old-fashioned schoolteacher. All the little soft curls had been combed flat. Her hair looked dark. Purple shadows circled her eyes. She did not take off her white gloves.

She appeared not to notice that I was in the room. We had not seen each other during the week-end. On Saturday morning, when Barclay and Riordan left, she had asked me to go, too. She was tired, she said. I had telephoned several times, both on Saturday night and Sunday, but she was always too tired to see me.

I was puzzled. This seemed a curious time for her to give me the brush-off. I asked myself a lot of questions, but the answers added up to a bright zero.

Noble Barclay took the oath. Everyone in the courtroom edged forward in his chair. Eleanor's white-gloved hands played with the pearls. I, Noble Barclay, swear to tell the truth, the whole truth, nothing but the truth. He was big, handsome, self-assured and earnest. He spoke in a mellow but clear-cut voice. There were no pauses, no evasions. He looked every juror in the eye and showed clearly that he was more than willing to co-operate with the officials.

Barclay admitted that he had difficulty in adjusting himself to the idea that his close friend and trusted assistant could commit murder. Although, Barclay added, he had been aware that in having relations with Miss Manfred, Munn had been playing with fire.

"Do you know certainly, Mr. Barclay, that she was Munn's mistress?"

"Does anyone in this room doubt it?"

Eleanor's necklace broke. Pearls rolled on the floor. There was a lot of talk and moving about. Officials, witnesses and attendants got down on their knees.

I kept my seat. So did Eleanor.

Barclay went on with his testimony. He was the only one in the office, he intimated, who had not been fooled by the lovers' ruses. We others, the wise and cynical, had let the wool be pulled over our eyes, had believed that affection was enmity, had been too blind to perceive that bitterness and slander were a disguise for shameful love.

It was a good, quick, glib explanation. Barclay's style was editorial with a strong *Truth and Love* flavor. I could almost see the titles: *Mystery Death of Secret Lovers—Was It a Suicide Pact?*

The alleged lovers were dead. Nobody came into the courtroom to deny Barclay's statements. Who would doubt a man of his reputation? His facts were as orderly as the alphabet. And Munn could not now be indicted and tried for murder. The case was closed.

At the end the crowd gathered around Barclay. Men waited in line to shake his hand. Ordinary, decent, law-abiding citizens felt it a privilege to meet the author of *My Life Is Truth*. Everyone was surprised and delighted to find the great man so humble and so sincere.

Down the block was a dirty bar. I chose a booth in the darkest cor-ner. Sitting alone, I ordered two double brandies. Eleanor had gone off with her father and the lawyer in the Barclay limousine. It was long and black and looked to me like a funeral car.

"Two double brandies?" asked the bartender.

"I'm expecting someone," I said. This was a lie, but I am not one of those sturdy souls who can share the truth with strange bartenders.

He brought the drinks. I had him set one before me, place the other across the table. He guessed that I was not expecting anyone, and as he returned to the bar I noticed that he was looking at my reflection in the mirror.

I raised my glass and drank a toast to Lola Manfred. This was more appropriate, I thought, than a wreath for her coffin.

The bartender was worried. I signaled and he came back to the booth. "I'm afraid my friend's not coming. Would you like it?" I pointed to the untouched glass. Lola would not have wanted good brandy wasted.

"Don't mind if I do. Though I'd rather've had bourbon."

"Have a bourbon on me, too." I threw five bucks on the table, saluted the bartender and left. He tapped his head.

Ten minutes later I walked into the office. It was 4 p.m., and the place should have been humming. Hardly a typewriter clicked. In the pri-vate offices, editors and sub-editors gossiped. In the Ladies' and the Gents' Rooms were gathered delegations of writers, readers, typists, office boys, and members of the Board of Religious Co-ordination. No one wanted to work. Too much had happened.

My fellow-workers crowded around as if I were Public Hero Num-ber One. They asked confidentially if it was true that the late E. E. Munn and the late Miss Manfred had been that way about each other. It was ridiculous. Anyone with eyes and ears should have known that these two were enemies. But Barclay had seen the reporters on Satur-day and stories had been printed in the Sunday papers. That made it authentic. Barclay employees who lived by the printed word believed in the printed word.

The human mind, as Barclay had informed Captain Riordan, is the greatest natural phenomenon of all time, the eighth wonder of the world. Henry Roe confided that he had always known there was something between Lola and Munn, and Tony Shaw rushed into my office to whisper that he was sure he had once seen them in a hotel in Atlantic City.

Presently Miss Eccles paid me a visit. Her chest heaved, her hands fluttered, her dry painted lips pouted girlishly. "Tell me, Mr. Ansell, aren't you just overwhelmed?"

"Overwhelmed is the word for it, Miss Eccles."

Beside my office door stood Miss Kaufman. Through rimless glasses she glared at Barclay's secretary. "He's busy, Grace. Don't bother him now. If you have any questions regarding business, send us a memo."

Miss Eccles turned her bony, indignant back upon the enemy. "This is business, Mr. Ansell. Tell me, have you seen *him* today?"

"Barclay? Of course. At the inquest."

"Did he say he was coming in?"

"He didn't honor me with his confidences. Nor make a statement to the press."

"Please, Mr. Ansell," lily-white hands were clasped in supplication beneath the sharp chin, "don't be whimsical. You know I have no sense of humor. There are vital questions to be answered. Office policy, you understand. Is Eleanor coming in?"

"She didn't confide in me either."

"But what are we to do about *Truth and Love*? With Miss Manfred passed on and Eleanor neglecting her responsibilities, how can the magazine ever go to press?"

"Who cares if *Truth and Love* never goes to press?"

Miss Kaufman laughed.

Miss Eccles gave me a stricken look. "I know it's not as important as life and death, Mr. Ansell, but the first rule in this business is that the magazine has to go to press on time."

"Perhaps they'll make you editor."

"Oh! Mr. Ansell! That's very flattering, but I haven't the editorial mind."

"You've been loyal," I said. "So loyal that you ought to be Supervising Editor. Maybe Mr. Barclay'll give you Munn's job. Shall I suggest it?"

"I doubt that I'm worthy," she sighed. But the look in her pale eyes showed that Miss Grace Eccles dwelt in a prophetic dream.

Miss Kaufman's voice disturbed the vision. "Quit bothering him now. He's got work to do."

Miss Eccles gave Miss Kaufman a glance which promised dismissal on the day that Barclay's secretary achieved new power.

When she had left. Miss Kaufman closed the office door, moved toward my desk and said, "It doesn't sound kosher to me. Does it sound kosher to you, Mr. Ansell?"

"Good for you, Kaufman. It cheers me to discover there's still some honest skepticism left in the world." I kissed her.

"None of that. I'm a respectable married woman. If it hadn't been for that bichloride of mercury, I wouldn't have believed it. But since I read that the ten thousand dollars he had on him was claimed by his sister who runs a beauty shop, I couldn't help putting two and two together."

"You sound like a manuscript that *Truth and Crime* would reject, Miss K. Which two and two and what's the sum?"

"Beauty shop operators use bichloride. They get it in tablet form and dissolve the tablets to use as antiseptics. Why couldn't he have got some bichloride tablets out of his sister's shop?"

"That doesn't tell us why he did it."

"Do you remember," Miss Kaufman asked as she cleaned my glasses with the square of pink cotton, "what Miss Manfred always answered when people asked how she dared say all those fresh things about Mr. Barclay? She used to say she knew where the body was buried."

"Whose body?"

"I wouldn't know," replied Miss Kaufman. She gave me back my glasses and marched out of the office.

For the rest of the afternoon she posted herself outside my door and told visitors that I was too busy to be disturbed. I spent an active hour drumming on the wood of my desk. Secured to the wall opposite my desk by four thumb tacks hung a picture cut from a woman's magazine. Miss Kaufman had put it there as a gag. The lettuce was green, the mayonnaise yellow, the shrimps pink . . . *can't be sure until we've got the analysis but I had another case that looked just life it. Bichloride*

of mercury. Or had the ambulance doctor never said it? Had my imagination, stimulated by too many crime stories, conceived the whole
thing? According to hospital records, to Noble Barclay, to I. G. Smith
of the Barclay Building Grille, I had eaten deteriorated shellfish. Can
such authority be contradicted? What proof had I, three weeks later,
that I had not eaten shrimps?

The darkness thickened. A gong sounded. Miss Kaufman popped
in to ask whether I would need her anymore that day. I told her to
hurry home to the wallpaper salesman. People passed, laughing and
talking, on their way to the elevators. Girls giggled. My fingertips were
numb and I quit beating rhythms on my desk.

Hinges creaked as my office door opened. I swung around in my
swivel chair. It creaked, too.

"Johnnie, are you still here?" asked Eleanor.

"What do you think?"

"Please don't be sarcastic. I've got to see you."

"You had plenty of opportunity over the week-end. I'd begun to
wonder if you weren't avoiding me on purpose."

She came a couple of steps into the office. I switched on the desk
lamp. The sudden light struck me between the eyes. I scowled.

"Sit down. Make yourself comfortable," I said.

She took the straight chair designed for new writers who come to
ask if the editor would be interested in an unusual story. She was still
pale but she had made an effort to liven her appearance with rouge
and lipstick. The purplish color made her skin seem frailer. She had
evidently stopped at the apartment, for she had changed the black
sweater for a frilled blouse.

I remembered the long week-end and grew angry. "What's wrong?
Why are you looking so tragic? Everything's turned out all right for
you, hasn't it?"

Eleanor raised her hand to her neck, gripped her throat as if she
meant to choke herself. Then her hand dropped.

"That was a wonderful performance your old man put on," I said.
"I'd have liked to congratulate him, but his admirers didn't give me a
chance. Let me congratulate you, though. You did pretty well yourself."

Her underlip trembled. "Johnnie . . ."

"Yeah?"

After a short silence she said, "I'm going away."

"Yeah? Where to?"

"I don't know. Anywhere. I've got to get away from here."

"Why?"

She did not answer. Her hands, still in the white gloves, tightened on her pocketbook. The pupils were so large that her eyes looked black. I remembered then what her father had told me about his first wife, Eleanor's mother. She had been tense, oversensitive, secretive. I thought of the chapter in the Introduction wherein Barclay described his young wife's suicide.

Eleanor sighed. "Don't make fun of me, Johnnie. I need help."

"I'd like to help you, but you make it tough." I wanted to show sympathy, but, at the same time, let her know that I was not going to stand for anymore lies or evasions. "The time for kidding's past. Either we've got to be completely honest with each other, or else."

In a muffled voice she said, "I didn't lie to you, Johnnie. I can't remember a single thing I said that wasn't true."

"You know more than you've told me. Maybe you didn't lie deliberately but you've deliberately withheld the truth. Isn't that so?"

She raised her head. Her stricken eyes asked for mercy. I fought off the urge to take her in my arms. Evasion and appeasement would only lead us around the same old circle, back to the point from which we had started. "Perhaps I oughn't to hold you responsible," I said coldly. "Perhaps you've never learned what honesty is. Your education seems to have been deficient. You've been taught to mold and twist your idea of truth to fit every convenient attitude. Apparently you've never learned that half-truths are worse than lies, more misleading. There's only one truth, and that's the whole truth, and unless we start with that, we'll never have a chance."

I heard muffled footsteps in the corridor. Someone sneezed. I jumped up, flung open the door. There was no eavesdropper, just a tired accountant who had stayed overtime to balance his books. He wished me a wan good night and trudged toward the elevator.

I closed the office door again. "It's okay. No one's there. You can talk now," I told Eleanor.

Her lips quivered. The effort at frankness made her tense and cautious. I waited. Impatience acted as an irritant and I felt my temper rising. On the stand beside my desk was a Thermos jug of green plastic and a glass exactly like the blue jug and glass from which I had taken a drink flavored with bichloride. The blue color had kept me from seeing that the water was tinted. Had that been considered when the mercury tablets were dropped into my Thermos carafe?

"Look," I shouted, standing above Eleanor and resting my hands on her shoulders, "you say you love me; you've promised to marry me, but you're either too scared or too stubborn to tell me what you know about Wilson's death and Lola's death and Edward Everett Munn. You've always been like that, stubborn and secretive. Maybe I'm a sucker, maybe I'm being used for something I don't understand. But I'm not going to let anyone try to poison me a second time."

"Poison you!" Her lips formed the words, but she did not speak them aloud. She pulled herself free of my hands and looked up at me. There was nothing false about her amazement.

I realized then that she was not the only guilty one. Mine was also a sin of omission. Along with the rest of the office, Eleanor had swallowed the shrimp story. I had not let her know the facts in the case, nor my suspicions. In my effort to keep it clean and pretty between us I had cheated her of the truth.

I told the story briefly, but gave her a complete picture of the argument over the Wilson story, the blue-carafe business and the ambulance doctor's first diagnosis. Then I described my interview with Noble Barclay, his promises and hints, and our conversation about the shrimp cocktail.

After I had finished there was a long pause.

She breathed heavily. Suddenly she said, "If I'd known, I'd have killed him."

"Your father?" I asked. The bitterness was intentional. I wanted to hurt her.

The look she threw at me was a challenge. Her jaw shot forward. Her eyes were narrow and pale in color. With her gloved hands she pounded softly on the desk.

Impatience burned in me like a fever. "Well, say it!" I shouted. "Don't be afraid. You can tell me. I don't run to the police with information. Say it, Eleanor. I know anyway."

"My father doesn't commit murder." The sudden dignity shocked me. She was an indignant lady who had been shoved by rude hands during a subway rush.

I sat back so suddenly that my chair almost tipped over. "Then why did he tell me that he suspected you? I thought it was to protect himself."

"Do you think I did it?" Her poise survived. She was still the aggrieved gentlewoman.

"No. I never did believe it."

This is what she had been waiting for. The society manner which she had used as a brake on her temper disappeared as completely as the fever and the tension. Black clouds were defeated by the sun; everything became normal again. She leaned over and kissed me on the forehead.

"Now that you've said that, Johnnie, I can tell you that I'm not entirely without blame. In a way I'm responsible for Mr. Wilson's death."

"What are you trying to say?"

"I brought the gun to Father's office. We'd been posing pictures at the Studio, and when I was sent for suddenly, I picked up the gun and carried it with me."

"What was in your mind?"

"I don't know." She looked down at her hands as if she wanted to avoid the question in my glance. "Perhaps it was unconscious. My wish to kill . . ."

"Don't go Freudian on me. You didn't know then, did you, that your father was calling you to talk about your date with Wilson?"

She shook her head. "But I knew it was urgent, that I was to leave my work and rush up there immediately. I guess I knew I'd be bawled out and that Ed would be there, smirking, waiting like an animal to pounce." She shuddered and held her arms around herself.

"Did you hate him so much that you carried a gun to a conference?"

"Were you ever afraid of anyone, Johnnie? Not sanely and consciously afraid but terrorized down deep in your bones? I didn't know I had the gun. I thought I was carrying my pocketbook. It seemed just an absent-minded mistake. I didn't even think about it until I heard that Mr. Wilson had been shot with the same kind of gun."

"And you thought your father did it?"

She nodded humbly. "I didn't know what to think. I was frightened dumb. Father had been so illogically angry about Mr. Wilson, it just didn't make sense. Honestly, Johnnie, I didn't know until that night, last Friday, that it was Ed."

"Why did Munn kill Wilson?" I asked.

"He thought my father wanted him to. He thought Father had asked me to bring the gun to the office. Believe me, my father didn't know anything about it until afterward. Ed Munn was crazy."

"Crazy like a fox."

"You didn't know him. He was . . ." she paused, groping for words. "He was like a dog that attacks people who seem to threaten his master. Father says it's partly his fault. He'd raised Ed too high, had given him too much power and responsibility for a man of his intelligence."

"A nice theory," I commented.

"He was scared," Eleanor said. "Afraid of everyone, of everything. Now that you've told me about being poisoned while you were working on the Wilson story, I'm beginning to understand. Ed probably thought you had something on him. He might even have thought you were working for the police. You came here after the Wilson murder, you know. Don't you see how it is?"

I saw, but my vision was blurred. Physical facts were clear but they had no meaning. So far as simple outward evidence was concerned, the Wilson mystery was solved. But the solution was too simple. The thing I dislike about detective stories is that in the end they tell you who did it and then try to brush you off with some sort of surface motivation. Even if I believed that seven million dollars had been hidden in the hollow leg of an antique chair or that the Siamese emeralds were worth twelve deaths, I'd want to know more about the things that went on in the murderer's mind when he dipped the arrow into that rare East Indian poison.

"You may be right about Munn's suspicions," I said irritably. "Guilt can drive a man crazy. But suppose I'd died that night, suppose the scrubwoman hadn't arrived in time? An autopsy would have shown the presence of bichloride in my body. There'd have been an investigation around here and somebody might have remembered that I was working on the Wilson story. Who'd your father have bribed then? And where does he fit in anyway?"

She turned away. I saw her small, neat, drooping back. The heat had been turned off and the air in the office had dropped to the freezing point.

"I know your father doesn't commit murders," I continued. "He merely condones them. Suppose I'd died that night. Could Noble Barclay have squared that one by suggesting a frustrated love affair?"

She whirled around. My wisecrack had hurt her. That had been the intention. I was sick and tired of the whole thing, weary of conflict, impatient of confusion.

"Don't look at me like that," I snapped. "I know I hurt you. I meant to. And damn it, I'll go on hurting you until I know where you stand, and whether you're on my side or your father's."

"I came here to ask your help." Eleanor's voice was unsteady. She fumbled with the clasp of her pocketbook. Finally she got it open and took out a manuscript typed on yellow paper.

"What's that?"

Wearily she brushed back the curls which clustered on her forehead. "I want you to read this," she said and gave me the manuscript. After a moment she raised her hand and pushed back her hair again. It was a desolate gesture.

Suddenly she turned and walked out, leaving me alone in the office with the yellow pages in my hands.

PART SIX

A Short History of Homer Peck

by Lola Manfred

"By the time I was thirty I was half blind, half deaf, half paralyzed and half alive. I had given up all hope of health and redemption, and my only interest was to find Nirvana in sodden drunkenness. And then, miraculously, I found the light! It was not the divine light of Religion nor the incandescent light of Science, but the simple homely candle-light of Truth."

My Life Is Truth
NOBLE BARCLAY

1.

Twenty-three years ago in a poor sanitarium in Arizona a young man lay dying. He was loved by everyone in the place, for his courtesy made duchesses of charwomen, and he treated the seedy orderlies as respectfully as if they were members of exclusive clubs. This generosity was the product of a rich imagination. The young invalid allowed fantasy free lodging in his mind, but kept it always in guarded chambers so that there was never any doubt in himself as to the hazy borderline between fiction and reality. He had enjoyed his thirty years and viewed with unconcealed apprehension the approach of death. An ambitious man, he disliked dying without having achieved fame. His name, peculiarly ill-suited to eminence, was Homer Peck, a name for a comedy character in a bad rube play. His was the American story, woven of the conventional homespun. Its elements, the village childhood, the jerkwater college, the early struggle could have been tailored to fit the biography of millionaire or gangster. He was eighteen when he went to work as a reporter on a Chicago newspaper.

In 1917 he was all on fire to save democracy, but Army doctors discovered that the fever of patriotism was less than his body temperature. They advised a year in bed. After sixteen impatient weeks he was at work again, this time in an advertising agency where his imagination was allowed even freer range than in the offices of a Chicago daily. In the first year of Prohibition, it was Homer Peck who ascribed to that burgundy-colored mouthwash "the tang of vintage wine." He was the first to write of perfume as "overture to romance" and to prove his theory with solemn statements from such connoisseurs as Norma Talmadge and Theda Bara. It was none other than Peck (this achievement falls spontaneously into the "none-other" class) who discovered that fifty-six per cent of the nation's people were, secretly, *C.C.*s.

C.C. Magic initials swept the country. Citizens afflicted with halitosis, pyorrhea and b.o. were mortified at sufferings that contrasted so trivially with agony endured by the C.C. Millions dragged their fetid carcasses into the nation's drugstores and asked for Liberia, the Fluid Freedom. Today, twenty-seven years later, the nation listens to news brought nightly through the generosity of the manufacturers of Liberia, the natural fluid essence that releases from his unendurable bondage the Colonic Cripple.

The scientific discovery of the appalling percentage of C.C.s among our citizens was not Peck's major contribution. He found a way to relieve mass suffering. Wrapped around each bottle of Liberia was a slender pamphlet written by Peck and named by him *Handbook of Freedom*. I doubt if any philosophical classic has attained wider popularity, or any political manifesto liberated more miserable slaves.

In the advertising offices of Michigan Avenue, the name of Homer Peck was spoken with reverence. The young genius might have commanded a salary of ten thousand a year. This did not satisfy Peck. When an obscure great-aunt died and left him what is known as a tidy fortune, on which he might have lived a tidy life with all the sunshine and leisure his illness demanded, he went into business for himself.

With Liberia he had offered freedom. In his own new business Peck offered success to the wistful thousands who, like himself, had been weaned on Horatio Alger, Jr., and dreamed each night of limousines and ocean greyhounds. Success, as a commodity, was no harder to merchandise than a cathartic. Peck knew that it was not the mild laxative Liberia which caused the testimonial letters to flow in by the thousands, but his *Handbook of Freedom* which, in spurious scientific language, taught the customer to overcome his fear of constipation. In his new venture Peck would expand the *Handbook* to a correspondence course; five dollars a month for fifteen months, a lesson every two weeks, and instead of freedom from costiveness, freedom from failure.

Peck wrote his course in the first person and in the cozy style which made the student feel that the master was his dearest friend. But who could follow a master named Homer Peck? Thus, in July, 1920, Warren G. Wilson was born, out of two presidential campaigns by a mail-order tycoon. In his lessons, his correspondence and even his collection letters, Wilson showed himself to be, not the fishy-eyed, cold-blooded capitalist, but a bluff, warm teacher who never stinted on the advice he gave his dear students. He was strict about monthly payments only because he wanted each student to respect the principles of honest business.

In spite of its high-sounding name and frequent allusions to a faculty, the Warren G. Wilson Foundation was a one-man institution. At the height of its life the Foundation employed six people, four of whom were typists, one an office boy, and Peck's devoted nineteen-year-old secretary.

After he had written twenty-two lessons the technicalities of commerce began to bore Homer Peck. He broadened Wilson's interests, told his students that business success was not all, millionaires were often the most miserable of men, and that success meant knowing "how to live." Lessons XXIII to XXX generously included essays on Self-Mastery; Freedom from Inhibition; Ego; the You in *You*; Fundamental Meaning of Truth; Looking at Yourself Frankly; and Purging the Mind, Heart and Soul.

By the time the thirty lessons were printed and bound in an imitation-leather cover, poor Homer's cheek was worn quite thin from the constant lodging of his tongue. This was the wrong spirit. A proper advertising man is awed by the virtues of the cold cream, the rye bread, the lubricating system he praises. But Peck had neither the piety nor patience to go on believing in the work which had cost so much of his time, his money and his health. Just when the business was about to bring a return of the money invested in printing, plates, overhead and advertising, Homer Peck quit. The office rent was paid, the furniture sold and Warren G. Wilson's glamorous career ended. Peck did not even try to sell the copyright, plates and good will.

His secretary was in love with him. When she was not working on Warren G. Wilson's sales and collection literature, the ardent, slender, dark-haired girl wrote tender quatrains dedicated to H.P. With Peck she drank cocktails out of coffee cups, danced to hot bands in basement night clubs, walked hand in hand on the Lake Shore, reciting Edna St. Vincent Millay, Shakespeare and Blake. The girl offered passionately to become his mistress, but Peck was tubercular. His only kiss was aimed at her right ear on the day he left for Arizona and she, with three hundred dollars of his money in her purse, went off to pursue the full life in Greenwich Village.

Peck found the Arizona sanitarium a drab place filled with hypochondriacs and sickly illiterates who enjoyed no conversation save the endless recounting of symptoms. He read. "I am interested," he wrote the girl in Greenwich Village, "chiefly in philosophy, religion and its history, psychology and psychoanalysis. I've read all the popular interpretations of the Viennese analysts, but the stuff is too highbrow. What this country needs is a good five-cent philosophy mixed with a liberal dose of old-fashioned mysticism. One cannot overestimate the power of suggestion."

This was in 1922 when the Coué craze had begun to sweep the country. "A new patient," Peck wrote to the girl, "has brought us the hopeful story of that Mrs. D. of Troyes who was cured of consumption in what appeared its final stages. Eight months later Coué had a letter from Mrs. D. She was not only cured but pregnant."

"'A miracle, Mr. Peck!' sighed our new patient, hoping to give a hopeless invalid a word of encouragement. Why not try autosuggestion? The same thing might happen to you."

"'Madam,' I said, 'it is conceivable that I may be cured of tuberculosis, but if I were to parallel the fate of Mrs. D. and also become pregnant, that would indeed be a miracle.'"

He was nevertheless interested in Coué's method and sent for a copy of *Self-Mastery Through Auto-Suggestion*. Its simplicity amazed him. As he studied the slim volume, he came to the conclusion that simplicity was the secret. Faith-healing had to be simple. The nature of the miracle rests in the nature of the man who seeks the miracle, not in the holy amulet, not in the hands of priest, witch or doctor, nor in the words of the prayer. It is by the strength of his belief that man heals himself.

Peck had made no scientific discovery; he was merely learning for himself a set of facts which orthodox medicine had long admitted. Faith cured those pains which, existing only in the mind, caused suffering as intense and symptoms as precise as organic infirmity. Psychoanalysts were exploring the buried causes of such self-induced suffering. But these men, in contrast to the faith-healers, were pedants who had constantly to check and recheck results, who treated a sick ego like fluid in a test tube, and more often than not tortured the patient by bringing to the surface those memories which the sick soul protected with an elaborate structure of pain. Only intellectuals were able to accept such treatment and only the wealthy able to pay for it. Worst of all, the psychoanalysts explained away the miracle, which practice frightened away many of the sorest sufferers.

Homer Peck found the seedy sanitarium a most convenient laboratory. It was not exclusively a resort for consumptives. Any patient was accepted if his relations could pay the monthly fee. Here Peck met women who preferred the invalid's couch to the marriage bed, men who could not endure the competitive struggle in a world in which it was worse than sinful not to acquire wealth. And there were others who indulged in secret, tortured desire for gratifications considered evil by their families and neighbors.

As he studied, Peck became sympathetic to the invalids whom he had at first snubbed. He became as intimate with their prejudices as with their pains, asked questions and received startling answers about parents, wives, husbands, bosses and sexual partners of one sort and another. All was dutifully recorded in his notebook. Had his intentions been honest, Peck might have made a solid contribution to the study of the contemporary neurotic.

But his education had been in the flamboyant schools of advertising. No less than Warren G. Wilson's dear students, Homer Peck was a victim of the urge-to-a-million. In this spirit he began the writing of his book. "In a way," he wrote to Greenwich Village, "it will combine the virtues of the Liberia *Handbook* with Wilson's dynamics. But it will include this added feature: the sufferer will be taught to cure himself by digging for the roots of his pain. It's the confessional made chummy, but there'll be no catalogue of sins, no prescribed penance. I shall call it *Confession and Suggestion*. There will be a formula which the patient—or novice—will repeat over and over until a sort of hypnosis is induced. I do not know whether I shall prescribe ten or twenty repetitions, although I shall probably choose some irrelevant and mystic number."

"Repetition of the formula will be the first step. The second is more exciting, the marriage of auto-suggestion to psychoanalysis. Having hypnotized himself with the formula, the patient lies on a couch, closes his eyes and babbles aloud. Anything that comes to his mind, uncensored, shameless, unrelated, and all leading to the core of guilt. It doesn't matter very much whether he ever gets to the roots. He probably won't. What matters is whether he can believe himself cured. Belief is the amulet, the touchstone, the magic."

"What name shall I sign to the book? Could anyone follow a Messiah called Homer Peck? Have you any suggestions? The author will have to be a mystery man for it would be fatal to reveal the fact that he has not been able to cure himself."

In December of 1923 the book was finished. The girl in Greenwich Village, the first to read it, could not believe that it was meant to be taken seriously. To humor the invalid she submitted it to three publishers who promptly rejected it, and then gave it for reading to a clever woman literary agent who refused to soil her hands with such trash.

While the girl chewed her fingernails and nibbled pencil stubs, wondering how to break the sad news to Homer, she had a wire from him. It said something of this sort:

GREAT NEWS STOP A MIRACLE HAS BEEN PASSED IN ARIZONA STOP MY METHOD SUCCESSFUL STOP INFORM PUBLISHERS I CANNOT CONSIDER LESS THAN

FIFTEEN PER CENT STARTING ROYALTIES STOP WHY
NO WORD FROM YOU STOP WILL SOON BE RICH MY
LOVE

HOMER

The girl thought he had fallen victim to his imagination, that he
had hypnotized himself into believing his poor lungs healed. She was a
flabby-hearted creature and could not answer his ecstatic wire with the
news that no decent agent or publisher would touch the book. There
was a man who wanted to marry her. He was going to Paris. Twelve
hours after she had got the wire she was married, and in another six
hours on her way to France.

The next morning her landlady cleaned the room. In the fireplace
she found a deposit of black ash. This was all that remained of Homer
Peck's bright dream, the book that was to have made him the new
Messiah.

2.

In believing that a confirmed materialist like Peck could perform a
miracle upon his unworthy flesh, the girl had shown herself a poor
judge of character. The book designed to bring health to the ailing cost
the author much of his own strength. He burned with a steady fever
and coughed until his lungs were a filigree of scar tissue.

This did not shatter his faith in his method. His strength was failing, his girl had deserted him, no word of encouragement had come
from the New York publishers, but Homer Peck had witnessed a miracle.

To the sanitarium had come a twenty-seven-year-old dipsomaniac
who believed the world would be a better place if he were out of it. He
was a young man of great charm who, when he had a mind to, could
have tempted St. Anthony to sin or wheedled the devil to saintliness.

His inebriate wickedness had broken his poor mother's heart, and had plunged his young wife into such desperate gloom that she had ended her life with a bottle of iodine.

His name was Noble Barclay.

In 1917, when all able-bodied young men were called to military service, Noble Barclay had been so far advanced along the road to hell that the Army would have none of him. For a while shame shocked him to sobriety. Embarrassed because he was not fighting, Noble explained that he was serving his country in a more important way. To give the lie substance and also to earn the fat money the war factories were then paying, he took a job which, otherwise, he would have considered beneath his dignity, his background and his class. Not the least of his gifts was a talent for believing whatever he heard uttered by his own voice, and it was not long before Barclay became certain that he was making greater sacrifices than the boys in khaki.

This attitude won him a wife. She was a pretty girl but serious, idealistic and overbred. Her people approved the bridegroom's appearance and name, accepted his explanation of the secret war job and celebrated with a costly wedding. Champagne was served. This was Barclay's undoing. He had been sober for half a year and he thought it would do him less harm to toast the bride than to confess his weakness. There were many toasts and Barclay, after drinking all the elderly kinsmen under the table, almost disgraced himself with a buxom bridesmaid.

Mary Eleanor was a modest girl. The story of the bridal night was never told, but it must have been an appalling one for the change in her was immediately marked. Her wild, rapt adoration became frozen acceptance. She lied to her parents and for a time succeeded in shielding from them the information that her bridegroom was almost constantly drunk. The family came to know it was a bad job when they discovered that his mysterious war work was a lie and that Noble Barclay tended a machine beside ignorant Italians and Poles and Czechs.

They were all relieved on that New Year's Eve when Prohibition became a national law. Barclay saw it as salvation and celebrated at a lemonade party with his wife's people who sacrificed their old port and their Rhine wine for his sake. He managed a year of sobriety, but when he lost his job and could not readily find another, he found solace in the speakeasy. As the liquor became worse the cost became higher. This did not keep him from drinking. Contrarily, he seemed to take perverse pleasure in spending his wife's allowance on bad gin.

During pregnancy Mary Eleanor had been spared her husband's love, but one night in May, when their daughter was three months old, Barclay demanded his rights as a husband. Mary Eleanor's submissiveness had ended. She turned on him like a wildcat. They fought. It was no quarrel, mind you, but a knockdown and drag-out fight which ended with his beating and then taking her. He left her cringing on the floor, laughing hysterically, and it seemed to him that her laughter followed him through the streets to the very door of the saloon.

He was discovered four days later, insensible, in the room of an angry whore, and told that his wife had killed herself. Her family would not let him come to the funeral, locked their doors and crossed to the other side when they met him on the street. For the next two years he worked intermittently and drank steadily. It amused him to torment his respectable mother-in-law, to ring her bell at odd hours, bring strumpets to her elegant drawing room, and to cause a semiannual scandal by suing for the custody of his daughter. In September, 1923, he brought himself to the attention of his wife's family by being discovered unconscious on the steps of the State Capitol where he had fallen into sodden slumber. When he had recovered from pneumonia, they shipped him off to Arizona.

The doctors who ran this sanitarium were less interested in curing patients than in keeping paying guests. Barclay's recovery was too rapid to prove a good investment; so the doctors supplied a daily dosage of bathtub gin which enabled them, conscientiously, to send his relations a monthly bill for room, board, treatment and extras. Had it not been for Homer Peck, they would have kept Barclay in the sanitarium until his liver rotted.

Noble Barclay was Peck's pet guinea pig. Barclay was desolate, lonely, guilt-ridden and grateful for a kind word. Peck told him about the new method, read him passages from *Confession and Sug-*

gestion. In the dim room with curtains drawn against the desert sun, the quiet so intense that it almost had substance, Barclay lay on Peck's bed, repeating the formula until his great body began to writhe, his lips to twist as he began to pour out the secrets of his tortured soul.

They were pitifully commonplace and sordid, the sort of thing the normal boy writes on a back fence. But Barclay's mother had named him Noble. In a room hung with Watts and Burne-Jones reproductions, she read to him from *Idylls of the King* and told him that the darkest of all sins is concupiscence.

She called it "that beastly thing."

When the boy arrived at puberty and joined the fellows in the alley, he listened wretchedly to their boasting. Enormous, gawky, muscular, but shyer than a village maiden, he wished his mother had named him Lust. Until he was eighteen he remained, miserably, a virgin and initiation convinced him that his mother had been correct in calling it beastly. This knowledge did not cool his blood and he became convinced that he was a sort of Jekyll-Hyde alternating between nobility and bestiality. In his first year of college he discovered alcohol.

Four colleges expelled Noble Barclay. He left Dartmouth only just ahead of the sheriff who wanted him on a rape charge, which was ironic, since the woman was a well-known prostitute. If the business had not been so tragic, it would have provided material for a hilarious comedy. This great swaggering Don Juan, so handsome that women on the street stared wistfully after him, was as ignorant of love as a Victorian babe. Believing the act beastly, he behaved like a beast. He had never attended a class in sex hygiene, nor read a book about it; had consistently played hooky from physiology classes and could not look at a skeleton without blushing.

A miracle was in order. Barclay was too convinced of his inherently evil nature to be cured by any simple explanation of the origins of his sins. Peck's method was tailored for his needs. It was the self-centered man's creed, a tidy inexpensive religion that did not bother itself with God.

And it worked. In Barclay's room the bottles of gin accumulated, untouched and undesired. Without alcohol's aid Barclay took into his bed a sensible, lusty nurse who considered it a privilege to assist in the education of the handsome patient.

Barclay's gratitude was enormous. No sacrifice would, at that time, have been too great for the expression of his devotion. Long after he was well enough to leave the sanitarium he lingered beside his friend. With no less eagerness than the author's, Barclay awaited the news that *Confession and Suggestion* had found a publisher. Barclay was a true believer; his tongue was never in his cheek; more than Peck, he believed the world was waiting for this great message.

At last Peck's patience was spent. Extravagantly he telephoned to the girl's boarding house in New York. The same landlady who had swept the ashes of his book into her dustpan informed Homer that the girl had married and gone off to Paris where, in the landlady's opinion, her sort belonged. Peck was stricken. He had never asked for the girl's devotion but he had believed her vows of love, and he was bitterly hurt at the discovery that she had treated his work with such flagrant irresponsibility.

In his hour of need Peck was comforted by his disciple. One week later Noble Barclay set out for New York with two hundred dollars of Homer Peck's money and the carbon copy of his book.

3.

When he boarded the eastbound train, it was Barclay's purpose to find a publisher, arrange terms that would profit Peck and to spread the good word. In gratitude for his salvation Barclay had offered to act as Peck's representative, and when Homer talked of a percentage, Barclay winced.

Like all new converts Barclay was possessed of the zeal to proselytize. This was spring and the eastbound train carried its quota of semi-invalids, homeward bound after a winter in the sunshine. While gentlemen told dirty stories in the smoker, the observation car was filled with ladies confiding to one another the subtleties of their various ailments.

This was fertile ground for Barclay. He had a way with ladies. Even in his unregenerate days, they had stared after him in the street. Now, healthy and buoyant, tanned by the sun, his waving black hair silver-frosted, he had only to tilt an eyelash and the strongest woman weakened. "If any other man had spoken with such lack of modesty, I should have screamed for help," wrote Miss Hannah Maierdorf (several years later) of the adventure on the train. "But Noble Barclay was more like a preacher than an adventurer. He told us the story of his wicked, wicked life without mincing words. All the ladies were moved and several of us spoke of matters which we had hitherto guarded as a Mason guards the secrets of the Shrine."

Miss Maierdorf was well qualified to speak in this manner as her brother was a popular Shriner of Mansfield, Ohio. For years Miss Maierdorf had been a victim of insomnia. "Neither the pills nor sleeping potions recommended by world-famous physicians nor the desert's deep quiet could bring me the tonic of sleep," she further confessed. "But that night, in spite of the shriek of the train whistle, the puffing of the locomotive, the jerks and starts, I slept like a baby." There was also on the train, according to Miss Maierdorf, an invalid tortured by asthma. "She quit wheezing then and there and has been a vigorous woman ever since."*

So impressed was Mrs. Horatio Beach of Kansas City that she implored the young man to stop over for a few days and help her get rid of sciatica. After considering the matter Barclay decided that a few days' delay would not injure Homer Peck, whereas the patronage of a wealthy convert might help him. Moreover, the dowager had an impressionable daughter with a name like a summer resort, Rosetta Beach.

The Beaches lived in a Norman castle set in a garden in which iron stags and marble goddesses were distributed generously among clipped box and privet hedges. The house was filled with mahogany, walnut, silver, ivory, ebony and teakwood. Standing before an impe-

---

* *Treasure Chest*, A Book of Testimony by the Followers of Noble Barclay, contains Miss Maierdorf's complete letter. The asthmatic lady has never been identified.

rial Chinese screen whose panels were embroidered with the symbols of Buddhism, Noble spoke to a select audience of Homer Peck, of the book that was to shake the world, and of his own mistakes, his misery, the suffering of his poor mother, his young wife's death, his relations with women, his drunkenness and degradation and finally of his regeneration. The frankness with which he spoke of the latter subjects so titillated Mrs. Beach's friends that many begged for private consultation. In all justice let it be recorded that Barclay's intentions were therapeutic rather than aphrodisiac. He could not help it if some of the women seemed "actually to stop breathing."*

As his experience increased and his technique improved, Barclay could not help noticing the contrast between the ladies' apathy when he paid tribute to Peck and their excitement when he told his own story. It was only natural that he began pruning those paragraphs of appreciation until presently his tribute to Homer Peck was as brief as it was perfunctory.

Rosetta Beach was the first to notice this. Once, when she was angry, she mentioned it. Barclay had spent an evening giving aid to one of Rosetta's best friends, a neurotic but handsome debutante.

"Presently, Noble, you'll leave Peck out of it completely and say you were the one who discovered Truth-Sharing."

He recoiled. "You misunderstand me."

"You hardly mention him anymore."

"I have never and shall never neglect to acknowledge my debt to my benefactor."

A few days later Barclay decided that he had dallied long enough in Kansas City. The time had not been wasted, for in putting Peck's theories into practice, Barclay had discovered certain weaknesses. "No wonder the book hasn't been published. It still needs a lot of work," he told Rosetta as, repentantly, she drove him to the station. "I intend to little more lecturing, work out a few more experiments before I bring it to a publisher.

"This," he added earnestly, "will be my small way of paying my debt to Homer."

---

* *My Life Is Truth*, Introduction, Page 38.

4.

When, two years later, Peck's old girl-friend returned, a divorcee, from Paris, she wrote a repentant letter, asking Homer to forgive her weakness in protecting him from the knowledge that no publisher would have his book. The letter was returned. On the envelope in blackest ink was written, "No longer with us."

Perhaps Barclay had also written to Peck at the sanitarium; perhaps his letter had been returned with the funereal scrawl; perhaps he believed Peck dead. It is charitable to assume that this is what prompted Barclay to sign the book with his own name, and it was indeed Peck's assumption when he discovered the fraud.

At that time the book had been out for more than a year and had sold three-quarters of a million copies. Peck had not heard of it because he had made a full retreat from the world. Disappointed by the girl's desertion, heartbroken when he failed to receive good news from Barclay, he had gone deeper into the desert. The sanitarium doctors had been glad to get rid of this troublesome patient who cured profitably incurable patients. Perhaps their wanton treatment of Peck's mail was the doctors' revenge; or since their place had always been sloppy and inefficient, it might merely have been carelessness that caused "No longer with us" to be written on all envelopes addressed to Homer Peck.

He had moved to New Mexico, lived in a lonely house on the desert and was attended by an Indian servant who was said to be a witch. One day on one of his infrequent visits to Albuquerque, he bought a copy of *The American Mercury*. Reading it in bed that night he came upon an article by J. S. D. Blankfort called *The Strange Phenomenon of Noble Barclay*.

Early the next morning his ancient Ford rattled to a stop before the bookstore and Peck hurried inside to ask an astonished clerk to order a copy of *My Life Is Truth*. The clerk had merely to stretch out his hand and take from a counter piled high with them a copy of Barclay's book. For the rest of the morning Peck sat in his parked car and read.

Barclay's best-seller was, substantially, Homer Peck's *Confession and Suggestion.* There were a few changes. Peck's apologetic, quasi-scientific, quasi-humorous foreword had been deleted. There was left no word of credit to scientists and faith-healers, and none of Peck's sly humor. The humor had been Peck's greatest error. Who could follow a facetious Messiah? One good laugh and *Confession and Suggestion* would fail at the first belch.

For Peck's foreword, Barclay had substituted that sensational Introduction which told the full story of his youth, his sins, his fall and his regeneration. From the text as well as the foreword all humor had been cut away. The jolly prose had become solemn. But the book had authority. Jerry-built foundations had become solid; the bastard had been legitimatized. And Noble Barclay was the father. With the richest, roundest adjectives he acknowledged himself the author of the book, the founder of the school of thought, the benefactor of mankind. Peck's timid, imitative title had been dropped and the name of his philosophy changed, simply and dramatically, to Truth-Sharing.*

As an erstwhile success peddler, a reformed racketeer of dreams, Peck recognized the improvements. Barclay's changes not only exalted Truth but served it up in a spicy dish flavored with the plums of evil and the almonds of sex revelation. There were no apologies, no evasions. There in Goudy old-style was the naughty word, and if while reading it, you were irritated by the slightest sense of shame, you had only to turn to Pages 10 and 11 of the Introduction and, like Noble Barclay, could blame your parents for failing to tell you that life is beautiful.

My Life Is Truth had not been put on the market by any old established publisher. Ordmann & Company, incorporated under the laws of the State of Maryland, was owned jointly by Noble Barclay (forty per cent) and the family of Henry Ordmann (sixty per cent). Before the Nineteenth Amendment, Ordmann had been in the distilling business. A man of stern conscience, he refused to evade the law of the country by manufacturing any of those substitutes such as pepsin-flavored wine (for stomach disorders) or unfermented grape beverage (do not

---

* According to her first deposition, Rosetta Armistead, née Beach, and not Barclay first used the phrase, Truth-Sharing.

expose to air as the mixture will ferment, which is forbidden by law). His daughter Janet had persuaded him that publishing was not only a legitimate but also a lucrative business. This was four weeks after she had heard Noble Barclay lecture in a small salon at the Bellevue-Stratford in Philadelphia, and three days before their elopement.

All of this Peck had learned from the Blankfort article. That night he wrote Barclay a letter. It was a stupid move, but Peck, like so many clever men, was generous in his estimate of others. He could not believe Barclay had intended to defraud him. Extenuating circumstances were not hard to find. No mail had been forwarded from the sanitarium.

Peck's letter was fair. It acknowledged Barclay's contributions to the book as well as his labor in its exploitation, and suggested a division of profits. Moreover, Peck wished to see his name on the jacket. In spite of that fatal sense of humor, Peck was proud of the book. It was a success and the aching for success still burned in the grown-up Alger boy.

Eight nervous days passed. On the ninth he received a letter on stationery engraved with the name of Noble Barclay. The original letter has been lost, but as Peck remembered, it ran something like this:

My dear Mr. Peck:

In reference to your communication of the 28th ult., let me assure you Mr. Barclay regrets that the press of business, out-of-town lecture engagements, etc., prevent him from replying personally. For your own sake, let the undersigned add that it is fortunate for you that Mr. Barclay is thus engaged. Were he to seek the advice of his counselors in regard to that letter, you would indeed find yourself in an unfortunate position.

Mr. Barclay has, however, forbidden me to make the accusation of fraud or blackmail. He does not wish to apprise Postal authorities of your action, since that would lead inevitably to consequences which it would be better for all concerned to avoid.

Mr. Barclay does not deny having been acquainted at one time with a person called Homer Peck. Mr. Barclay even remembers that on one or two occasions he discussed with this Mr. Peck the precepts which he later elaborated in his immortal work, *My Life Is Truth*. He might even have asked Mr. Peck's advice in regard to a triviality. Mr. Barclay adds, regretfully, that Mr. Peck's suggestions were usually too facetious to be taken seriously.

Mr. Barclay's slight acquaintance with Mr. Peck and the facts stated above do not, however, give substance to your absurd claims. It is hardly possible for you to be the same Mr. Homer Peck with whom Mr. Barclay had these discussions, inasmuch as the aforementioned Mr. Peck has passed on.

It is my personal opinion that Mr. Barclay has been more than liberal in his attitude toward your claim, and it is my suggestion that, for your own sake, you refrain from further pursuit thereof. In case you are not aware of it, the Post Office Department extracts heavy penalties of those who use the mails to defraud.

Yours very truly,
EDWARD EVERETT MUNN
Secretary to Noble Barclay

There was but one answer possible for a man of Homer's temperament. He knew that Mark Twain would have winked at the plagiarism when he wired: THE REPORT OF MY DEATH HAS BEEN GROSSLY EXAGGERATED WHAT DO YOU OFFER YOU PHARISEE.

The next morning he received a reply signed by Munn: DO NOT ACKNOWLEDGE YOUR CLAIM ARRIVING MONDAY TO DISCUSS SITUATION DO NOTHING UNTIL THEN.

The next three days were given to plans for battle. Peck did not hire a lawyer. Truth was on his side and he believed that truth would prevail. He studied *My Life Is Truth*, recalled conversations with Barclay, made copious notes with which to confront Barclay's representative.

Late on Monday afternoon a stranger knocked at the door of Peck's bungalow. The stranger was a tall man with the high, bony legs of a stork, but he was mean and shifty-looking, a stork who leaves babies at the wrong houses. His name, engraved on a new calling card, introduced Edward Everett Munn.

"I have come in the interests of Mr. Noble Barclay."

"What's your proposition, Mr. Munn?"

"There's no reason why we should offer a proposition. Your claims are groundless."

"Except that I wrote the book."

"Mr. Barclay is grateful because you listened while he read certain portions of the manuscript aloud, and later discussed the ideas with him. As he has been successful with the book and is an extremely generous man, he would like to have you share in his good fortune. For your small services at the time, Mr. Barclay is willing to pay you what I consider a most generous amount. I, personally, advised against it, but . . ."

"You son-of-a-bitch! I wrote the book and Barclay stole it."

"Careful, Mr. Peck. Blackmail is a penal offense."

Peck paced the screened porch. "Barclay wrote it? Why, Barclay was so sodden drunk he couldn't write his name. Sometimes he couldn't even remember it. Ask him who cured him of the drink habit. Ask him how he discovered why he had to get soused all the time. Ask him who told him about the birds and the bees . . ."

"You'll find it all in the Introduction. Let me refer you to the section entitled Rebirth . . ."

"You mean where he sits out all night in the desert, considering his sins, digging down into the roots of shame, and finally in desperation, whips himself into a frenzy and forces himself to talk about it . . ."

"The greatest document ever written on human despair."

"I was the one who whipped him. I used my knouts, my kurbashes, my rawhide on his spirit until he quivered with unendurable pain. He begged me to quit, but I was inexorable," Peck declaimed as though word and memory were unquestionable proof of his claims.

"He is willing to pay you two thousand five hundred dollars."

Peck's temperature rose. "Trying to bribe me, huh? Twenty-five hundred dollars. Think I'm crazy? I'll drag this through every court in America . . ."

"I've been empowered to offer you a more generous sum," Munn said cautiously, "to keep you from doing yourself injury. Blackmail is a serious offense. The Post Office Department . . ."

Munn paused. The juxtaposition of the words blackmail and Post

Office Department had dramatic value. Through the screened wall of his porch, Peck appeared to be studying the coral and aquamarine of the desert sunset, but he saw what Munn intended him to see, the stone walls of Atlanta and Leavenworth.

Because he had nothing better to say he repeated, "I wrote the book."

"Have you any proof, Mr. Peck?"

"I wrote it, do you understand? The idea was mine." Peck's voice trembled and his words were run together.

"Have you a copyright? Or a manuscript which two or more reputable people saw you write?"

"Writing isn't a spectator sport, Mr. Munn. Although there were people in the sanitarium, if I could find them . . ."

"Have you the manuscript?"

"There were nurses, patients, orderlies. I'm sure I could find two people who saw me writing."

"And the manuscript?" Munn's eyebrows rose in polite skepticism. His voice remained level. "I'm sorry, Mr. Peck. If you insist upon making this claim, tangible proof is necessary."

Peck stuck to his guns. The evening chill descended. Peck's temperature climbed and he began to cough.

"Proof," Munn kept saying. "Have you any proof that would be acceptable in a court of law?" He had not studied law but he had memorized the glossary at the back of a book on Business English, and his phrases had a grim, legal sound. "Better to settle out of court, Mr. Peck. If you had proof to substantiate your claim, I should offer advice of an opposite nature. But in your position, let me assure you, the wisest course would be to accept Mr. Barclay's offer."

Chills alternated with Peck's fever. Like most consumptives he was of an extremely volatile disposition. Golden elation and black depression alternately possessed him. As the cold shadows fell across the desert, as he shivered and coughed, as the images in his mind grew grimmer and his imagination became peopled with a ruthless lot of Post Office inspectors, judges and jailers, his will weakened and he listened as though Munn were his friend.

"How high will Barclay go if I promise not to pursue my claims?"

"Five thousand. That's maximum, Mr. Peck. Otherwise we shall be obliged to bring this case into court ourselves. Blackmail is not a light offense. And unless you can show adequate proof . . ."

Proof, proof, proof. The reiteration of that word was like the dripping of water that drives the lonely prisoner insane. Peck agreed to settle. "Come around in the morning," he said, thinking of his comfortable bed and warm blankets.

"I'd like to leave tonight. I can get the Limited out of Albuquerque if I get there by eleven." He looked at his watch. "What is there to wait for?"

Outside a Ford waited. The driver was not only a notary public but one of the Sheriff's deputies. Munn had only to open the screen door and say, "Come in and witness a signature for us, will you?" and there was the law itself, ready to pounce if the word blackmail was spoken aloud. There was a typed document, too. It began, "I, Homer Peck . . ."and continued in legal-sounding phrases to state that the claims made in his letter of the 28th ult. were without foundation. Moreover, Homer Peck promised not to pursue said claim inasmuch as he was fully aware of the status of such action.

Peck asked for several changes but Munn was firm. Once he had got the upper hand, the smoothness was gone from his voice and manner. With the deputy sheriff as his ally, he had become a second-class tyrant. And Peck was a sick man. He felt that he had not long to live, and above all, he wanted peace. Munn handed him a gold-banded fountain pen and he signed.

When his visitors had left, he looked at his hands as though they had been soiled by the five crisp thousand-dollar bills.

5.

Homer Peck did not die. Perhaps it was his own (or Barclay's) system working backwards. Certainly Peck was not the sort of invalid who could be cured by holding the good thought. He could not accept any philosophical or religious attitude which separated man's immortal spirit from his material body; and after much study and observation, he decided that those who were most contemptuous of it were, also, most enamored of their living flesh.

At any rate he began slowly to improve. His will to survive was strengthened by a firm belief that he would someday find proof of Barclay's deceit and be vindicated. Faith prevailed.

One day, while looking for something else in an old trunk, he came upon a dusty copy of his forgotten works, the Warren G. Wilson course in Business Dynamics. He glanced over it, amused by the pompous dishonesty. From those dusty sheets a fact emerged and smote him full upon the forehead. He groaned aloud and grew furious at the lameness of his memory. On the night Munn had come to pay his visit and demand proof of Peck's claim, Peck had forgotten Lessons XXIII to XXX. He had forgotten Self-Mastery; Freedom from Inhibition; Ego; the You in *You*; Fundamental Meaning of Truth; Looking at Yourself Frankly; and Purging the Mind, Heart and Soul. In Lesson XXV he had suggested confession as tonic to the sick spirit. This entire chapter, word for word, had been included in *Confession and Suggestion*. In other words Barclay had plagiarized a plagiarism. But Peck's plagiarism had been legal; he held the copyright.

Better evidence he could not have possessed. The law does not admit the theft of an idea, for an idea is too unsubstantial to be claimed wholly by any writer. But sentences, phrases, paragraphs, all in print, all protected by copyright, are tangible property.

This time Peck wrote no letters. Nor did he file suit for plagiarism. During lonely nights in the desert he had enjoyed visions of revenge as lush and tasteless as De Mille spectacles, but he was far too sensible to seek such garish satisfaction. To destroy Barclay would have been as impractical as killing the goose without receiving his share of the golden egg.

At this time Barclay, the publisher, had started to flourish. On every newsstand in the country his new magazines flaunted their crude colors. He had become a public figure; he was interviewed when he returned from European voyages, photographed with Congressmen and comedians on Florida sands, received in the White House by President Hoover. His name was used in cross-word puzzles and its synonym was Truth. Nothing could so effectively destroy Noble Barclay as proof of dishonesty.

For Homer Peck, Lessons XXIII to XXX were the infusion that gave him blood to carry on. No one was more aware than Peck himself of the irony in the fact that Barclay's five thousand dollars, untouched until now, financed the journey designed to unearth additional evidence of fraud. From *Treasure Chest*, which its publishers called *A Book of Testimony by the Followers of Noble Barclay* but which was actually a pamphlet used in mail-order campaigns, Peck learned of Miss Hannah Maierdorf and of the Beaches who, on the eastbound train, had heard Barclay's first lectures. Unfortunately for Peck, Miss Maierdorf had gone to live in Majorca (her brother, the Shriner, had died and left her a pleasant income); Mrs. Beach was dead and Rosetta married to a cotton broker in New Orleans. She was loath to have her name used and consented to give evidence only after Peck promised that the affair would never be mentioned to newspapermen. She signed an affidavit, telling the circumstances of her meeting with Barclay on the train, of his treatment of her mother, of the cure, and of his subsequent stay at their home. She remembered clearly that Barclay had begun by giving Peck entire credit for his credo, but had later skimped on his gratitude to such extent that in mockery she had suggested that he take entire credit for himself.

From New Orleans Peck traveled west again, this time to California where he found one of the doctors who had owned the seedy sanitarium. Dr. Fillmore Macrae was not well-disposed toward Peck. He still cherished the old grudge against the patient whose cures had been more effective than his fake palliatives. But cash had always been Dr. Macrae's favorite medicine and a thousand dollars cured his resentment. He, too, signed a deposition.

To Butte, Montana, Peck traced the good-natured nurse who had assisted so practically in Barclay's education. She recalled the adventure with such gusty detail that Peck was obliged to edit her memories. But he was grateful to her descriptions of those tortured sessions in Peck's darkened room, for her indignation at the fraud, her refusal to accept money for her affidavit, and the home-cooked meal she had insisted upon preparing for him.

His final witness was his old sweetheart, the girl who had failed to find a publisher for the original manuscript. She was no longer slim, and her dark hair had been dyed an alarming shade of pink. Peck had found her name signed to a bit of light verse in a popular magazine, had written in care of the magazine and had received, ten days later, a telegram expressing surprise at his being alive.

One evening her doorbell rang. "Homer!" She flung her arms about the neck of the gaunt, sunburned visitor.

He pulled away gently, for he was still zealous in avoiding any contact that might give the tubercle bacilli a new home. "I'm not Homer Peck," he told her. "I'm Warren G. Wilson."

"Have you gone crazy?"

"I've changed my name," he confessed. Knowing the woman would laugh at the tale of his quixotic decision, he told the story humorously. Homer Peck had signed a letter acknowledging that his claim against Barclay was fraudulent. He had accepted five thousand dollars as the price of silence. But Warren G. Wilson was free to prosecute Barclay; Warren G. Wilson's name had been signed to the paragraphs that Barclay had plagiarized.

The next morning he called at Barclay's office. Strangers were not readily admitted. The alleged creator of Truth-Sharing had to be protected from the gratitude of his followers. But Wilson had planned his entrance. He offered a card bearing the name of Dr. Fillmore Macrae, Macrae Institute of Chiropractic, Los Angeles. Barclay could not have forgotten the doctor who had cared for him solicitously in the old days. Barclay supposed that Dr. Macrae wanted an interview in *Truth and Health* and his Institute of Chiropractic endorsed by the so-called medical board of that magazine.

"Dr. Macrae" was admitted to the private office. Barclay went white when he recognized the visitor.

"My name," the visitor said with dramatic emphasis, "is Warren G. Wilson. You may have heard of my course in Business Dynamics. Chapters Four, Five, Seven and Thirteen of *My Life Is Truth* are identical with my Lessons Twenty-three to Thirty."

Barclay spoke into a box on his desk. As though he had sprung out of the oak paneling of the walls, Edward Everett Munn appeared. He was no longer Barclay's secretary. By virtue of his dirty work he had acquired the titles, Supervising Editor, General Manager and Assistant to Noble Barclay. He was cozily established in a private office and he knew that his job was insured for life.

The drama appealed to Wilson and he spun it out in florid fashion. "You need no longer sympathize with me because I lack proof that my work was stolen and published under another author's name. Gentlemen, I now have such proof that, were I to introduce it in court, I could not only recover millions in damages but I could also ruin your career, wreck the very foundations of your lucrative business and have you sent to the penitentiary, but also make you, the symbol of truth, the very image of deceit and falsehood."

"If you've got such good proof," sneered Munn, "why don't you take it to a lawyer instead of coming here with these implausible threats?" Turning to Barclay, he commented, "It's extortion. He's trying to hold you up for more money."

Wilson turned his back on Munn. The snub was tactical. Only Barclay merited Wilson's attention. "I'm no fool, although you've played me for one for a long time now. My evidence could easily wreck you, but it would also destroy your business and lose a lot of money which rightfully belongs to me. After killing the truth it could not easily be resurrected. I propose a settlement."

Munn tried to speak.

Wilson cut him short. "I don't propose to negotiate with anyone but Noble Barclay. This time I'm in a position to make terms. I want a million dollars."

"Don't listen, Barclay. He's trying to bluff you," Munn advised.

Barclay said nothing. He sat as though his ornate desk were a barricade protecting him from the reality of Wilson's attack.

"I consider this most reasonable," Wilson continued. "You've already made several millions out of my idea, and while you might have wasted some of the money on bad investments or magazines that have failed, the fact remains that you made the money and that I have the right to demand my share of your profits. In addition . . ."

"It's all a bluff," Munn interrupted.

Barclay raised his hand for silence. The movement was uncertain, like the first movement of a hand that has recovered life after paralysis.

Wilson saw that Barclay was frightened. "In addition," he said with growing assurance, "I demand my share of the credit. I'm not going to ask you to confess that you stole my idea, Barclay. The price would be too high. All I ask is that you acknowledge your debt to me as your teacher, and state that my instructions were the source of your philosophy. In all further editions of the book, in all advertising and exploitation, I demand credit as founder of the system which has made you famous. That's my proposition. We can discuss the details later."

"Should I call the police?" Munn moved hopefully toward the telephone.

Barclay made another pained gesture.

For the first time Munn spoke courteously to Wilson. "Would you mind giving Mr. Barclay time to consider your proposition?"

"You gave me no time," Wilson reminded him.

"A million dollars is a lot of money. Even Mr. Barclay isn't rich enough just to write a check."

Barclay nodded weakly. Wilson was reminded of the old days, the mornings of hangover, the look of defeat in Barclay's sick spaniel eyes, the insane mumblings of remorse, the wild vows of abstinence. It was absurd for Wilson to feel pity for a man who had so ruthlessly defrauded him, but Wilson was the victor now and felt that he could afford compassion. He let them know that a suitcase in his hotel room was filled with affidavits and documents which could ruin Barclay, and with characteristic magnanimity, offered to defer action.

He thought he was being firm and severe. "Tomorrow morning at eleven promptly, I'll visit you again. If you do not then accede to my terms I'll take the documents to my attorney and have him file suit. This, I know, will prove costly to us all but I may find compensation by selling the story of the fraud to one of your competitors. Several publishers, I am sure, would jump at the privilege of financing my suit." He rose. "Until tomorrow at eleven."

Munn purred like a cat. Barclay looked as if the Governor had signed a last-minute reprieve.

That evening Wilson and his old sweetheart drank prohibition champagne and decided that they would live on the income from Barclay's million in Capri or Mentone or St. Tropez. The woman had married a second time and her husband refused to divorce her, but they did not think this would matter much in Mentone or Capri. Wilson saw a life of luxury and culture, of poetry and champagne, imagined himself and the woman stretched in long chairs on a green terrace that overlooked the Mediterranean.

All in a glow he returned to his hotel room. At the first glance he thought its disorder an illusion born of prohibition champagne. Someone had opened the dresser drawers, gone through the closets, examined the desk and rifled his luggage. His documents had been stolen along with his copy of the Wilson course and the affidavits he had so expensively gathered. He called the hotel manager who summoned the house detective. They sent for the police. A thorough investigation was promised, but its first steps revealed nothing. No elevator man, no chambermaid had seen a stranger enter Wilson's room, nor had the desk clerk given out his key.

It was a severe blow. Wilson was short of money. The Depression had cut his income to a sum that would barely keep a cat in tinned mackerel, and most of the five thousand had been used in the search for evidence against Barclay. The theft of his papers deprived poor Wilson of everything, the million dollars, the Riviera, the dream, the champagne and the poetry.

The next morning, promptly at eleven, a reception clerk announced that Mr. Warren G. Wilson had called to see Mr. Barclay. Swinging his stick and carrying his Stetson as though he were as ready as ever to embark on his voyage to the Riviera, Wilson entered the private office and seated himself in a high-backed chair opposite Barclay's desk.

"Have you considered my proposition?" he inquired.

Barclay cleared his throat and looked obliquely toward Edward Everett Munn who stood with his thumbs thrust into his vest.

"Your claim is fraudulent," Munn asserted. "We know there's nothing to it. What proof can you produce that Barclay stole your idea? Either you withdraw everything you claim or we hand you over to the police."

Barclay smiled. He had recovered with remarkable speed from his

paralysis of die previous day. "You seem to be suffering from an obsession, Mr. Wilson. It's true that I once knew a Homer Peck," he uttered
the name with delicate sarcasm, "and I don't deny having once or twice
discussed my theories with him. But to say that my philosophy was
your idea, your creation, is worse than fraudulent; it's just plain crazy. I
don't like to prosecute, and so I advise you, for your own sake, to forget
the whole thing."

Barclay's earnestness astonished Wilson. That a man could
appear so artlessly honest while flagrantly lying seemed so incredible that Wilson stammered and sputtered as if he were the liar. The
knowledge of right did not uphold Wilson. Emotion robbed him of
self-assurance.

"Will you leave now, Mr. Wilson?" asked Munn in a voice greasy
with triumph. "Mr. Barclay is a busy man; he has more important . . ."

Wilson rose. Inwardly he quivered. "Very well, gentlemen, if that's
the way you feel." In the voice of Caspar Milquetoast he added, "I shall
have my attorneys file suit at once."

"I thought you were going to bring it to the attention of certain
publishers. You seemed so sure yesterday that they would finance your
suit," gloated Munn.

Wilson stood silent for a moment, leaning upon his stick. It took all
of his strength to carry out the bluff. "I'm afraid, Mr. Munn, that there
will be quite enough notoriety without seeking sensational publicity.
Last night I had the opportunity of giving my story to reporters, but
I withheld it. Certain valuable papers were stolen from my room." He
paused, noting the glance that traveled between Barclay and Munn.
His courage quickened. "I prefer to handle the matter in the conventional way, through my attorneys. Incidentally, you gentlemen have
either had faulty legal advice or . . ."

"We have the best lawyers in New York," Munn boasted.

"Perhaps you neglected to acquaint them with all the facts. Surely
they must know that, merely by writing to the Register of Copyrights
in Washington, any citizen of the United States can institute a search
into the status of a copyright. The cost is one dollar."

"What good would that do?" asked Munn, licking dry lips.

"I don't believe it would be difficult for said citizen to obtain copies of those passages of the Wilson course which, as I informed you yesterday, are identical with Mr. Barclay's writings."

"Wait, Homer," Barclay commanded as Wilson strolled toward the door. "Perhaps we'd better talk this over."

"What is there to discuss?" queried Wilson, nonchalantly flourishing his stick.

Barclay was taking no chances. "Even though I think you're bluffing, I don't like the idea of a lawsuit. We may not seek publicity, but we're sure to get it. And since my career and my reputation are founded on a belief in truth, it won't do me any good to be involved in such a suit, even though I'd be sure to win it."

Munn was dissatisfied. He mumbled something at Barclay who frowned and snapped, "Sit down, Ed. Let me handle this."

Wilson sat down, too. "What's your proposition, Noble?"

"I'm not ungrateful for the help you once gave me," Barclay began. "While it isn't as important a part of my book as you seem to believe, I'd like to reward you for the assistance. Do the right thing by you, Homer. Maybe even better than the right thing." He leaned back in his chair, working earnestly at the role of philanthropist.

Wilson saw that Barclay was genuinely alarmed, and the knowledge gave him the effrontery to bargain. They settled for twelve hundred dollars a month. It was a lot of money, particularly at that time, but only a splinter off the bulk of Barclay's income.

6.

As time went on, Wilson succeeded in raising his monthly income to two thousand dollars. It was not that he needed the money so much as that he enjoyed the game of extortion. In the old days when he had promoted correspondence courses he had invented fictions for fleecing suckers of five dollars a month; now he used the same methods, but the stakes were higher.

There was always great mystery surrounding the payments. Each month Wilson was obliged to meet Munn in a crowded hotel lobby, railroad station or department store, where the two should not be conspicuous. Munn never came to Wilson's rooms. On several occasions, when illness prevented Wilson from keeping the appointment, the money was sent (in a plain wrapper) by messenger. And when he was in Maine or Florida, it arrived by registered mail.

Wilson acquired expensive tastes, patronized the best tailors, enjoyed rare wines and became a collector of first editions. These did not satisfy him. The game of extortion began to bore him and he found easy living poor ointment against the itch of frustration. He envied Barclay's fame, resented the rosy glow of righteousness that surrounded the publisher of the *Truth* Magazines. With masochistic energy Wilson tormented himself by reading Barclay's sensational love and crime stories.

"Every month he gets worse. I'd like to expose him," Wilson frothed.

"Yeah? And what'd you do if people stopped buying his magazines? Where'd your pleasant two grand a month come from?" his old friend asked.

During the depression she had become a literary whore, selling her talent and experience to the various publishers of cheap love magazines. It was inevitable that she should wind up in Barclay's office. She stayed there, Wilson often said, to torment him. He had offered a number of times to share his ill-gotten income, but the woman refused. This was not because she scorned his method of getting a living, but from a perverted sense of independence. They had once tried living together, but she had become a slut and Wilson a fussy old maid, and all that remained of their love was a skeleton's shadow. They quarreled furiously, let months pass in sulky loneliness. Invariably one or the other suggested forgiveness, reunion was celebrated, they drank too many toasts and quarreled again.

At one such feast Wilson announced, "I've decided at last. I'm going to write a book about Barclay. I've got to tell the whole story. As long as I keep silent, I'm as bad as he is."

"Isn't this attack of conscience striking you rather late in life, Homer?"

"All the more reason for my wanting to expiate my sins."

"You've made your gutter and you'll have to lie in it."

"I'm going to publish all the evidence, prove all the facts. In my chapter on the theft, I'll have the Wilson course printed on the left-hand pages, Barclay's *Truth* on the right."

"Think of your carcass, dear. And your plush-lined, *foie-gras* consuming gizzard. Think of that poor frayed lacework that used to be your lungs. How long could you survive in a real gutter?"

"You can help me," Wilson said. "I want to find out about Barclay's private life, about his home, his wife, his children . . ."

"You know what your trouble is, Homer?" She would never use the new name. "You lie in bed too late in the morning. Idling there, contemplating your navel, you fall victim to morality. If you'd leap out of bed, do fifty nip-ups, drink a tall glass of hot water and the juice of two lemons, you'd never worry about such things. Consider Barclay; he doesn't smoke Coronas or drink *Liebfraumilch*, and certainly he never disturbs his metabolism by thinking. 'Yond Cassius . . .'"

"I'm serious, damn you."

"What is it you want to know, Homer? About those adorable twins, presented by Gloria, the Perfect Mother. Perhaps you'd like to learn the truth about the second marriage . . ."

"I know all about that."

"Who told you?"

"Janet."

"Oh! Where'd you meet the second Mrs. Barclay?"

"I made it my business. She's quite willing to help me with the book. The period just after he started lecturing on Truth-Sharing and then got her father to back him in publishing the book is Janet's. She hasn't forgotten a detail."

"Janet, I take it, nurses an asp in her bosom. Did Noble ever confess to her, in the dark reaches of the night that he'd swiped his credo?"

Wilson shook his head. He had asked this question of Janet and she had assured him that Barclay had always acted as if Truth-Sharing had come as divine inspiration.

"Janet's furnishing me with material on the transition period. Messiah-to-publisher in one easy jump. She's got all the dope on the early days of the magazines, but I need information on his present life, not only what I glean from his magazines, but what it's actually like. Truth in a Fifth Avenue duplex. Do you know the present Mrs. B.?"

"Gloria? She'd be as helpful as a *Truth and Beauty* editorial."

"How about the daughter?"

"A lovable kid," the woman said. "Completely bewildered because the world isn't what Father told her. She's like a child brought up in orthodoxy and beginning to wonder whether she'll commit herself to eternal hellfire by daring to question it."

"She's the one for me then. I want you to arrange a meeting."

"You're cooking your goose, my dear man, and I'm not going to add to the seasoning."

Wilson paid no attention to the woman's protests. He knew what he wanted. "You must arrange a meeting, but don't introduce us. I want the girl to trust me . . ."

"How you flatter me. Homer. Eleanor's downright fond of me. I've been a radiant influence since she's come into the office. Just at present I'm trying to help her decide to own up to Father that she's revolted by the creature he's chosen for a son-in-law. She's touchingly respectful of my opinions."

"Just the same she must know you're anti-Barclay. I want my friendship with her to be unsmirched by the enemy hand."

"You needn't think I'll help you."

"I have an idea. You take her to dinner some night, not here, we're too well known. Have you ever gone to Jean Pierre's? I eat there sometimes; the food is remarkably good. You take her there and in the midst of dinner, remember some engagement and excuse yourself . . ."

"What a loathsome idea! I'll do no such thing."

A week later she took Eleanor to dine at Jean Pierre's, saw but did not recognize Wilson at the next table, remembered erratically that she had forgotten the young admirer who, even now, waited hungrily in the lobby of the Lafayette, asked Eleanor to forgive her and dashed off.

The next morning in the office Eleanor confessed to the woman that she had let herself be picked up by a middle-aged man of the world. Throughout the winter the girl continued to dine with Wilson, to visit his apartment, listen to his records, look at his books and pictures, and, in the office, to boast of her friendship with this cultured and unusual man.

The woman, petulant because she imagined Wilson in love with the young girl, drank too much and accused him of seducing Barclay's daughter. Wilson lost his temper and reminded her that drunkenness and promiscuity did not enhance her charms. They parted enemies and saw each other only once again.

They met on Fifth Avenue in front of the Public Library. The woman said, "It's ages since we've seen each other. What the hell are you sulking about?"

"Why should you want to see me? As long as there's a young fool and a bottle of cognac to amuse you, what need have you for my company?"

"It's so delightful seeing you, Homer. You say the sweetest things. How's young love?"

"Don't be an idiot." He tucked his arm under the woman's. "You know I'll always love you, you alley-cat. Come along and have dinner with me."

"I have a date."

"Leave him waiting in the lobby of the Lafayette. I'm in a sentimental mood."

They dined in the Oak Room of the Plaza and Wilson talked about his book. He expected to have it finished within a month. "I want to thank you for arranging that meeting with Eleanor." He spoke cautiously, aware that the girl's name might cause a torrent of jealousy.

"Has she been useful?"

"Wonderful. She's grateful to have someone like me, disinterested, with no preconceived Barclayan prejudices, to talk to."

"You're really a rat, Homer, taking advantage of her girlish confidences. She doesn't know about the book, does she?"

"Only that I'm writing one. But I haven't told her what it's about. I told her the title, but that can't mean anything to her."

"Oh," said the woman, affronted. "You've never told me the title."

"I haven't seen you since I decided on it. *The Autobiography of Homer Peck*. How do you like it?"

Later, while they were drinking coffee, the woman said, "I wish you hadn't told her about the book."

"Why?"

"She might talk about it. Remember what happened to your papers that other time."

"Nonsense. There's nothing to worry about. As soon as the book's finished I'm going to put a copy in a safe-deposit vault. Did I tell you I'd finally persuaded Mrs. Armistead to make another deposition?"

"Who? Oh, Rosetta Beach, the summer-resort girl who first called it Truth-Sharing. So she's agreed to reveal her scarlet past? Probably old enough now to enjoy talking about it."

"The book'll be a sensation. In a way I'm pleased that those first documents were stolen. This will be a mature work, not written in the white heat of anger, but upon calm reflection . . ."

"With fewer clichés, I hope. And what do you propose to live on when the monthly income ceases?"

"The book will make money."

"Not that much."

"What do I care? It's more important for me to get the truth told at last. I've saved a little and there are my books; they're worth quite a nice little sum. I'll have enough to last me . . ." He paused, and with a brief shrug, added, "I haven't long, you know."

He said it coolly as a man might say that he expected rain by morning. The woman was moved. She had been inconstant, but she had never been fonder of another man. Because she could not let him see her distress, she laughed a little. "Before you throw away your lovely income, will you buy me a double Courvoisier?"

"I'll buy you a bottle."

That was the last gift and the last time she saw him. When, on the following Sunday night she heard that Warren G. Wilson had died as the result of a shot in the back, she drank the rest of her good brandy. When that was gone she drank an inferior kind, and when she had finished that she drank bad whiskey. To have gone to the police and told what she knew of Wilson and his plans for exposing Barclay was too great an ordeal. Her courage was of a low order and her stomach weak. She had no real evidence, only the history of a man's life and the knowledge of an old secret. The police would have asked questions and the woman, in answering, would have been obliged to review the ugly past and look full upon the spectacle of her failure.

Frequently at night a specter visited her bedroom. It was not the shade of Homer Peck, but the seedy ghost of the woman's integrity. More than once she vowed on the empty bottle to tell what she knew of Wilson's life and the causes of his death. By day the ghosts faded, alcohol diluted her courage, the woman clung desperately to the livelihood she loathed. She became petty and childlike in hinting of dangerous knowledge.

At first skeptical, the murderer grew more and more nervous. Of late he has attempted appeasement, flattered the woman, sent roses and come to pay court at her home. It has begun to look as if he wanted people to suspect an affair between Lola Manfred and Edward Everett Munn.

PART SEVEN

The Terrace

"For the mystery man or woman, the person in whose burdened heart a secret is borne, I have no less pity than for the incurable invalid. Secrets are illness, secrets are festering sores . . ."

My Life Is Truth
NOBLE BARCLAY

From Eleanor to John

New York, May 29

DEAREST:

How does it feel to be grass-widower? Are you eating lonely dinners in the kitchenette, thinking wistfully of the little woman, or are you doing the town, like the rest of the Hollywood husbands, with one of those glamorous blondes? At the risk of becoming a repulsively possessive wife, darling, I entreat you to scrounge all possible dinner invitations from happily married friends, or work at night or read good books. Cold baths, exercise and a bland diet are also said to be helpful.

As for me, I started missing you before I kissed you goodbye, and since then I've been breathing in a vacuum. There are one hundred and forty million people in this nation, but when you're not around, the continent seems uninhabited. Aside from that, it was a comfortable trip and you were probably right in insisting that I come and face it.

Well, Johnnie, I've faced it. I saw Father today. If my typing is uneven, it's not the machine. My hands still don't work right and when I hold out my arms, my fingers wave like Old Glory in a spanking wind. All that I regret is that I decided to save money by staying here instead of taking a room at a cheap hotel. A drawer in a filing case would be preferable. Visiting here is like spending a holiday in a state penitentiary.

Not that luxury is lacking. I have the nursery suite, the twins and the nurse having been sent by Gloria to the country place. It makes me feel rather like the princess in the tower, for the place is guarded by everything but bloodhounds. Father is alleged to be off on some secret mission of national importance, for it would not be appropriate to suggest that a man of his energy would merely retire. And to hint of the true conditions would be the basest heresy.

The elevator man (a new one since we left) stared suspiciously when I named my floor. When I told him that I was Mr. Barclay's daughter he consented to take me as far as the foyer and press the bell for me, but he remained on guard until the apartment door was opened by a character who looks like a private detective in butler's livery. Finally I was inspected and passed on by . . . But guess! None other, as she would say, than our old friend Eccles. At the sight of me she burst into tears and put on such a show of bathos that I almost lost my expensive breakfast.

Grace took me upstairs to my rooms. As soon as we were safe behind the locked door, she began a whispering campaign directed against Gloria. "Her lack of faith, Eleanor, is shocking. She employs doctors, conventional medical men who haven't the slightest concept of the true cause of your poor father's desperate situation."

"When a person's ill, it's quite natural to call in medical men. Besides," I reminded her, "the cause of Father's stroke is quite obvious. Even though he quit drinking long ago."

Grace interrupted with a sigh. "*Et tu, Brute.* His own daughter. No wonder Caesar has fallen."

"What's your diagnosis, Grace?"

Her hands traced a pattern in the air. "Far, far beyond the comprehension of those medical artisans who look for causes of physical maladjustment in the body."

This was so reminiscent that I almost laughed aloud. "I suppose you believe he could be cured by digging out secrets, cleansing the festering sores, applying the sharp, clean antiseptic of Truth."

"If only he could." She sighed again. "That's the tragedy and the irony. To think of him, the prophet of Truth-Sharing held prisoner by some guilty secret. What could it be, Eleanor? How could a man who has led an irreproachable life, who has never faltered at confessing his sins, how could he have cause for self-reproach or guilt? Sometimes, Eleanor, I'm tempted to rebel at Fate. It's all so unfair."

There was a knock at the door. I opened it and Gloria's cool lips were pressed against my cheek. Her words of welcome were honeyed calculation. "Your father's resting. As soon as he wakes, he'll want to see you. But come along, dear, I want you to meet someone." She led me by the hand along the corridor to the sitting room.

A man rose and bowed, like an old-fashioned courtier, from the waist. I gave him only half an eye, for I was fascinated by a piece of furniture which had been brought into the room. There, displayed boldly in my father's house, stood a cellarette, its open doors displaying an assortment of bottles and glasses. As I recovered from the shock of this strange sight, I realized that my hand was being pressed in a warm, moist palm.

"So this is the daughter," he said with an accent so faint that I could not determine its origin. "No wonder your dear Papa was so eager to have me meet you. But you did not tell me, Gloria, that she was beautiful."

I regained possession of my hand and backed away. The man took the tall chair which Father used to like best. He was of medium height but thickset with a look of shagginess about him, unkempt thick hair, leonine eyebrows, tweeds too bulky for a man of his build.

"A drink?" asked Gloria, nodding toward the cellarette. As though I had demanded explanation, she added hastily, "We have it here for General Podolsky. He does so much of his work here now. Your father likes to keep in touch. Intensive brain work demands moderate stimulation."

I laughed. Podolsky's narrow red-brown eyes measured me coldly. There was a long silence. Presently he got up and started pacing the floor, head bent, brow wrinkled, hairy hands clasped behind his back. The whole thing was a show, every effect predetermined. With his back to me, he asked about you, Johnnie. He said that he had heard you were one of the most brilliant young men Father had ever hired, a natural-born editor. I agreed enthusiastically with all the flattery and was about to add that you have character as well as intelligence when

Podolsky whirled around, faced me and suggested that you and I come back to work for Barclay Publications.

"I am speaking for your father, and I know it is his dearest wish that you and your husband join our staff again."

Whether this magnanimity toward us black sheep was ever actually suggested by Father, or whether Podolsky was following the general pattern of Barclay bribery, I could not be sure. But I suspected at once that he knew more than he hinted of Father's secrets.

But this man is no Munn, Johnnie. He might have been willing to step into that vacant office and play at being stooge until the time came for Father's shadow to take over the substance, but there the resemblance ends. Ed Munn was stupid and a fool. I am sure that Father chose Podolsky in preference to his other yes-boys because he did not want to make the same mistake again, and put a dull man in a job that demanded brains. What happened today has made me wonder whether Father would not have been better off to put Henry Roe or Dr. Mason in the Munn vacancy.

Naturally I turned down his offer. But Podolsky is not easily rejected. He wondered whether I ought not to consult you before making a decision, described the changes in the organization, offered salaries that made my head whirl, mentioned interesting work, the chance to travel and the opportunity to influence public opinion. With the Barclay reputation and distribution outlets, *Truth Digest* has grown so phenomenally that it now has the second largest circulation of any digest magazine.

I listened patiently, but always gave the same answer.

"You're a stubborn little girl," he said. "Does your husband allow you to make decisions in this high-handed way?"

"My husband and I don't allow each other to do anything. We consider each other capable of making decisions. Moreover," I said proudly, "my husband expects to sign a contract with a major picture studio." I kept my fingers crossed while I lied, Johnnie. I had to show off before this upstart.

"Isn't that lovely?" cooed Gloria.

Podolsky raised his eyebrows. And Grace Eccles came in to tell me that Father was awake and waiting for me to come down to him.

On the staircase she put her arm around me and said, "You must gird yourself, dear. It'll be hard at first. The fallen eagle."

At every step my knees grew weaker and the blood in my veins became more watery. As we entered Father's study I remembered the last awful evening there, with Father and Ed arguing about the gun that killed Mr. Wilson. The French doors were open now, the sun gilding the white plaster hands that grasped black plush drapes. In that bright light the room had lost its incongruity and horror.

Father was waiting on the terrace. I did not immediately look at him, but at the white iron furniture, the geranium red awning and cushions, and at the new iron fence. When I last saw the terrace, there had been only a low coping.

I had expected greater change in Father's appearance, had heeded Grace's warning and girded myself for the shock. He is thinner, of course, but the bones of his head stand out in all their powerful modeling and he has the color of vigor, a deep, glowing suntan. He walked toward me and my heart stood still. He drags his right leg and holds his arm in a rigid half-parenthesis.

I ran toward him, put my arms around him and kissed him. He began to tremble and I was afraid that he would fall. My weight was not enough to brace him and I staggered back. Suddenly, from nowhere, a male nurse appeared and helped him into his chair. I saw then that my father was crying.

With his left hand he indicated that I was to sit near him and I pulled up one of the red-cushioned chairs and sat there with my hand in his. I talked quickly and breathlessly with no pauses between sentences and ideas. I told him about us, our little apartment, our work, our hopes, about the climate, the canyons and the seashore. After a time I became exhausted and could only wait for his silence. The pressure of his left hand grew heavy. His mouth contorted. He cannot speak at all; he can only utter curious, aborted sounds so deformed that one can barely recognize their kinship with human speech.

Beyond the iron terrace railing stretched Central Park, all liveliness and sunshine, flowering syringa, baby carriages and roller skates. In the clean light Father's suntan was no more convincing than a Hollywood make-up. Suddenly the virile left hand jerked me forward, the brown fierce eyes commanded my attention. He tried, with eyes and brows, with the muscles of his cheeks, the tension of his fingers, the crippled voice to communicate with me. I think I knew what he was trying to say. Had I kept Lola's manuscript? Where was it? Had you read it? Did we plan to use it against him?

"May we interrupt this happy reunion?" Podolsky's voice cut like acid through the fatty unction of his words. "Feels good, doesn't it, Barclay, to talk to one's child again? Doesn't Eleanor look lovely?" he asked with jaunty familiarity.

Father uttered a curious, protesting, animal sound. I followed the direction of his troubled eyes. Podolsky carried a highball. He set the glass on the low coping below the iron rail and stretched his thick legs on the cushions of a chaise-longue.

Gloria crossed the terrace. She walked with conscious affirmation of her womanly charms, wriggled her hips under the flowing pajamas and thrust out her breasts. The wind played with her chiffons. As she passed his chair, Father extended his good hand. Gloria avoided it and moved toward the rail.

"A lot of questions you'd like to ask Eleanor, eh, Barclay?" Podolsky lifted the glass and savored the whiskey's bouquet. "Has she told you anything interesting?"

Purple blotches like birthmarks stained Father's artificial suntan. A vein throbbed in his forehead; his useless right arm seemed to quiver and his head wobbled. I could almost feel the throbbing and hammering of his heart, the clotting and stagnation of blood in his brain.

"Are you worried?" continued Podolsky with such irritating blandness that my own blood pressure rose. "Do you think your own daughter would betray you?" Podolsky had designed his cruelty to fit the pattern of Father's suffering. He never made a statement, but only asked questions of a man who could not answer. "Hasn't Eleanor her own interests at heart? Isn't she to inherit a portion of your estate, Barclay? Wouldn't it be wise to warn her that her interests and yours are identical?"

Father was watching Gloria. She turned from the rail to catch a message from Podolsky. It was all very subtle, no more than the twitch of an eyelid, but the flavor of conspiracy was mingled with the scent of Gloria's cosmetics. I thought of secrets whispered in dark bedrooms, and wondered if Father had ever indulged in indiscreet Truth-Sharing with his beloved wife, and if Gloria, finding the burden of secrecy too great, had whispered, too.

"I hope you understand, Eleanor, that this visit is to be guarded with utmost secrecy. It would be disillusioning to his millions of followers if they were to discover that Noble Barclay is unable to heal himself through the practice of his theories." Podolsky laughed and gestured with the hand that held his empty glass. Then he ordered Gloria to fetch him another highball.

She obeyed at once, floating across the terrace in her flying chiffons, offering temptation to the General, avoiding her husband's outstretched hand. Poor Father's face had become bloodless; his lips were pale mauve and the lids closed over his anguished eyes. He sighed, and the sound of it, the only recognizable human sound he had been able to utter, was so painful that I could stand no more of it. I rushed across the terrace, tore blindly through the study and up the stairs.

I locked the door, threw myself across the bed and tried to cry. But I must have fallen asleep, for the nightmare returned. Although there is a rail on the terrace now, my nightmare rocks had grown sharper, the mountain pass narrower, the cliff steeper. He tossed me into blankness and I died hideously. When I woke I was shivering and sweating ice.

Has the nightmare stayed with me because I lost my courage at the inquest, Johnnie? But I didn't actually lie that day. I answered the questions that were asked and it wasn't my fault that these questions never came within guessing distance of the truth. What else could I have done, Johnnie? He was my father. That, more than any fears for the Barclay name and fortune, kept me silent. It was, I suppose, the old habit of loyalty, the habit that had been bred into my bones. You must remember how I cried in your arms when you hurried to my house after reading Lola's story, and how I begged you to wait a while before doing anything with the knowledge inherited from my dead friends.

You told me then that I'd be tormented until I had gained revenge or saw justice done. But I find neither revenge nor justice in the cruel irony of my father's suffering. He has been hurt enough, it seems to me, and I don't want to wound him more. His glory, his name and position are still his pride, Johnnie. When I woke up after the nightmare, my room was hot and I opened the window. It looks out on the terrace. There sat my father, motionless in his chair, and beside him, her head bent in happy servitude, the faithful Eccles.

She was reading to him out of *My Life Is Truth*.

I was tempted to call out of the window or rush downstairs and promise to destroy Lola's manuscript, vowing that I would never betray his confidence, nor reveal his guilt. The thought of you kept me from it. I know how you feel about this and I have decided to make no promises, strike no bargains, show no pity until I hear from you.

What are we to do, darling? Must we tell? Is revenge necessary? Will justice be done if we destroy the little that is left to this broken man? The murders are forgotten now, the murderer dead. Can't we let this one truth stay buried?

Please write to me immediately. I'll do whatever you say. I trust you more than anyone in the world and I need you desperately. And I hope that someday I can do something big enough to show my gratitude for all that you've done for me.

With all my love,
Yours,
Eleanor.

From John to Eleanor

Hollywood, 6/1/46

My sweet:

You're in a bad way, aren't you? As soon as I'd finished reading your letter I called the airport and asked for an emergency reservation. I even divulged the fact that I am Noble Barclay's son-in-law which, you must admit, is going pretty far for Ansell. No seats were available and none for tomorrow or the day after.

In a way I'm glad I couldn't make it. This is your problem, kid, and the time has come for you to face it, alone and unsupported. This may sound tough, but I believe you've grown strong enough now to realize that it isn't enough to quit being Barclay's daughter just to become Ansell's wife.

Your nightmare comes back, I think, because you still feel guilty about our lack of action after the discovery of the Manfred manuscript. This is not wholly your guilt, darling. I've procrastinated, too, refused to push you into a situation which would cause you to suffer. This is a weakness in me. I love you and I want to save you from pain and turmoil. I still can't forget the way you looked that night you came to my office with the manuscript. Your father certainly succeeded in scaring me when he told about your mother's suicide and hinted that you had inherited her instability. That was a ruse for scaring me off the Wilson story, and while it never worked out the way he planned, it helped to keep his secret.

This sounds as if I had little faith in you, but I couldn't help worrying about the series of shocks and disillusionments that hit you all in one week-end. It was bad enough for you to learn of Lola's death and to discover that your ex-fiancé had killed her, but the worst blow was the discovery that your father was a fraud. Revenge and justice, I said, because I saw the need in you for hurting your father as he had hurt you, and for vindicating poor Lola's memory.

It's not revenge that we seek, neither you nor I, Eleanor. When I was a pipsqueak editor, forcing issues to assert my authority, I might have sought vindication for my hurt pride. And if revenge were all you wanted, you could easily accept the fact that the gods have contrived a neat form of punishment for your father. But honest men are also stricken with apoplexy. If punishment is involved, the pattern of it is psychological. It may be that your father seeks refuge from Truth-Sharing. The need for confession may have grown so pressing that, unconsciously, he prefers dumbness. The circle is vicious. Noble Barclay can't share the truth because he can't speak or write; and conversely, he can't recover from his paralysis because he is unable to share the truth.

I may be wrong about this. I know so little. What I do know is that for you and me, it is not a simple matter of revenge. Or of punishment. You paint a touching picture of the broken eagle in his Fifth Avenue eyrie, but let's not become too deeply touched or we, too, will be paralyzed.

The murders matter no longer. Nor the old swindle involving the discovery of Truth-Sharing. But the truth has to be told. Not for the sake of vindicating poor Lola of the charge of having been loved by Munn, not because Homer Peck's ghost will haunt us until we tell the world how he paid for his sin of creating a religion that had no god, not for abstract justice, either.

Your father may be helpless and inarticulate, but his influence goes on, the swindles, the lies, the fakes perpetrated in his name. After I read your letter, I wanted to think this out and I took a long walk. Do you know what sight shocked me out of my reverie? A newsstand gaudy with magazines, six of them published by Barclay.

I bought them. I read them. I used to think them vulgar but comic. Now, after six months away from the pious atmosphere of Barclay conferences, I find evil in the magazines. Time and distance make it clearer to me that these periodicals mislead and misinform good, gullible citizens who believe implicitly in the printed word. In the name of Truth, fact is distorted, rumor spread, crackpots glorified, authority given charlatans and crooks.

Do you know Podolsky's history? Your E. E. Munn was a piker by comparison. Munn lost his head and committed a couple of puny murders. There are worse crimes. This may sound like heresy, but after a war and the perfection of the atomic bomb, individual murder loses its criminal dignity.

Last December at a conference, I reminded your father that Podolsky's political lies had been exposed by the New York newspapers. It was common knowledge that he had been the best pal of a big Nazi agent and that he made a good living by creating political myths and disseminating international falsehood. As the usurper in your father's domestic life Podolsky is not nearly so formidable as the occupant of his office.

In our time, darling, we have seen a weak king and an old, tradition-bound chancellor welcome dangerous upstarts for the sake of protecting ancient realms and profitable attitudes. Perhaps the analogy is exaggerated. I make this association after studying the back cover of *Truth Digest* and noting the languages into which it is translated, and the countries into which it brings the Podolsky point of view.

Not that I consider the Barclay-Podolsky axis any worse than the rival combinations that spread misinformation so generously among our countrymen and friends. There are others who conduct the important, social business of publishing periodicals in a loose, anarchic fashion. The crime is commonplace. But this does not condone it. Are murderers let off because homicide happens every day?

What a sermon! You ask for help and I give you editorials. But you must see this objectively, just as if your name had never been Barclay. The thing that is tearing you apart is the conflict between two bone-deep desires. You know your father's guilt and still you hope to protect him. For he is still your father, he is old and sick, and you were not born with a serpent's tooth.

We ask little, Eleanor, but we do want our chance to live honestly. The nightmare has to be exorcised or we shall be sacrificed to the old and evil, to the dishonest and the dying. We daren't go on cherishing fables for the sake of the paralyzed and moribund, nor for the protection of oily stooges and cuckolding conspirators. It is for our own kind, the young and healthy, that we have to speak out.

Think about this when you sit with your father on the terrace or when you see him, helpless and impotent, mocked by his wife, humiliated by the usurper. And when you open your window and look down upon that touching sight, Noble Barclay finding solace in his faithful follower and in the philosophy which he probably believes he created, remember that the creed cannot cure him.

Whatever your decision may be, I'll keep on loving you. But it would be unfair not to tell you that I believe that we can never remain honestly ourselves unless we tell the truth wholly. Now that Wilson and Lola are dead, there are no others who know the story so intimately nor who can tell it so honestly as you and I.

Have you the courage, Eleanor?

My love to you,
John

The End

www.ingramcontent.com/pod-product-compliance
Lightning Source LLC
Chambersburg PA
CBHW030252200626
46816CB00002BA/606